LITTLE,
BROWN

175
L B
YEARS

LARGE
PRINT

A complete list of books by James Patterson is at the end of the book. For previews of upcoming books and more information about James Patterson, please visit JamesPatterson.com or find him on Facebook or at your app store.

NYPD Red

James Patterson
AND
Marshall Karp

LITTLE, BROWN AND COMPANY

LARGE PRINT EDITION

Copyright © 2012 by James Patterson

Excerpt from *Merry Christmas, Alex Cross* copyright © 2012 by James Patterson

Little, Brown and Company
Hachette Book Group
237 Park Avenue, New York, NY 10017
littlebrown.com

First Edition: October 2012

Little, Brown and Company is a division of Hachette Book Group, Inc., and is celebrating its 175th anniversary in 2012. The Little, Brown name and logo are trademarks of Hachette Book Group, Inc.

The publisher is not responsible for websites (or their content) that are not owned by the publisher.

The Hachette Speakers Bureau provides a wide range of authors for speaking events. To find out more, go to hachettespeakersbureau.com or call (866) 376-6591.

Library of Congress Cataloging-in-Publication Data
Patterson, James.
  NYPD Red / James Patterson.
      p. cm.
  ISBN 978-0-316-19986-5 / ISBN 978-0-316-22413-0 (large print)
  1. Detectives—New York (State)—New York—Fiction.
  2. Murder—Investigation—New York (State)—New York—Fiction.
  3. Motion pictures—Production and direction—New York (State)—New York—Fiction. I. Title.
  PS3566.A822N96 2012
  813'.54—dc23
2012019537

10 9 8 7 6 5 4 3 2 1

RRD-C

Printed in the United States of America

Cheers to Charlene Black, Donna Cucchiara, Joan Fitzgerald, Lea Marie Ripa, Mary Lou Venuto, and Priscilla Weed. — JP

For Howard Schiffer and Vitamin Angels, a man and a cause that changed my life. — MK

PROLOGUE

THE CHAMELEON

One

FADE IN:
INT. KITCHEN—REGENCY
HOTEL,
NEW YORK CITY—DAY

It's the height of the breakfast rush at
the Regency's world-famous You-
Can-Kiss-Our-Ass-If-You're-Not-Rich-
and-Powerful dining room. THE
CHAMELEON slips quietly into the
busy kitchen. His sandy hair is now
dark, his skin copper. He blends right
in, just another nameless Puerto

Rican in a busboy uniform. He goes totally unnoticed.

THE CHAMELEON HAD stared at those words in his script hundreds of times. This morning they were coming to life. His movie was finally in production. "And action," he whispered as he entered the Regency kitchen through a rear door.

He did not go unnoticed.

"You!" one of the black-tied, white-jacketed waiters yelled. "Get out there and top off the coffee cups at table twelve."

Not exactly what he'd scripted, but so much better than he could have hoped for. Like most New York actors, The Chameleon knew his way around a restaurant kitchen. He filled one chrome carafe with regular coffee, another with decaf, and pushed through the swinging door into the dining room.

The cast of characters was even better than he had expected too. Today was the start of Hollywood on the Hudson week, the city's all-out push to steal more film production business from LA. So in addition to the usual East Coast power brokers, the room was chock-full of Hollywood assholes chewing on multimillion-dollar deals and hundred-dollar breakfasts. And there, holding court at table twelve, was none other than Sid Roth.

If you could go to prison for destroying careers, families, and souls, Sid Roth would be serving a string of consecutive life sentences. But in the movie biz, being a heartless prick was a plus if it translated into the bottom line, and over the past three decades Roth had turned Mesa Films from a mom-and-pop shop into a megastudio. The man was God, and the four other guys at the table were happily basking in His aura.

The Chameleon began pouring coffee when Roth, who was regaling his tablemates with a Hollywood war story, put a hand over his cup and said, "Get me another tomato juice, will you?"

"Yes, sir," The Chameleon said. *One tomato juice and a featured cameo coming up for Mr. Roth.*

He was back in less than three minutes with Roth's juice. *"Muchas gracias, amigo,"*

Roth said, and he emptied the glass without giving his waiter a second look.

And vaya con Dios *to you.* The Chameleon went back to the kitchen and disappeared through the rear door. He had ten minutes for a costume change.

The men's room in the lobby of the hotel was posh and private. Cloth hand towels, floor-to-ceiling walnut doors on each stall, and, of course, no surveillance cameras.

Half a dozen Neutrogena makeup-removing wipes later, he went from swarthy Latino to baby-faced white boy. He traded the waiter's outfit for a pair of khakis and a pale blue polo.

He headed back to the lobby and positioned himself at a bank of house phones where he could watch the rest of the scene unfold. It was out of his hands now. He only hoped it would play out half as exciting as writ.

INT. REGENCY DINING ROOM—DAY

Camera is tight on THE VICTIM as he feels the first effects of the sodium fluoroacetate. He grabs the edge of the table, determined to fight it off, but his legs won't hold him. Panic sets in as his body goes into catastrophic betrayal and his neurological center goes haywire. He experiences a full-blown seizure, vomiting violently, flailing his arms, and finally crashing face-first into his mushroom-tomato frittata.

"How do you know he'll order a frittata?" Lexi had said when she read it.

"It doesn't matter what he orders," The Chameleon said. "It's a placeholder. I just had to write something."

"Oatmeal would be better," she said. "Maybe with some berries. Much more cinematic. How do you know he's going to do all that...what did you call it? Catastrophic betrayal?"

"It's a guideline. I won't even know who the victim is till the last minute. Most of it is improv. All we want is for the guy to die a miserable, violent death."

7

* * *

Sid Roth delivered. The vomit, the panic in his eyes, the spastic seizure—it was all there. Instead of falling facedown, he took a few blind steps, crashed into a table, and cracked his skull on the base of a marble column when he hit the floor. There was lots of blood—a nice little bonus.

A woman screamed, "Call 911!"

"And cut," The Chameleon whispered.

All in all, a brilliant performance.

He texted Lexi as he walked toward the subway. **Scene went perfectly. One take.**

Fifteen minutes later, he was on the F train reading *Variety*, just another blue-eyed, fair-skinned, struggling New York actor heading to his next gig—a 9:00 call at Silvercup Studios.

Two

THE FILM BUSINESS in New York needs chameleons, and he was one of the best. It was all on his résumé—the Woody Allen movies, *Law and Order,* the soaps—at least a hundred features plus twice as many TV shows. Always in the background. Never saying a word. Never upstaging. Blending, blending, blending.

Not today. He was sick of being a face in the crowd. Today he was the star. And the producer, and the director, and the writer. It was his movie—the camera was in his head. He pulled a handful of script pages from his pocket.

INT.
SOUNDSTAGE—SILVERCUP
STUDIOS—DAY

We're on the set of another piece-of-crap IAN STEWART movie. The scene is a 1940s wedding reception. Ian is THE GROOM. THE BRIDE is DEVON WHITAKER, all tits, no talent, and half Ian's age. The happy couple steps onto the dance floor. A hundred WEDDING GUESTS look on, trying to act happy for them. EDIE COBURN, playing the jealous EX-WIFE, enters the room. She's filled with rage. The guests are horrified. The camera moves in close on one of them. It's the real star of this scene. It's The Chameleon.

His cell phone vibrated, and he grabbed it. Lexi. Again.

"Guess what?" she said.

"Lex, you can't keep calling me every five

minutes," he said. "I'm in a no-phone zone. The AD is a total hard-ass about it."

"I know, I know, but I had to call," she said. "It's all over the Internet that Sid Roth is dead."

"Baby, it's been three hours," The Chameleon said. "Some guy at his table was tweeting it before Roth hit the floor."

"Yeah, all the stories say 'apparent heart attack.' But TMZ just said he was poisoned."

"TMZ is full of shit. They're a bunch of tabloid trashmongers. Everything they print is a lie."

"But it's true."

"They don't *know* that it's true," he said in a harsh whisper. "They won't know anything till the autopsy. But they don't care. They just put out whatever garbage will get eyeballs on their website."

"I didn't mean to upset you."

"It's not your fault. It just screws up the flow of my script. The way I wrote it nobody is supposed to know about the poison till tomorrow. It's a bigger payoff for the Ian Stewart–Edie Coburn thing."

"How's that going?"

"Lexi, I can't talk now. I'm on the set."

"Not fair," she said, turning on her pouty voice. "If I can't be there with you, at least keep me in the loop."

"I am keeping you in the loop. I texted you a picture of me in wardrobe."

"Oh, great. So now I have a screen saver of you dressed up like one of those goombahs in *The Godfather*. But I still don't know what's going on."

"That's the problem, Lexi. Nothing is going on. Nothing. Nada. There's like a hundred extras sitting around since nine o'clock, but we haven't rolled a single frame of film."

"Did they tell you why?"

"They don't *tell* us anything. But I heard Muhlenberg, the director, bitching to somebody on the phone. Edie refuses to come out of her trailer."

"Probably because she's pissed at Ian. It was all over TMZ that he's been cheating on her."

The Chameleon took a deep breath. Lexi was smart. Dean's list four years running at

USC. But brains took a backseat to her constant obsession with trivial crap like horoscopes, Hollywood gossip, and Internet chatter.

"It doesn't matter if he's cheating or not," he said. "If Edie doesn't come out, Ian won't come out either."

"They have to come out," Lexi said. "It's in our script."

The Chameleon laughed. "I think Muhlenberg is in Edie's trailer right now telling her it's in *his* script."

"Hey, asshole. You with the cell phone in your ear."

The Chameleon looked up. It was the prick AD.

"No phones on the set means no phones on the set."

"Sorry. I've been sitting around here forever. I got bored."

"You're an extra," the AD said. "You get paid to be bored. Lose the phone or get off the lot."

"Yes, sir." He cupped his hand around the cell and whispered, "Lex, I've got to hang up. No more phone calls, okay?"

"Oh, crap," she said. "Then how am I supposed to know when you've finished the scene?"

"It'll be all over TMZ," The Chameleon said. "Guaranteed."

BOOK ONE

THERE'S NO PEOPLE LIKE SHOW PEOPLE

Chapter 1

I WOKE UP angry as hell. It was still pitch-black except for the glowing 3:14 on the digital clock. I would have liked to catch another three hours, but the only sleep aid I had in the apartment was the loaded revolver on my night table, and I'd much rather have used that on the dumb son of a bitch who put my partner in the hospital.

I turned on the light. There was a rolled-up purple yoga mat under the dresser, and I decided thirty minutes of *sukhasanas* and downward-facing dogs would stretch my muscles and ease my stress.

It worked.

By 4:15 I was showered, dressed, and nursing a cup of green tea. It's not my drug of choice, but Erika, my yoga instructor, swears it will heal my chakras and help my body handle the physical and psychological pressures of life. I told her I'd give it a shot for a month. But only behind closed doors. If anybody at work even smelled tea leaves on my breath, I'd get laughed off the job.

I'm Detective First Grade Zach Jordan, NYPD.

There are thirty-five thousand cops in New York City, and I'm one of the lucky seventy-five assigned to the High-Profile Victims Response Team.

The unit was our mayor's idea. He's a hardcore business guy who believes running a big city is like running an airline—you cater to your Platinum Frequent Flyers. In New York that means the superrich, the supremely powerful, and the ridiculously famous.

Every day I get to serve and protect Wall Street billionaires; sports stars with seven-figure contracts; and the movers, shakers, and divas of show business. That last group keeps us the busiest. Probably because most of them are either so desirable they're stalked, so rich they're robbed, or so despicable they're murdered.

Of course the name High-Profile Victims Response Team practically screams out that we have a special task force dedicated to the needs of the city's crème de la crème. True, but politically damaging. So the mayor has asked—make that ordered—us not to use it.

They call us NYPD Red. And for a cop in New York, it's the ultimate cool job.

My tea had gone cold, so I added sugar and put it in the microwave. Thirty seconds later it was hotter and sweeter, but it was still tea. I sat down at my computer and checked my email. There was one from Omar. All it said was Hey, Zach—today's the BIG DAY. Break a leg. LOL. Omar.

I hit Reply and wrote back. I'm glad one of us thinks this is funny.

Omar Shanks is—make that *was*—my partner, until last week. The NYPD softball team was playing the fire department in our annual fund-raiser when some asshole fireman slid into second trying to break up a double play. What he broke was Omar's left ankle, and he tore up his ACL. According to the docs, Omar will be off the grid for at least four months. So this morning I'm getting a new partner.

Her name is Kylie MacDonald, and we've got something most partners don't have. Baggage. More than I want to get into now, but I can offer a snapshot.

It was my first day at the academy. I was sizing up the other recruits when a tan, golden-haired goddess walked out of a Beach Boys song and into the room. There was a defibrillator on the wall, and I was pretty sure I was going to need it. She was too beautiful to be a cop. She'd do much better as a cop's wife. Mine.

At least half a dozen guys had the same thought, and in seconds she was in the middle of a sea of testosterone. I ignored her on the theory that girls like Kylie are more attracted to guys who don't fawn, pant, or drool. It took a week, but it worked.

"I'm Kylie MacDonald," she said to me one day after class. "We haven't met."

I grunted. "Yeah. I've been avoiding you."

"What? Why?"

"The shirt."

"What shirt?"

"The one you wore the first day. The one with the Mets logo."

"Let me guess," she said. "You're a Yankees fan."

"Die-hard and lifelong," I said.

"I wish I'd known," she said. "I'd have worn my Yankees T-shirt for you."

"I seriously doubt you have a Yankees shirt," I said.

"Five bucks says I do."

"You're on."

She took out her cell phone and scrolled through the photos. Finally she found the one she was looking for and handed me the phone.

It was a picture of Kylie and an annoyingly good-looking guy who had his arm around her. He was wearing a Mets hat, and sure enough Kylie was wearing a T-shirt that said "Yankees" right across the front. And right below "Yankees," it said "Suck."

"Pay up," she said.

Beautiful and smart. How could I not fall in love with her?

I gave her the five bucks. What happened after that is a long story filled with laughter and tears, happiness and heartbreak. Like I said—baggage that I'd rather save for another time. But I can explain how it ended. Big church wedding. Kylie and Spence Harrington—the guy in the cell phone picture.

That was almost ten years ago. Now Kylie and I are about to team up. It's never easy breaking in a new partner. Even harder when you're still hopelessly in love with her.

And that, if you haven't already figured it out by now, is what woke me up in the middle of the night.

I dumped half a cup of green tea into the sink. To hell with my chakras. I needed coffee.

Chapter 2

GERRI'S DINER IS on Lexington Avenue just around the corner from the 19th Precinct and directly across the street from Hunter College. Breakfast was in full swing when I got there, but at 5:00 in the morning there's zero risk of bumping into any college kids. It was mostly cabbies, construction workers, and cops, one of whom has a PhD instead of a gun.

Cheryl Robinson is a department shrink. In addition to her extensive understanding of human behavior and her finely tuned listening skills, Dr. Robinson has something that sets her apart from other psychologists I've met.

She is drop-dead gorgeous. Despite the fact that she swears she's ninety percent Irish, she has the dark brown eyes, jet-black hair, and the glorious caramel skin of her Latina grandmother.

I won't lie. I've been attracted to Cheryl since the day we met at a hostage negotiations seminar. But she was married, and, for me, that meant off-limits. Recently her marital status had changed, but the ink was barely dry on her divorce papers. This morning she was sitting alone in a booth, and judging by her body language and the soulful look in her eyes, she was still wrestling with the ghost of her failed relationship.

For some guys that's an open invitation. They see a woman in full-blown rebound mode as an easy target, ready to compensate for the emptiness in her life with a night of uncomplicated, no-strings-attached sex. But I'm not one of those guys. At this point, Cheryl and I had become good friends, and she looked like she needed a friend more than a fling.

I bought two large coffees to go, bagged one, and opened the other. "Do you mind if I join you?" I said, sliding into the booth across from her. "You have Damsel in Distress oozing out of every pore, and I have this hyperactive White Knight gene."

"I thought all cops had that problem," she said. "But you're the first one to come over and try to cheer me up."

"That's because you also have Department Shrink oozing out of every pore," I said. "They're afraid if they sit down and talk, you'll start analyzing them."

"What's to analyze?" she said. "They're all crazy, so they became cops, and they're all cops, so they stay crazy."

There were a bunch of open sugar packets on the table in front of her. I picked one up. "Having read the entire Hardy Boys series as a kid," I said, "I'm guessing that based on the amount of sugar you've gone through, you've been here about forty minutes."

She looked at her watch. "An hour."

"I guess even shrinks have problems that wake them up in the middle of the night," I said.

"Same problem, different night," she said. "Fred."

"I thought your divorce came through a couple of weeks ago. Based on the laws of the state of New York, isn't he officially no longer your problem?"

"He emailed me last night. He's engaged."

"Hmm," I said, nodding my head thoughtfully and slowly, stroking the imaginary goatee on my chin. "Und how does zat make you feel?"

She laughed. "That's the worst Dr. Freud impression I've ever heard."

"Actually, it was Dr. Phil, but you're deflecting the question."

"Look, I don't care if the bastard remarries, but I'd feel better if it took him more than fourteen days to get over me."

"You're right, Doc," I said. "He could at least have held off till you got over him. Oh wait, you are."

She laughed. "I hit the wall with Fred two years before the divorce."

"So now some other woman gets to suffer. Win-win."

"Thanks a lot," she said. "Now I get to play doctor. What woke you up so early?"

"It's going to be a crazy week. A bunch of

free-spirited Hollywood types are about to descend on New York, and I wanted to gird myself for their arrival."

"I see," she said. "And it has nothing to do with the fact that today's the first day you're partnering up with your ex-girlfriend."

Cheryl Robinson knew all about my history with Kylie. It happened one night at a retirement party. Cheryl was a good listener, and I was just drunk enough to open up. I had no regrets. In fact, it was kind of therapeutic to be able to talk to a professional and still keep it off the record.

"You know, I think you're right. Kylie does start today," I said. "And hey, I never thanked you for helping her get the job."

If I had to zero in on the most beautiful part of Cheryl Robinson, it would have to be her smile. It's like she has an on switch, and the second it's flipped, the dark eyes, white teeth, and full lips all light up at once. My snide little remark, which might have backfired with someone else, tripped that switch, and I got a dazzling, thousand-megawatt smile.

"Nicely done, Detective," she said. "Make

me the heavy. But no, I didn't help Kylie MacDonald get the job. She did it on her own. Captain Cates asked me to take a peek at her P-file off the record. It was stellar. Apparently, the fact that you two had a go at it didn't hurt her career."

I raised my coffee cup. "Here's hoping it doesn't hurt my career."

She rested her hand gently on mine, and I swear I almost dropped my cup. "Zach," she said softly. "Stop feeling sorry for yourself. Let the past be the past and start fresh."

"That's good advice, Doc," I said, laying my hand on top of hers. "For both of us."

Chapter 3

THE DOWDY REDBRICK building with bluestone coping and terra-cotta trimming on East 67th Street between Third and Lexington has been home to the 19th Precinct since the 1880s. It's a sprawling old beast, five stories high, with room inside for the more than two hundred uniforms and dozens of detectives who cover Manhattan's Upper East Side.

It's also the perfect location for NYPD Red, which has citywide jurisdiction. We're tucked away along the north wall of the third floor, out of the mainstream, but with lights and sirens, not far from a big chunk of the city's five boroughs—and an occasional glimpse of the Chrysler Building, to my eyes the most beautiful and grand of all New York's landmarks.

I was at my desk when I heard it.

"Yo! Six."

I'd know that voice in my sleep. I turned around and there she was—flowing blond hair, sparkling green eyes, and an infuriating gold band on the fourth finger of her left hand. Kylie MacDonald.

"K-Mac," I said.

"What's the matter, Six? Did you forget my number?" she said, wrapping both arms around me and giving me a hug.

"How long are we going to keep playing that stupid number game?" I said, inhaling the familiar scent of rosemary-mint shampoo.

"According to the terms of the bet, for as long as we both shall live. Or if we happen to meet in hell, longer than that. How you doing, Six?"

Kylie and I are both natural-born competitors, and a few days after we met and she beat me out of five bucks, we made the granddaddy of all bets. We were each so hell-bent on outperforming the other at the academy that we agreed that after graduation the winner could call the loser by his or her class ranking. Out of 275 recruits, I finished sixth.

"I'm fine," I said. "How you doing, One?"

"Ah, so you do remember my number," she said.

"I don't think you'll ever let me forget it."

"And now that we're partners, I get to remind you every day. I'm so psyched. I can't believe I got tapped for NYPD Red."

"I totally believe it," I said. "You had a major page-one arrest."

"That bust sold a lot of newspapers, but it pissed off the brass." She smiled a killer smile. "And don't tell me you don't know the details, Zach."

"I might have heard a few things, but if you promise to keep using my name instead of my number, I won't ask you if they're true."

"Cough it up. What did you hear?"

"You went undercover and nailed a guy who had raped half a dozen nurses."

"That was in the papers," she said. "Quit dodging."

"You weren't assigned to the case. You did it on your own. Rogue cop. Maverick. Loose cannon."

"The third woman he raped was my friend Judy. She's a nurse at Coney Island Hospital. She finished her shift at two in the morning. She's walking to the subway when this guy jumps her, punches her in the face, and rapes her. She doesn't even call 911. She calls me, hysterical. I reported it, then spent the night with her in the hospital. Next day I asked to be assigned to the case."

"And they said no, because you've got a personal bias," I said.

"Show me a female cop who doesn't have a personal bias against a serial rapist," she said. "The guy in charge of the investigation was old, lazy, and stupid. He never would have nailed the perp."

"So Number One decides to go after him on her own."

"It wasn't rocket science," she said. "The guy's MO never changed. He kept the attacks localized to Brooklyn, and even though he'd switch hospitals, he'd always pick one where there was a long dark walk to the subway."

"So you dressed up as a nurse and started walking from the hospital to the subway station. How many nights did you go out there?"

"I had seventeen strikeouts. I got him on the eighteenth night."

"Did you have backup?" I said.

"Zach, I didn't have any authority, so no, I didn't have any backup. All I had was my badge and my gun, and it worked."

"Lucky for you."

"Lucky for a lot of nurses. Loose cannon or not, I got the job done. If I bent a few rules, tough shit. I have no regrets."

"Maybe that's why they sent you here," I said. "We bend rules all the time."

"*We*, Detective Straight Arrow? I know you, Zach, and you are definitely not a rule breaker. You're a Capricorn to the core. Organized, loves structure, not driven by impulse, a master of restraint."

"Hey, we can't all be cowboys."

"Which is probably why they partnered us up," she said. "Yin-yang, point-counterpoint—"

"Sane cop, crazy cop," I said.

"Tell me about your partner, Detective Shanks," she said.

"Omar? He's not as pretty as you. Or as crazy."

"You know what I'm getting at. How's his leg, his knee, whatever? I'm only here on probation. When he comes back, they're going to cut me loose. I want to know how much time I have to impress the hell out of Captain Cates so she keeps me on."

"You have a few months," I said. "But I have to warn you, Cates doesn't impress easily."

"On the other hand, if you piss her off you'll be gone before lunch."

We looked up. It was our boss, Captain Delia Cates.

Kylie stuck her hand out. "Detective Kylie MacDonald, Captain."

Cates's cell phone went off. She checked the caller ID. "It's not even eight o'clock, and the Deputy Mayor in Charge of Annoying the Crap Out of Me has called four times." She took the call. "Bill, give me five seconds. I'm just wrapping something up."

She fist-bumped Kylie's outstretched hand.

"Welcome to Red, Detective MacDonald. Morning briefing is in ten. Jordan, I need you in my office before that."

She pressed the phone to her ear and took off down the hall.

Kylie just stood there. I knew what was going through her head.

"Don't try to analyze," I said. "Cates is all business, no foreplay. If you expected a cup of tea and some girl talk, it's never going to happen. You said 'hello,' she said 'hello.' Now get to work. And don't think about trying to impress her. She vetted your file. You wouldn't be here if she didn't think you could do the job."

"That helps," Kylie said. "Thanks."

"Hey, that's what partners are for."

Chapter 4

HENRY MUHLENBERG CLAMPED his hand down hard over Edie Coburn's mouth. She sank her teeth into the soft flesh of his palm and threw her head back, but he didn't let go. The last thing he needed was for some idiot to walk past her trailer and hear her screaming.

Her body convulsed. Once. Twice. Again. Again. She shuddered and went limp in his arms.

He eased his hand off her mouth.

"Get me a cigarette," she said. "They're on the counter."

Muhlenberg slid off the sofa and padded naked to the other side of the trailer. He was twenty-eight, a German wunderkind who made edgy films that critics loved and nobody went to see. Fed up with driving a ten-year-old Opel and living in a one-bedroom flat in Frankfurt, he sold his soul for a Porsche 911, a house in the Hills, and a three-picture film deal.

The first picture had tanked, the second made six mil—a home run for an indie, but in big-studio-speak a colossal failure. If this one didn't blow the roof off the multiplexes, he'd be back in Deutschland shooting music videos for garage bands.

It was his final at bat, and now that bitch Edie Coburn was screwing it up. He had come to her trailer to negotiate a truce between her and her asshole husband, Ian Stewart, who unfortunately was also her costar. Negotiate? More like grovel.

"Edie, please," he had said. "We've got a full crew and a hundred extras standing around with the meter running. It's costing the studio a thousand dollars for every minute you refuse to come out and shoot this scene."

"Ian should have thought of that before he started banging that brainless bundle of silicone and peroxide."

"You don't know that for a fact," he said. "The rumor about Ian and Devon is just that—a rumor. Probably started by some flack at the studio to get advance buzz about the movie."

"I don't know about Germany, Herr Muhlenberg, but here in New York, all rumors are true."

"Look, I'm not a marriage counselor," he said. "I know you and Ian have problems, but I also know you're a professional. What'll it take to get you into wardrobe and onto the set?"

She was wearing a short royal blue kimono with a busy floral and peacock design. She tugged on the sash and the kimono fell to the floor.

Revenge fuck. Muhlenberg complied.

At a thousand bucks a minute, the sex cost the studio fifty-four thousand dollars. Edie wasn't nearly as good as the underage star of his last film, but if you had to bang a forty-six-year-old diva to save your career, you could do a lot worse than Edie Coburn.

He lit the cigarette for her. She sucked in hard and blew it in his face. "I hope you're not waiting for a standing ovation," she said. "This was strictly business."

"Right," he said. "Then I can tell Ian we can expect you on the stage in thirty minutes."

"Yeah. You might want to put some pants on first."

Chapter 5

"HEIL HITLER," IAN said, throwing his right arm in the air as Muhlenberg entered his trailer.

It wasn't funny the first time. It wasn't funny the hundredth. The director forced a smile.

Without makeup, Ian Stewart looked every day of his fifty-six years. He was a womanizing shit heel with a short fuse and a giant ego. "Russell Crowe Without the Charm," one tabloid had called him. And Muhlenberg's career was riding on him.

"I had a little talk with Edie," Henry said.

"Little talk? You were in her trailer for nearly an hour. What'd you have to do?" he asked, rolling his tongue over his lips.

"Give me a break, Ian. This is your big scene. The one you insisted on. It added over three million dollars to the budget," Henry said. "I did whatever it took. She's ready to shoot. Now please, get into makeup before she changes her mind."

Ian clicked his heels. *"Ja, mein Direktor. Danke schön."*

As far as Muhlenberg was concerned, the scene he was about to shoot was a total piece of shit. A black-tie wedding reception. Ian was the groom. Devon Whitaker, the twenty-two-year-old blonde Ian was banging, was the bride. Edie was the ex-wife. She crashed the wedding, gun in hand, and shot the happy couple.

But wait—it was all a dream sequence, so the big ham got to die dramatically on camera and still come back for the rest of the film. All it did was muddy up a script that already had the life sucked out of it by four different writers. But Ian wouldn't make the movie without it. *Wanker.*

"Hey, did you hear about Sid Roth?" Ian asked.

"Yeah, I heard he dropped dead over breakfast at the Regency. Heart attack."

"More like poison if you believe the rumor mill." Ian laughed. "Doesn't surprise me. That bastard had so many enemies, it's a wonder nobody killed him sooner."

"I can see you're all broken up about it," Henry said.

"I'm thrilled," Ian said. "With Roth dead, I move up another notch on the list of most hated people in show business. Three more and I'll be in the top ten."

"Well, if it's any consolation, you're number one around here," Henry said. *"Heil Hitler."*

Chapter 6

CAPTAIN DELIA CATES is NYPD to the core. Born and raised in Harlem, she's a third-generation cop with a career path that puts her on the fast track to becoming the city's first female police commissioner—Columbia University, four years in the Marine Corps, and a master's in criminal justice from John Jay College.

She's somewhere north of forty, quite attractive, with dark brown eyes, flawless cocoa skin, and a warm, easy smile. Inside, she's tougher than a three-dollar steak. She's also a born leader and the best boss I've ever had.

It's not every day she summons me for a one-on-one, and this morning's invitation caught me off guard. I walked into her office at 7:55.

It was a typical no-nonsense Cates meeting. She spelled out what she wanted, I responded with a few well-placed "yeses" and "Captains," and I walked out at 7:56 only slightly more conflicted than when I went in.

I headed for the briefing room and took a seat with Kylie and eleven other detectives. Cates walked in at 8:00 on the nose.

"Good morning, ladies and gentlemen," she said. "As you all know, the mayor has rolled out a red carpet three thousand miles long in the hopes of winning the hearts and wallets of Hollywood's movie moguls. Our job is to make them feel welcome and safe. Basically, it's the same drill we go through every day, but this week we have five times as many people to serve and protect. A lot of the goings-on will be behind closed doors. Meetings, lunches, tours of production facilities—all in controlled environments, a lot of them with their own rent-a-cops.

"But there's also going to be a number of

high-visibility public events, and that brings out the stalkers, the fans, the paparazzi, and a shitload of other crazies. The biggest one is a red carpet shindig tonight at Radio City. I just spoke to the DI at Midtown North, and people are already starting to camp out. We'll have at least a hundred uniforms working the crowd, plus another thirty in plainclothes, including all of you. The bad news is that this is going to be one damn long day. The good news is that the mayor loosened the purse strings, and there's plenty of overtime money in the budget.

"Tuesday and Wednesday, there'll be fewer public events, but you know these folks like to party after a hard day, so take your cell phones to the bathroom with you. Then on Thursday—"

Her cell went off. "See what I mean?"

We all recognized the ring tone. Cates called it her "bat phone." Anyone who had that number took priority over whatever she was doing at the moment.

She answered. "Captain Cates." She listened stone-faced for fifteen seconds, then said "We're on it," and hung up.

"We're off to a bad start," she said. "We have a dead Hollywood producer on the floor of the dining room of the Regency—Sixty-first and Park. Possible homicide. Jordan and MacDonald—get on it."

I can't quite explain what happened next. Kylie was up and heading for the door. But I just sat there processing the reality of what had woken me up in the middle of the night. Kylie and I were a team, and we were going out on our first case together. It was quite a rush. It couldn't have been more than three seconds, but it was three seconds too long for Cates.

"Jordan," she barked. "Go."

I went.

Cates snapped right back to the briefing. "For those of you who haven't met her, Jordan's new partner is Detective Kylie MacDonald. She's on temporary assignment—"

Temporary assignment.

It's the last thing I heard before I got to the door, but I no longer had any idea how I felt about that.

Chapter 7

THE REGENCY WAS only five minutes away from the precinct.

"I can't believe Cates threw me a homicide on Day One," Kylie said as soon as we got in the car.

"Possible homicide," I said. "And I can't believe we invited all these Hollywood heavyweights to New York and one of them is dead before lunch."

"What did Cates want when she called you in to her office?"

"Nothing important."

"Cates is too busy to call you in for nothing

important," Kylie said. "If you don't want to tell me, don't tell me, but don't dodge the question."

"She wanted an update on Omar. I gave it to her." It was a lie, and a pretty lame one at that.

Kylie didn't buy it. "Zach, I'm on trial here. Cates wants to know if I'm going to cut it. The best way she can do that is to tell you to keep tabs on me and report in to her."

"That's bullshit," I said. "Cates makes all her own decisions."

"Yeah, but you're going to be with me twelve, fourteen hours a day. She's going to want your input."

Which is exactly why Cates called me in to her office.

We caught a red light at 63rd and Park, and I turned to Kylie. "I hope you're not going to spend twelve, fourteen hours a day over-thinking shit like this."

"Look, you don't have to tell me anything. If she did ask you, she probably *told* you not to tell me anything. And if it makes you feel any better, I hope she did ask you."

"Why?"

"You already know I'm a better cop than you are, so I don't care if you get a vote." She laughed. "As long as she doesn't ask my husband. Spence is dead set against me getting this job on a permanent basis."

The committee inside my head called an emergency meeting. *Spence knows you never got over Kylie. You're a threat. He doesn't want you spending sixty hours a week with his wife.*

As far as I was concerned, the answer was clear, but I needed to hear it for myself. "What's Spence's problem with this assignment?" I asked.

"He wants me to get pregnant," she said. "I was just about ready, but when Red came along I told him it was my dream job, and if I got it full-time, we'd have to put the baby on hold for a few years."

The committee regrouped. *Spence isn't in competition with you. He's in competition with the job. If she stays on as your partner, she doesn't get pregnant. Now what are we going to tell Cates?*

There was a line of limos parked in the No Parking zone in front of the hotel. I had to hit the siren three times before the driver at the front of the line even looked at me, and twice more before he reluctantly gave up his spot.

We got out of the car.

"What's the drill?" Kylie said. "You're the senior. You want me to stay in the background, or jump in with both feet?"

"There are no senior partners or junior partners," I said. "You're here because you're a good cop. Besides, Cates said the vic was a Hollywood producer, and you have the extra bonus of being married to a guy in the biz, so you understand what makes these people tick."

Kylie shook her head. "I've got news for you, Six. Nobody knows what in the hell makes these people tick."

Chapter 8

"SETTLE DOWN, PEOPLE," the assistant director bellowed. "Picture is up. Roll sound."

Henry Muhlenberg took a deep breath. He was finally back in control. Thirty feet away, looking elegant in a vintage *Casablanca* black shawl-collar tuxedo, The Chameleon had the same thought.

"Speed."

The clapboard snapped shut, and the assistant director called out, "Background action."

The Chameleon and ninety-nine other wedding guests slid into character, chatting, laughing, drinking, all without making a sound.

"And action," Muhlenberg called.

The bride and groom, Devon Whitaker and Ian Stewart, stepped onto the dance floor, and the assembled guests stopped pretending to talk and pretended to be enthralled as the happy couple began to dance.

The band pretended to play. The music would be added to the sound track in post-production. Ian and Devon twirled around the room.

"Dancing, dancing, dancing," Muhlenberg called out, waiting for the couple to hit their marks. "And now!"

Edie Coburn stepped into the scene wearing a pair of wide-legged, high-waisted Katharine Hepburn trousers and a loose-fitting chocolate brown silk blouse.

"Well, well, well!" she screamed, pointing a nine-millimeter SIG Pro at the couple. "The former Mrs. Minetti finally gets to meet the current Mrs. Minetti."

The crowd reacted with appropriate horror. Muhlenberg looked at the video monitor on the close-up camera. Edie Coburn was calm and cold on the outside, but seething with rage on the inside. Hardly a stretch for her to play the jealous ex-wife, Muhlenberg thought, but still, she was brilliant.

Ian turned to her, his eyes filled more with anger than fear. "Put the gun down, Carla. If this is another one of your stupid melodramatic—"

Edie fired at the bride. Once. Twice. Blood stained the lace front of the wedding gown, and Devon collapsed to the floor. Ian let out a wail and charged toward Edie. She fired again. Blood spread across his white shirt. He staggered, and she fired again. Arterial spray spurted across the dance floor, and Ian fell down hard.

It was a spectacular film death, and Henry had it covered with four cameras. "And cut!" he yelled. "Brilliant."

The assistant director helped the bloodied bride to her feet. "Ian, you need help?" he asked.

Ian Stewart didn't answer. He gasped for air and let out a groan that turned into a full-throated wet gurgle as blood gushed from his windpipe and onto the parquet floor.

The special effects guy was the first to figure it out. The blood squibs on the wedding gown had exploded right on cue, but the blood pouring out of Ian Stewart was very real.

"Live fire!" he shouted as he barreled his way onto the set, grabbed Edie Coburn's arm, and wrestled the gun from her hand.

Henry Muhlenberg was right behind him. He dropped to the floor and lifted the actor's head. The blood had slowed to a trickle. Ian's face was contorted, mouth agape, eyes wide open, seeing nothing.

"Get a doctor!" Muhlenberg screamed, knowing it was futile.

The extras were on their feet, some stunned, some crying, some shoving their way to the front to get a better look.

The Chameleon stood in their midst, motionless, just another horrified face blending in with the crowd.

Chapter 9

KYLIE AND I entered the lobby of the Regency Hotel, and three men pounced on us. The general manager, the executive chef, and some guy from corporate. The manager informed us that one of their guests had suffered a heart attack, and Mr. Corporate said they were there to help in any way they possibly could.

In another era, the lead detective would have squared off with them and said, "Bullshit—you want the cops and the dead guy out of your dining room as soon as possible so you can get on with lunch and pretend this never happened."

Today's NYPD is different. We practice CPR—Courtesy, Professionalism, Respect. I thanked them for their help, exchanged business cards, and politely asked for their indulgence while my partner and I took a look at the deceased.

"We have a defibrillator on hand," the manager said, like this was a dry run for the insurance investigation. "But it appears to be one of those sudden but deadly coronaries. There was no time to save him."

The corporate guy, who was probably the vice president in charge of covering shit up, said, "I wouldn't be surprised if he was a heavy smoker." Then he assured us that all the resources of the hotel were at our disposal to help resolve this tragedy in a timely fashion.

Short of tossing the body on a baggage cart and tucking it out of sight behind the bell desk, I couldn't for the life of me imagine what resources he had in mind.

I have no idea how they describe the Regency dining room in their brochures, but I'd call it Old Money Posh. Thick carpeting, heavy drapes, silky fabric on the walls, and upholstered chairs, all in various shades of gold.

In stark contrast to all those golden hues was a brownish red puddle and the splayed body of a man who was definitely not flying back to LA first-class.

"His name is Sidney Roth, Bel Air, California, age fifty-three."

It was Chuck Dryden, a crime scene investigator with a keen eye, remarkable instincts, and zero personality. With Chuck, there's never any of the usual how's-it-going cop banter. They call him Cut And Dryden because he gets straight to the point, without any mirth, without any chin-wagging.

I introduced him to Kylie, which I'm sure was a total waste of six seconds of his time.

"What's the COD?" I said. "The hotel brass are pushing heart attack, but I'm sure they'll be happy with any God-given untimely death that indemnifies them."

"Heart attack victims don't usually crap their pants," Dryden said. "I think he was poisoned, but we won't know for sure till we do an autopsy and a tox screen."

"Thanks," I said.

Chuck nodded and went back to work.

"Did you hear that?" Kylie said. "He said poison."

"He said he thinks it was poison."

"I hope he's right," she said. "I've never worked a poison homicide before."

"In that case, can I give you a little free advice?"

"Sure."

"A lot of people are watching us. Try not to look quite so happy about it."

Chapter 10

NOTHING CLEARS A crowded restaurant like a bleeding corpse. We were told that someone yelled "Call 911!" when Roth hit the floor. After that, everybody yelled out "Check!"

By the time the two uniformed first responders showed up, most of the witnesses had left the building. Luckily, this was the Regency and not a Starbucks, and Philippe, the very buttoned-up and genuinely helpful maître d', assured us he could refer to his seating chart and reconstruct the entire population of the dining room from the minute it opened to the minute Roth died.

"Mr. Roth was at table twelve with four others," Philippe said. "Two of them are still here."

He pointed to two men in their early thirties sitting at a table in the corner, a silver carafe and two coffee cups between them.

I looked up, and one of the men grinned and started waving.

"He seems to be taking Roth's death rather well," I said to Kylie. "What the hell is he waving at?"

"Me," she said. "I know him. He's a friend of Spence's."

We walked over, and the man stood up. "Kylie," he said. "I knew you were a cop, but what are the odds?"

"This is my partner, Detective Zach Jordan," she said. "Zach, this is Harold Scott."

"My friends call me Scotty," he said, shaking my hand.

He introduced us to the other man. "This is Randy Pisane. We were having breakfast with Sid Roth when he died."

"Thanks for staying," I said. "Can you tell us what happened?"

"One minute Roth is fine. He's telling us

war stories. I mean this guy worked with everybody—Eastwood, Newman, Brando— the biggest of the big. I've got to tell you, even if half of that shit was true—"

"Scotty," Kylie said. "What actually *happened?*"

"Anyway, to make a long story short, all of a sudden, bam—he's standing up, puking, having some kind of a seizure, and then down he goes. Smashed his head open, bled all over everything. It was gruesome. I mean, you see a lot worse on film, but in real life, it's—I don't know—it's real. It sucks."

"Did Roth grab his chest or his arm or his shoulder?" Kylie asked.

Scotty shrugged. "I don't know. It was kind of fast, and I was pretty grossed out by all the vomiting."

"You mean did he grab his chest like he was having a heart attack?" Pisane asked.

"Yes."

"No, there was none of that," Pisane said. "Look, I'm no doctor, but I wrote for *CSI: Miami* for two seasons, and what happened to Roth played out like an episode we shot where the guy was poisoned."

"You mean like food poisoning?" I said.

He looked at me like I was stupid. "No! Poison, like murder. Don't you watch *CSI: Miami*?"

"So you're talking about a homicide," I said. "Do you know if Mr. Roth had any enemies?"

Both men laughed.

"It would be a lot easier if you asked if he had any friends," Scotty said.

"Scotty's right," Pisane said. "Google him. He was a ruthless son of a bitch, but everybody wanted to work with him because he made a bitchload of money."

We thanked them and found Dryden, who was still busy photographing table twelve.

"One of the witnesses corroborates your theory," I said. "He says that the symptoms Roth displayed just before he died make it look like he was poisoned."

"Is he a doctor?" Dryden said.

"A writer for *CSI: Miami*."

"It's crap. Never watch it."

Philippe had had the good sense not to clear Roth's table. There were still five plates, five coffee cups, five waters, and one empty juice glass sitting on the table.

"This is Rafe," Philippe said. "He was Mr. Roth's waiter."

"Where was Roth sitting?" I asked.

Rafe pointed toward the juice glass.

I turned to Dryden. "Chuck, you can bag and tag it all, but do me a favor, when you run it through the lab, start with the glass."

"And you might want to test everything in the kitchen," Kylie said. "Just in case someone was targeting the whole dining room and Roth was the first to drink the Kool-Aid."

Chuck moved his head imperceptibly in something that looked like agreement.

"Rafe," I said, "did you bring Mr. Roth the juice?"

"No. There was a busboy—a new guy, Latino. I asked him to top off the coffee. When he got to the table, Roth asked him for the tomato juice, and he brought it."

"What's this busboy's name?"

"I don't know," Rafe said. "Like I told you, he was new."

"Where is he now?"

Rafe shrugged. "I don't know. He's not here. He's not in the kitchen. He probably went home."

I turned to Philippe.

He shook his head. "We don't have any new busboys today. This is a busy week. I have all my regulars—nobody new. The one who brought the juice—I don't know who he is."

My cell phone rang. It was Cates.

"Give me an update," she said.

"We're at the Regency. The Possible Homicide is looking more like a Probable Murder One, but we have to give the lab rats time to dust and dissect. We're going to head back to the precinct."

"Don't," Cates said. "I need you at Silvercup Studios. There's another body. Ian Stewart, the actor."

"What went down?" I asked.

"He was shot," Cates said.

"Anybody see anything?"

"There were about a hundred witnesses," Cates said, "and if none of them are any help, we've got the whole thing on film."

Chapter 11

I GAVE PHILIPPE my email address and told him to send me a list of everyone who was in the dining room. "And put the two guys who had breakfast with Roth and bolted before the cops got here at the top of the list."

I thought about asking Rafe the waiter to sit with a police artist and come up with a sketch of the busboy, but I know a waste of time when I see one. No sense circulating a picture of a generic male Puerto Rican who looks like half a million guys from East Williamsburg to Spanish Harlem.

I thanked Philippe and motioned Kylie toward the exit. As expected, the Regency's unholy trinity was waiting in the doorway.

"Do you have any surveillance cameras in the dining room?" I asked.

The manager looked at me like I'd asked if they had peepholes in the guests' bathrooms.

"This is the Regency," he said. "Our clients come here for discretion and privacy."

"How about the back of the house? Do you keep an eye on the kitchen staff?"

"We did, but..." He looked at the executive chef. "Etienne had the cameras removed when he came here two years ago."

The burly chef gave a wave of his hand to let me know that he had no regrets. "I find them offensive, distracting," he said.

The old me would have said something like *Makes it easier to spit in somebody's bouillabaisse if they piss you off,* but my sensitivity training kicked in and I went with, "We'll need a list of everyone who worked here this morning."

"Fine," Chef Etienne said.

Not so fine with the guy from corporate. "Detective, is that really necessary? It's a heart attack."

"It's a police investigation," I said. "My partner and I have to go. We'll be talking to you."

"Wait!" It was *le chef.* "We have to set up for lunch. How long before that, that..." He pointed at the dead man on the dining room carpet, which I'm sure he found offensive and distracting.

"I'm sorry it's taking so long," I said. "He'll be out in a few minutes. Thank you for being so patient." It was the classic bullshit response waiters are trained to give customers when the dinner they ordered an hour ago still hasn't come out of the kitchen.

I seriously doubt if Chef Etienne appreciated the irony.

Chapter 12

KYLIE WAITED TILL we were in the car before she said a word.

"For a couple of homicide detectives, we didn't do a lot of detecting," she said.

"Technically, there's nothing to detect yet. The only guy who confirmed that it's a homicide writes crime fiction for a living. Chuck Dryden knows it's poison, but he won't commit till he's back in the lab with a test tube full of proof."

"Give me a break, Zach," she said. "He could have made the call right there on the scene. If you ask me, some cops are too damn thorough."

"You're faulting him for being *thorough?* Kylie, the guy is more scientist than cop. His job is all about being…"

She grinned. At least it started out as a grin, and then it blossomed into a full-blown stupid girly-girl giggle. "Gotcha," she said. "Do you really think I have a problem with cops who do their jobs by the book?"

"Sorry, but you do have a reputation for working off the reservation."

"That was the old me. The new me is practically a Girl Scout. My mission is to play by the rules, impress the hell out of Captain Cates, and get to ride with you for the next couple of years."

And not get pregnant.

I turned east onto 59th Street, drove past Bloomingdale's, and crossed Third Avenue. The 59th Street Bridge to Queens was straight ahead.

"Clearly we're not going back to the office," Kylie said.

"Cates called. There was a shooting at Silvercup Studios."

"Oh my God. Spence is there."

When I first saw Spence Harrington's picture on Kylie's cell phone back at the academy, he was a struggling television writer and her ex-boyfriend. Ten years later he's an executive producer with a hit cop show that he shoots right here in New York.

I wish I could tell you I hate his guts, but Spence is a decent guy. Kylie had dumped him back then because she had a career in law enforcement, and he had a daily coke habit. But Spence wasn't about to give her up that easily. Without saying a word, he entered rehab. Twenty-eight days later, he showed up, detoxed and desperate, and asked Kylie to give him one last chance. She did, and the transformation was remarkable. A year later they were married.

As soon as I told Kylie there was a shooting at Silvercup, she went from tough cop to anxious wife.

"Sorry, sorry," I said. "The vic is Ian Stewart. I didn't realize Spence was working at Silvercup."

"He's developing a new series," she said as the tension drained from her face. "It's another cop show, and a damn good one. He's screening the pilot for the Hollywood glitterati on Wednesday night. It's all part of the joys-of-shooting-in-New-York attitude the mayor is trying to hawk."

"The mayor is in deep doo-doo," I said. "The joys of shooting in New York just took on a new meaning."

She pulled out her cell phone and hit the speed dial. "Hey, babe, it's me. Are you okay?"

I didn't have to be a detective to know who babe was.

Kylie turned to me. "Spence is fine."

I nodded. "Say hello for me."

"Zach says 'hi.' Did you know there was a shooting at the studio?" Pause. "Then why didn't you call me so I wouldn't worry about you?" Longer pause. "Oh, I didn't check my email. Next time, call. Zach won't mind."

"I won't mind what?" I said.

"Spence didn't call because it's my first day on the job, and he didn't want to bother us."

"No bother, Spence!" I called out.

"Zach and I are in the car," she said. "We're on the bridge. Are you ready for this? We caught the Ian Stewart shooting."

There was a long pause while Spence did the talking.

"Good advice," Kylie responded. "Thanks. I love you too." She hung up.

"What kind of good advice did Spence give you?" I asked.

"He said the buzz is all over the lot that the shooting was an accident, but he doesn't buy it."

"Why not?"

"He said assholes like Ian Stewart don't get shot by accident."

Chapter 13

BEFORE BECOMING THE center of film production in New York City, Silvercup Studios was a bakery. I'm not kidding. Until the early 1980s Silvercup White was one of those spongy, marshmallow-soft sandwich breads made mostly of flour, water, and air that was a staple of my parents' generation.

But as one newspaper punster said back then, someone finally realized there was more dough in making movies than in making bread. Was there ever, because thirty years later, Silvercup is now the largest film and television production facility in the Northeast.

The only remnant of its past glory is the ageless Silvercup sign that still dominates the skyline as you cross the bridge into Queens. All they did was change the word "Bread" to "Studios."

I turned right off the exit ramp and cruised past the storage facilities, auto repair shops, and the rest of the industrial ugliness that defines Long Island City. Three squad cars from the 108th were already parked in front of the sprawling complex on 22nd Street, and one of the uniforms waved me through the front gate.

Bob Reitzfeld was waiting in the parking lot. Bob is a former NYPD lieutenant who likes to tell people that the only thing he ever failed at was doing nothing. He retired on a full pension, tried golf, tennis, and fishing, hated them all, and within three months signed on as a security guard at Silvercup for fifteen bucks an hour. Two years later he worked his way up to the top spot.

I got out of the car, and he shook my hand. "Zach, I'm glad you're here. We're in short supply of people for the mayor to crap on."

"I'm sure he's not happy," I said.

"Understatement. This is Day One of Hollywood on the Hudson week. He's screaming that he's going to change the name to Homicide on the Hudson," Reitzfeld said.

"Do you know for sure that it's a homicide?" I asked.

"The only thing I know for sure is that we're on the East River, not the Hudson, but I'll be damned if I'm going to correct His Honor when he's on the warpath."

Kylie got out of the car. Reitzfeld did a quick double take. Then his cop brain instantly put the pieces together. "I heard Omar was on the DL. Don't tell me this is your new sidekick."

"You guys know each other?" I said.

"I only know this young lady as Mrs. Spence Harrington, but I've heard a lot about Detective Kylie MacDonald," he said. "So, how do you like NYPD Red?"

"It's my first day," she said, "but I'm keeping busy."

"Brace yourself for a baptism of fire. The body is at Studio X. It's a two-minute walk. I'll give you the highlights." He turned and headed toward the Forty-third Avenue side of the main lot. Kylie and I flanked him.

"The vic is Ian Stewart. Everything you read in the tabs that says he's a total asshole is true. He's pushing sixty, should be getting ready for the grandpa roles, but he still thinks he's leading-man sexy. Can't keep his dick in its holster—straddles any young thing that comes along—and rumor has it he's not necessarily gender-specific. He's been banging Devon Whitaker, his young costar, which pissed off Edie Coburn, his other costar, who also happens to be his latest wife. Edie threw a hissy this morning, locked herself in her trailer, and shut down production for a couple of hours. The director finally pried her loose with his crowbar, and when I say crowbar, I think you get my drift."

"Who's the director?" Kylie asked.

"Some whiz kid out of Germany, name of Henry Muhlenberg, nickname The Mule, which—and again, this is rumor—is not so much about him being stubborn as it is an anatomical reference. Since he was banging the victim's wife just a few hours ago, he's an automatic person of interest, but he's a powderhead, so you won't get much out of him till his nose is clean."

"What can you tell us about the shooting?" I said.

"The armorer on the set is an old pro— Dave West. He's been handling prop guns for twenty years. He gave Edie a nine-millimeter SIG Pro that was supposed to be loaded with blanks. She took two shots at Whitaker, no problem. Two more at Stewart and, as if by magic, she gets to kill the whoring, cheating bastard she's married to and still claim that she didn't know the gun was loaded."

"Do you think she did?" Kylie said.

"No. She was hiding out in her trailer all morning. Besides, there's no amount of money that would convince a guy like Dave West to put real bullets in the gun. I think someone on the set got ahold of it and switched mags."

"How is that possible?" I said.

"It's not, if Dave's doing his job by the book," Reitzfeld said. "But his wife's been sick and his head's not always in his job. Last month I caught him leaving a gun cabinet open, and I tore him a new one. He swore it would never happen again, but like I said, his wife's sick and his focus isn't where it should be."

We stopped in front of the elephant doors at Studio X. "It's all my fault," Reitzfeld said. "If I'd kept a tighter watch on Dave, this wouldn't have happened."

"Bob, there are a thousand people wandering around here," I said. "You can't be responsible for all of them. How can you blame yourself?"

"Zach, I'm head of security, which includes firearms safety," he said. "It doesn't matter if I blame myself or not. Somebody will. This is show business. Shit floats up."

Chapter 14

I'VE BEEN HANGING around soundstages ever since I was a kid. My mom was a makeup artist, and there were a couple of years when I decided I was too old to need a babysitter and she decided I was too young to be left home alone, so after school I'd meet her on the set of a commercial, music video, or feature.

Early on she taught me everything I needed to know to understand people in show business. "They think their poo smells like sugar cookies," she said. "It doesn't. But it makes them feel good if you pretend it does."

Working for NYPD Red, I meet a lot of people who are convinced they're God's gift to the world. I can smell their shit a mile away, but Mom's advice helps make my job a lot easier.

Kylie, Bob, and I walked through the stage doors of Studio X, which is about a city block long and almost as wide—no big deal in Hollywood, but pretty impressive by New York standards.

There were about forty people behind the camera, all of whom eyed us carefully as we navigated our way around cables, light stands, and sound carts. We stopped at the edge of the set, a banquet hall, where a semicircle of tables was decked out with fine china, crystal stemware, and exotic flowers. At least that's what they'd look like on film. In reality they were all plastic. At the center of the main table sat an ornately decorated five-tiered wedding cake, which I knew would be Styrofoam, because buttercream would never hold up under the hot lights.

"Come meet the groom," Bob said. "He's on the dance floor."

About a hundred extras, all in black tie and long gowns, had been talking as we showed up. The chatter died down to a whisper as we slipped on paper booties and trod carefully between the pools of blood.

Ian Stewart was on his back, the final emotion that had surged through his brain frozen on his face. It appeared to be a combination of OMG and WTF, but I might have been reading too much into it. Dead is dead, and Ian was very.

There was a different CSI waiting for us. Maggie Arnold is younger, prettier, and much friendlier than Chuck Dryden. We'd flirted at past crime scenes, and she gave me a big smile when she saw me. I introduced her to Kylie and asked for a top line.

"Top line is pretty much going to be the same as the bottom line," she said. "He took two nine-millimeter rounds, one to the chest, one to the neck. Bled out fast."

"The armorer says he loaded the magazine with blanks," Kylie said.

"I believe him," Maggie said. "We dusted the gun. The outside is covered with prints, which will probably match up with the prints we get from the armorer and the shooter, Edie Coburn. But the magazine and the rest of the bullets have all been wiped clean. If the armorer was the last one to handle the gun, his prints would be there."

"So Dave is telling the truth," Bob said. "Somebody swapped mags."

"And that somebody could still be here," I said. "How soon after the shooting did you seal off the studio?"

"Not soon enough," Bob said. "First there was chaos. Then they called 911. It was nearly ten minutes before I got the call on my walkie and ordered a total lockdown. The guy we're looking for had plenty of time to slip out."

"I'm not really sure it makes a difference," I said. "Whoever switched mags could have left long before the shooting."

"I doubt it," Kylie said.

"Why's that?" I said.

"Look at this," she said, sweeping her hand around the elaborately decorated room, past the hundred dressed-to-the-teeth extras, finally letting it come to rest with one finger pointing down at the blood-drenched body. "This is classic cinematic drama. It's too big a spectacle to miss. I'll bet you five bucks that whoever put real bullets in that gun stayed to watch Ian Stewart die."

I didn't take the bet. One thing I learned about betting with Kylie over the years: she almost always wins.

Chapter 15

DAVE WEST HAD kind eyes. He was about fifty, an African-American with a thin wisp of a mustache and even less hair on his head. He had a soft, round face that I'm sure lit up when he laughed, and brown eyes that were tinged with sadness and bewilderment. But the kindness came through still.

I offered Kylie a shot at taking the lead, but she passed.

"Not here," she said. "Not now."

West was sitting at a table at the rear of the studio, an untouched cup of coffee in front of him.

Kylie and I introduced ourselves, and I sat down across from him. She stood to the side.

"I know you're upset," I said. "Can we talk?"

"It's my fault," he said. "I screwed up."

"Dave!" It was Reitzfeld.

I threw him a look. He held up both hands. "Sorry. I just can't let him incriminate himself."

"Mr. West," I said. "Just answer the questions as I ask them. How long have you been an armorer?"

"I got my BFA license twenty-three years ago last month."

"BFA?"

"Blank Fire Adapted," he said. "There's prop guns and real guns. The props are harmless, but not too authentic. So most directors like to use a real gun that fires blanks."

"And you supply the guns?"

"Sometimes yes, sometimes no. But I have total control over all BFA guns on the set, and I have the absolute final say on whether a gun is safe to use in a scene or not."

"And what happened today?"

"It was a nine-millimeter SIG Pro. The movie takes place in the forties, and I needed a period piece. The gun's got some years on it, but it's in mint condition. I cleaned it and loaded the magazine with blanks."

"Sorry to interrupt," I said, "but you're sure they were blanks."

A hint of a sad smile. "Yeah. Like I said, I've been a gun wrangler for twenty-three years. It's hard to confuse blank cartridges with real bullets. You're a cop. You ought to know. Blanks have no lead at the tip. The ones I used had a red cotton wad inside the casing. Totally harmless, unless you fire the gun at extremely close range, but I met with the director, and I knew Edie would be a good ten feet away."

"What time did you put the blanks in the magazine?" I said.

"I guess about nine, nine fifteen. We were supposed to shoot at nine thirty, but something happened with Edie and we wound up sitting around for a couple of hours."

"And where was the gun during that time?"
He hesitated. "There's a lockbox."
"Did you lock it up?"

His bottom lip trembled and his eyes watered up. "I set it down on the prop table. I kept thinking we were going to roll camera any minute."

"Could somebody have come in here and tampered with the gun?"

He nodded. "Look at this place," he said. "They call it the prop room, but it's not a room. There are no walls, no doors—it's all open, and it's twenty feet from the craft table. Anybody could walk over and tamper with anything, but I was sitting right—" He stopped, and it wasn't hard to figure out why.

"Was the gun ever out of your sight?" I said.

"Two, three . . . maybe five minutes."

"How long would it take to switch the magazines?"

"Five seconds. But why would anybody do that?"

"Let's say somebody did," I said. "How would they know in advance to have the right magazine—one that fits the gun you were using."

"Production notes," he said. "Everything we do is documented on paper and distributed all over the place. The SIG Pro was on the prop list since way back in preproduction. Anybody could've seen it."

"At what point did you give Edie Coburn the gun?" I asked.

"Eleven thirty, I think."

"Did you check to see that it was the right gun?"

"Yeah. I looked at the serial number, and then I took out the magazine and checked that too, but—"

He picked up the cold coffee from the table in front of him and took a sip.

"But what?" I asked.

"This mag for the SIG Pro—you can only see the top two cartridges. I looked in and saw two red tips. How was I supposed to know the rest would be live? But I was stupid. I was too trusting."

"When Ms. Coburn fired the gun, what happened?"

"She took two shots at Devon Whitaker, the bride," he said. "That's what was in the script. Bang, bang. So Devon got the blanks. Her blood squibs go off and down she went. Then Edie fired two more at Ian. Soon as I heard it, I knew. Blanks don't reverb like that. I froze in my seat. Luckily, Alan, the special effects guy, ran over and wrestled the gun from Edie's hand, but by then..." He buried his face in his palms and his body shook as he wept quietly.

One thing was clear. Dave West wasn't a killer. He was a patsy and he was about to take the fall for a sadistic killer. Reitzfeld had said that Dave's wife was sick. But not once did he whine about her or use her illness as an excuse. He had taken his mind off his life-or-death job, and he was willing to own his mistake and suffer the consequences.

He stopped sobbing and looked me square in the eye.

"I'm sorry," I said.

"Go ahead," he said and put both hands behind his back. "It's your job."

"Dave West, you're under arrest for negligent homicide in the death of Ian Stewart," I said.

I read him his Miranda rights while Kylie and Bob Reitzfeld looked on.

I've never felt so bad about arresting anyone. And then something happened that made it even worse. It hit me in the pit of my stomach. Kylie was right. The shooting of Ian Stewart was too big a spectacle to walk out on. And whoever switched the harmless blanks for deadly bullets was in this room right now, silently watching me slap a pair of handcuffs on an innocent man.

Chapter 16

YOU MIGHT THINK that a wide-eyed, su-peralert, extremely talkative person would be an ideal witness to interview. Not when all that hyperactivity is induced by cocaine.

Henry Muhlenberg, the young hotshot director, was useless. Even if we'd missed the dilated pupils and the runny nose, all it took was one question to realize he was too coked up to help.

The question was "Can you tell us what happened?"

"What happened was somebody put real bullets in the gun," he said, talking at race-car speed. "Bang. Edie shoots Ian. He's dead. I'm dead. You know what I mean when I say I'm dead? She might as well have pointed the gun at me, because I'm finished. Over. Kaput."

We couldn't shut him up, so we sat him down and walked out of earshot.

"He wasn't nearly this whacked-out when I first got here," Reitzfeld told us. "He probably decided to get rid of whatever blow he had on him before the cops showed up, and why waste it by flushing it down the toilet?"

"Forget about him," Kylie said. "Here comes the real boss."

Shelley Trager strode through the doors of Studio X. He's that rare breed of producer who's made it big in New York. A scrappy Jewish kid who used his fists growing up in the rough-and-tumble Irish neighborhood of Hell's Kitchen and his brains navigating the ego-driven world of show business.

"The only difference," he's fond of saying, "is that in Hell's Kitchen, they stab you in the front."

He was strikingly handsome in his prime, but now, closing in on sixty, he's fighting a losing battle with both his waistline and his hairline. But time has only improved his reputation. He's one of the acknowledged good guys in the entertainment business, and his company, Noo Yawk Films, has provided jobs for tens of thousands of actors, writers, and production people who would otherwise be waiting on tables.

A longtime friend of the mayor, Trager is one of the biggest supporters of bringing more of LA's film business to the city. And since he owns a piece of Silvercup Studios, what's good for New York is good for Shelley.

"Zach," he said when he saw me.

I met him a year ago when I put away a wacko who was stalking one of his young stars. It came as no surprise that he remembered exactly who I was.

Kylie, of course, knows him personally, but there were no hugs, no air kisses—just a brief exchange of head tilts, and Trager got right down to business.

"How can I help?" he said.

"The armorer says somebody got to the gun and switched the blanks for live ammo," I said. "For starters, we'll need the names of everyone on the set. And I know they're on the clock, but I'll have to ask you not to release anybody till we get statements from every one of them."

"Done," he said immediately. "What else?"

"We're told the shooting was all caught on film," Kylie said. "We need to see it."

He took a little longer on this one. Finally, he said, "Under one condition. NYPD and nobody else. When you're done, I want the footage locked up. God forbid it should show up on YouTube."

"Thank you," Kylie said.

"I heard you arrested Dave West," Shelley said. "Is it really necessary? The poor guy's got a sick wife."

"We had to," I said. "I doubt if the DA will be tough on him, but it would help if he had a lawyer."

"I've already hired one," Shelley said. "Perry Keziah—you know him?"

I nodded. Everybody knew Perry Keziah. He wasn't just a lawyer; he was the best of the best. Dave would be home in time for dinner.

"Excuse me," Trager said.

He walked onto the set and stood over Ian

Stewart's body. Everything else stopped. Nobody on the stage moved. Nobody talked. All eyes were on him.

He lowered his head and mouthed a silent prayer.

Then he walked back and stood face-to-face with Kylie and me.

"This is a tragedy," he said. "But if what they're saying about the death of Sid Roth is true..." He paused, as if speaking the words out loud would make them real. "If what they're saying about the death of Sid Roth is true," he said, dropping his voice to a whisper, "then it's a conspiracy."

Chapter 17

KYLIE AND I stood there and let Trager's words sink in. A major producer is found dead in the morning—probable homicide. An above-the-title actor is shot a few hours later—probable homicide. It's a pretty big coincidence, and homicide detectives don't believe in coincidences.

"I hit a hot button, didn't I?" Trager said.

Kylie stared at him. "What do you mean?"

"You're both lousy poker players. I can tell by looking at the two of you that Sid Roth, who was ten years younger and in ten times better shape than I am, did not suddenly keel

96

over and die of a heart attack on the first day of Hollywood on the Hudson. The rumors are true. He was poisoned, wasn't he?"

"Shelley, you know we can't answer that," Kylie said.

"Fine. The mayor can. I'm the guy who helped him deliver a thousand Hollywood big hitters to New York. I'm the first guy he'll call if he thinks the other nine hundred and ninety-eight are at risk." He took out his cell phone.

"Put it away," Kylie said. "We're waiting for the lab results, but it looks like Sid Roth was poisoned."

"Son of a bitch," Trager said. "Are we talking about a serial killer?"

"Not yet," I said. "There's no pattern. Except for the fact that both men were in show business, there's no link between the two of them. We have to investigate each case separately."

"Which means we have to talk to Edie Coburn," Kylie said.

"Give her a break," Shelley said. "She's in shock."

"That's what happens to people who witness a murder," Kylie said. "We know how to talk to her."

"She's in her trailer," Trager said. "I'll take you there."

Edie Coburn was in a lot less shock than advertised. She was smoking a cigarette and sipping clear liquid out of a tall water tumbler. I doubted it was Evian. Shelley introduced us as Detectives Jordan and MacDonald from NYPD, but he left out the part about his connection to Kylie through Spence Harrington. He told her we had a few questions about the "unfortunate accident."

"I didn't know the gun was loaded," she said. Actually, she didn't just say it. She delivered it. It was like she'd rehearsed the line all afternoon, and the camera started rolling as soon as the cops walked in.

"You know that's a line from a song," Trager said.

She smiled. Of course she knew.

"We're sorry for your loss, Ms. Coburn," I said. "Can you talk about what happened on the set?"

"Let's not pretend," she said. "I was a naughty girl. I held up production all morning because I was furious at Ian. He's a serial adulterer. I ought to know—the first time I slept with him he was married to someone else. So I married him with my eyes wide open. He cheats; I look the other way. But this one was too much. Did he really have to fuck the girl the two of us would be doing a scene with? And worse than that, the bitch told everybody. All proud of herself, like it was some sort of big conquest, like Ian was the Holy Grail."

She took a swig from the tumbler. "I knew how important this scene was to Ian, so I went into my diva act and refused to come out. I decided to let him sweat for a while."

"What motivated you to finally do the scene?" Kylie said.

"Oh, you're cute," Edie said. "You wouldn't ask that question if you didn't already know the answer. The director came to my trailer. Let's just say he's very persuasive. He convinced me." Another gulp from the glass. "Convinced the hell out of me."

"And when you got to the stage, were you still angry at your husband?" Kylie said.

"What do you think?"

"And were you uncomfortable with the fact that a lot of people on the set knew he was having an affair with Devon Whitaker?"

"No, sweetie. I'm uncomfortable when my panty hose ride up. When I walked out on that stage in front of all those gossiping extras, I was mortified. But how I felt and what I did are two different things. The prop guy gave me the gun. I didn't know there were any real bullets in it. If I did, I would have fired the two blanks at Ian and put the entire clip into Devon Whitaker. She's the one who told the cast and crew that she was screwing my husband."

"Thank you for talking with us," I said. "Again, we're sorry for your loss."

"I called Ian's brother Sebastian in London," she said. "They agreed to let us have a memorial service in New York for his fans. Then they want his body sent back home as soon as possible."

"The medical examiner should be finished with the autopsy by tomorrow or Wednesday," I said. "The family can claim his remains after that."

"Thank you," she said, draining what was

left in her glass. "Shelley, would you mind staying after the detectives leave."

Kylie and I took our cue and exited the trailer.

"If we're looking for someone with a motive," I said, "she's got one with a capital M."

"She's a bitch," Kylie said, "but she's innocent. Ian Stewart was a world-class skirt chaser, and Edie knew it. He'd cheated on her before, and she figured he'd cheat on her again. I'm sure she wanted payback, but more on the order of a nice little bauble in a robin's-egg blue Tiffany box, not a dead husband. She didn't do it. She didn't set it up."

"You sure?" I said. "Whatever happened to 'hell hath no fury like a woman scorned'?"

"It doesn't apply here," Kylie said. "A lot of these people sleep around, but in show business, adultery isn't a motive for murder; it's a lifestyle."

Chapter 18

THE CHAMELEON WANTED to scream. It had all been going so well, and suddenly the two detectives had pulled the rug out from under him.

His cell phone vibrated. Another text from Lexi: Ian is a trending topic on Twitter. Congrats. UR242.

He hated all that childish text lingo. He'd mastered ROTFLMAO and a few others, but this was a new one. It took him a while to parse this one out: you are two for two.

He was, but he wasn't happy. He had switched magazines on the SIG Pro—as writ. The armorer gave the loaded gun to Edie Coburn—as writ. Ian Stewart was lying in a pool of blood—as writ.

But the next scene was the one he'd been waiting for all day. It was a turning point in his script.

INT. SOUNDSTAGE—SILVERCUP STUDIOS—DAY

The Chameleon waits his turn as the detectives interview the extras. He knows all about the elite task force they call NYPD Red. He was looking forward to jousting with them. They'd try to trip him up a hundred different ways, but he was ready. They were smart. But he was smarter.

When he wrote the script, The Chameleon had no idea who the lead detectives would be. All he knew was that there would be a dead man on the floor, he was the killer, and he would be standing face-to-face with two of NYPD's smartest cops. Staring them down. Dodging their obvious trick questions. It was great theater.

But it wasn't happening.

The two detectives talked to the whacked-out director, then they walked off with Shelley Trager. *Walked off.* He wanted to scream out at them, *I'm the killer! Grill me. Suspect me. The audience will love it. It's fucking drama, you assholes.*

But no, they simply left the studio—disappeared—leaving him to answer dumb questions from a bunch of unsophisticated, low-level bozos in blue uniforms. They would lump him in with ninety-nine other extras, none of whom were worth two seconds of screen time.

His cell vibrated again. He read the text: **Jonesing 4 ice cream. Bring home sum Rocky Road. Luv u. CU46.**

He smiled. CU46. His favorite text of them all: See you for sex. It would have to be fast. He was only 242. If Lexi paid a little more attention to the script, she'd know that by the end of the day he was planning on being 343.

Chapter 19

"EFFECTIVE IMMEDIATELY, AND until further notice, the entire unit is operating RTC," Captain Cates said. "Repeat—all of NYPD Red is on duty round the clock. You can shower in the gym, and if you insist on getting any sleep, we're setting up cots on the fourth floor."

It was 5:00 p.m., and we were all back in the briefing room. The mood was a lot more somber than it had been nine hours ago.

"Since this morning we've had two high-profile homicides," she said. "Sid Roth, an LA producer in town for Hollywood week, collapsed and died at breakfast at the Regency Hotel. The lab found traces of sodium fluoroacetate in Roth's juice glass, and the ME just confirmed that the same poison was found in much greater quantities in Mr. Roth. We have a primary person of interest—a male, Latino, about thirty, who was dressed as a busboy. That's a vague enough description to start, and because the suspect was in disguise, it's also possible he was using theatrical makeup to cover up the fact that he's white. There were no prints on the carafes that were handled by the suspect, and the only prints on the glass belonged to the victim.

"A few hours after Roth was murdered, Ian Stewart was shot dead at Silvercup Studios with a gun that was supposed to have been loaded with blanks. There were approximately a hundred and fifty people working on that soundstage, any one of whom could have switched the blanks for bullets. For the record, sixty-three of them are women, but I'm not ready to eliminate anyone because of age, race, or gender. Also, there's no guarantee that someone didn't walk in from another part of the lot. So far, statements from the cast and crew taken at Silvercup have added up to one big fat zero. And if you're thinking of how many of those people have restaurant experience, the answer is a hundred of them are film extras—so, all of them.

"Based on what we can pull up so far, there's no obvious connection between Roth and Stewart. They never worked together, but operating on the Six Degrees of Kevin Bacon theory, it's not hard to imagine that somebody worked with each of them and hated them enough to kill them both on the same day.

"There were no signatures linking the two killings, but with two dead bodies on Day One of Hollywood week, I don't care if there's a connection or not. We're acting as if somebody out there is going after these high-profile targets and is not planning on stopping.

"As I said to the mayor just a few minutes ago, there's no way that this unit could have prevented a bogus busboy from slipping poison into someone's juice, or someone on a crowded soundstage from putting real bullets in a prop gun," Cates said. "He didn't like hearing that, but he accepts that it's true. However, we are now on high alert, and we can—we must—prevent any more attacks. There's a major red carpet event at Radio City Music Hall tonight. It's the big celebrity-packed kickoff to Hollywood on the Hudson week. The mayor will be there, the governor will be there, the paparazzi will be there, the fans will be there, and we will be there.

"We were already scheduled to work the event, but now we've been beefed up with re-inforcements. We've got metal detectors and screeners at every door, K-9 will be out there with bomb sniffers, we'll have air coverage, and we'll have another three hundred uni-forms on the streets. Detective Jordan will be in charge of the Command Center on Sixth Avenue. The rest of you will be in plain-clothes working the crowd. Except you, De-tective MacDonald. I want you in not-so-plainclothes working the theater from the inside," Cates said. "I assume you were going to be there anyway."

"Yes, Captain," Kylie said. "My husband and I are invited."

"Good," Cates said. "Then the department doesn't have to spring for a dress. All right, people. There's a madman loose out there. Go find him. Dismissed."

Chapter 20

THE CHAMELEON LAY spread-eagle on top of the crumpled sheet. He had positioned the floor fan at the perfect angle and the perfect speed for a gentle breeze to softly caress his naked body.

He stared up at the ceiling, closed his eyes, and focused on his breathing. He inhaled deeply, exhaled slowly, trying to get his brain to stop ruminating about his upcoming scene. Meditation was not his strong suit.

He was almost there when his cell rattled against the birch veneer of the Ikea night-stand.

He propped himself up on one elbow and reached for the phone. It was a text: **6 wuz gr8. Luv Lexi**.

The sex *had* been great. And when he rolled over exhausted, she hopped out of bed, and padded naked to the kitchen. Leave it to Lexi to take her cell phone so she could text him from twenty feet away.

This is why he adored her. She was smarter than any girl he'd ever known, but she still did wonderfully stupid things like text him from the kitchen to tell him the 6 wuz gr8. He texted her back: **4 me 2. Wherz my ice cream?**

A few seconds later the answer came back: **Scoopin fast as I can.**

He sat all the way up in bed so he could watch her scooping.

Scooping is what she was doing the first day he met her—only it wasn't ice cream. She was selling popcorn at the Paris Theatre, one of the last single-screen movie houses in New York.

"You must be a big Hilary Swank fan," she said, ignoring the prefilled bags and dig-

111

ging deep into a batch of hot, fresh-popped corn.

"Not really," he said.

"This is the third time you've come to see the movie this week," Lexi said. "It can't be the popcorn."

He laughed. "You know the scene in the beginning where the guy at the bar tries to hit on her, and she blows him off? That's me."

"Get out of here," Lexi said. "You're acting in the movie that's playing right here at the Paris? Just for that I'm giving you a medium popcorn and you only have to pay for the small."

"Thanks," he said. He didn't even want the small one. The popcorn sucked, but he kept buying it so he could talk to the popcorn girl.

"One question," she said. "Why do you stay for the whole movie if you're only on in the beginning?"

"My name is in the end credits. 'Jerk at the Bar—Gabe Benoit.' That's me."

"Hey, Gabe, nice to meet you. I'm Lexi Carter—Jerk at the Popcorn Stand."

He stayed and watched the movie two more times until Lexi got off work. Then they walked over to the Carnegie Deli on Seventh Avenue and split one of their foot-high celebrity sandwiches—an artery-clogging, towering pile of corned beef and pastrami called the Woody Allen.

"Wouldn't it be cool if one day you got so famous that they named a sandwich after you?" Lexi said.

"I have a better idea," he said. "They can name half a sandwich after me and the other half after you."

They took the subway downtown to her apartment for coffee.

"I lied," she said as soon as she locked the door. "I don't have any coffee."

"What've you got?" he said.

She peeled off her T-shirt, stepped out of her jeans, and stood there naked.

God, she was gorgeous. Lexi was one of those women who actually looked better naked than she did with clothes on. Thick auburn hair, bottomless blue eyes, and creamy white skin all the way down to her frosted pink toenails.

"You have the most incredible body I've ever seen," he said.

"You're just saying that."

"No, really. I mean it."

"Thanks. Most guys prefer tits the size of volleyballs. Mine work better if you like tennis."

"They're perfect," he said.

"You know what my mom always said—the perfect breast is just big enough to fill a champagne glass."

The next night he bought her a gift. Two Baccarat champagne glasses. Since then, she used them for everything. Diet Coke, M&M's, sunflower seeds—it didn't matter. It was, she told him, the best present she ever got.

Right now the champagne glasses were filled with ice cream. She twirled out of the kitchen, a glass filled with Rocky Road in each hand. She gave him one and plopped down on the bed next to him.

"Go ahead," she said, digging into the ice cream. "Vent."

That was part of their deal. When he got home, the first thing he had to do was share all the best parts of his day with her. She gobbled up all the gloriously horrid details. Then she bubbled over with questions. What was Roth wearing? *Blazer, yellow shirt, no tie.* What did he finally end up ordering for breakfast? *Smoked salmon platter, toasted bagel.* Were there any movie stars at the Regency? *Just me.*

When she finally ran out of questions, they made love. After that Lexi was happy to listen to him bitch and moan about whatever went wrong during the day.

"There were two detectives from NYPD Red," he said. "It's pretty obvious that whoever switched the magazines could still have been right there in the studio. So you'd think they would question me. But no. They just walked off, and I got interviewed by some young Chinese-Japanese-Korean cop."

"Don't be a racist," Lexi said. "It's not nice. They're called Asian."

"I thought Asians were supposed to be smart. This guy was an idiot. He asked me questions like 'Did you go anywhere near the prop table?' It's the same as saying 'Did you put real bullets in the gun so it would kill Ian Stewart?' Of course I'm going to say no.

I think he took one look at me and decided I wasn't even worth the trouble. Like, you're not good enough to be the killer. You're just some extra who sits in the background and mumbles walla-walla-walla all day long for two hundred and twenty-five bucks. You know what, Lex, he's the goddamn racist."

"It doesn't matter," she said. "Tonight you'll show them who the real star is. You're gonna rock. I got your wardrobe and your makeup all ready."

"Thanks."

"Gabe..."

He knew by the way she said his name what was coming next.

"No," he said. "Out of the question. Not this scene. It's too dangerous. You can't come with me."

"Please," she said. "It's no fun sitting around wondering what's going to happen."

"You can watch it on TV," he said. "Just turn on the E! channel and you'll see it all."

"But I want to see it with you."

"Put the DVR on and record it," he said. "When I get home, we can watch it together."

She lowered her head and sulked. "Not as much fun."

He dipped his finger into her champagne glass, scooped out a small dollop of cold creamy chocolate, and rubbed it gently against her left nipple. He leaned into her and slowly, tantalizingly, ran his tongue around her breast until he finally arrived at the sweet chocolate center. He sucked it off and she squirmed.

"I promise you'll get to do a scene, but this one is too chancy," he said.

"You promise I'll get one?"

"I swear."

She kissed him. "You want dinner when you come home?"

"I'll bring back pizza," he said. "All you have to do is wash out those champagne glasses."

"For what?"

"Champagne," he said, kissing her other breast. "Tonight, we'll be drinking champagne."

Chapter 21

KYLIE AND I were in our office on the third floor. And when I say "our office," I mean the flat gray, high-ceilinged half a football field, filled with two long rows of institutional desks, very few partitions, and even less privacy.

Being a cop has its perks, but luxurious accommodations have never been one of them.

"The captain has me on the inside, you on the outside," Kylie said. "Are you okay about splitting up?"

For a second I thought she was kidding, but she wasn't. We were partners, and for

Kylie that meant working as close to each other as possible.

"It makes sense," I said. "We'll be fine."

"I can't believe this is my first day at NYPD Red, and I'm going to work in an evening gown," she said.

"Let's not tell Omar," I said. "I wouldn't want him to get jealous."

"You realize I'm going to have to explain to Spence that I'm wearing a wire," she said. "I can't just talk into thin air."

"Actually, he'll be good cover for you," I said. "You can talk to the Command Center, but it'll look like the two of you are just having a normal conv—"

I heard her heels click-clacking on the tile floor, and then I saw her walking toward my desk. Cheryl Robinson. She saw me see her, and she smiled—second time today, that killer smile that lights up a room, even one as drab as this.

"Hi, Zach," Cheryl said. "This must be your new partner, Detective MacDonald."

She reached out, and the two women shook hands. I don't know why I felt uncomfortable, but I tried not to let it show.

"Cheryl Robinson, department psychologist."

"Kylie MacDonald, NYPD Red probie. I hope you're not here to pick my brain, because it's on serious overload, plus I have to get home and make sure the gown I'm wearing tonight covers my ankle holster."

"I'm guessing you're working the crowd at Radio City," Cheryl said.

"The in crowd," Kylie said. "It was part of my plan for the evening anyway—one of the joys of being the wife of a TV producer. Now I'm getting paid to do it, and if we're lucky, Zach and I will catch our first madman together. Win-win. It's nice to meet you, Cheryl, but I've got to run home and suit up."

"Break a leg," Cheryl said.

We watched Kylie leave. "In case you hadn't noticed," I said, "she loves being a cop."

Cheryl just nodded.

"Come on, Doc, if you're going to make a house call, give me a little more than a head nod."

"I'm off duty," she said. "I just stopped by to see you personally."

"Oh . . . well, here I am." *Still uncomfortable. Still not sure why.*

"When we had coffee this morning, we were both looking at a tough day. I did pretty well with mine. And you helped. I just wanted to say thanks for the advice."

"It was good advice. I wish I'd thought of it myself."

"I know I'm the one who said it, but you're the one who helped me hear it. So thanks."

"Any time."

"I really did stop by just to say thank you," Cheryl said, "but as long as I'm here, how's the new-partner dynamic going?"

"We had two homicides in less than eight hours, so even if I wanted to dwell on the past, I don't have the time."

"I guess there's an upside to everything," Cheryl said. "Maybe that means you'll get a good night's sleep."

"We're on high alert tonight," I said. "The way things are shaping up, I'm not sure if I'll get any sleep."

"In that case," she said, turning on the million-dollar smile, "I'll see you at the diner in the morning."

Chapter 22

NYPD HAS DOZENS of command posts on wheels. The one parked on the corner of 50th Street and Sixth Avenue is the biggest, baddest one in the fleet. It's a joint product of American, British, and Israeli ingenuity— a two-million-dollar, forty-eight-foot-long rolling nerve center affectionately known as Copzilla.

"Hard to believe we need all this hardware to catch one guy," Captain Cates said.

"If it is one guy," I said.

Cates had changed from her civvies to her dress blues and stopped by before heading out to spend the rest of the night within screaming distance of the mayor, who wanted to be—quote—*kept in the goddamned loop every goddamned step of the goddamned way.*

"I just spoke to Mandy Sowter at the Public Information Office," Cates said. "Ian Stewart led the evening news. Mainstream media is still calling it a 'tragic incident that's under investigation,' but the tabloids are hitting hard on the Jealous Wife Shoots Cheating Husband in Front of Hundreds of Witnesses angle."

"Technically, they're both right," I said.

"Sid Roth's autopsy isn't public yet, so most people haven't connected his death with Stewart's. But the bloggers have picked up on TMZ's poison story, and now the social networks are buzzing with serial-killer rumors. You'd think that the threat of a murderer on the loose would keep people as far from the red carpet event as possible, but look at that mob out there."

"Die-hard fans," I said. "If their favorite celebrity is going to get gunned down, they don't want to miss it."

"Even if a couple of stray bullets come their way?" Cates said.

"Like I said, die...hard...fans."

Cates left, and I sat down at the console with Jerry Brainard, a civilian dispatcher who knew every inch of Copzilla's hundreds of miles of microfiber.

"My partner should be in the lobby of the Music Hall," I said. "Can I get a picture?"

Brainard cued up the corresponding camera and zoomed in on Kylie. She was wearing a silky, cream-colored, jaw-dropping gown that hugged her waist, then flared out to the floor—an absolute fashion must for anyone wearing an ankle holster. I had no idea who the designer was, but the handsome guy at her side was definitely Spence Harrington.

I keyed the mic. "Command to Yankee One," I said.

A big smile spread across her face and she shook her head in obvious protest to the code name I'd assigned her. "This is *Yankee* One."

"What are you looking at so far?" I said.

"It's like DEFCON One in here," she said. "There are more cops than Rockettes. So far there have been metal detectors, radiation detectors, and four-legged bomb detectors. If the mayor is looking for security, he's got it."

"And if they gave out awards for best undercover wardrobe, you guys would win. You both look terrific," I said. "How's Spence doing? Is he okay with this?"

"Are you kidding? He does cop shows for a living. Now he feels like he's in one."

"Just make sure he doesn't try to do any of his own stunts," I said. "Command out."

I turned to Brainard. "Pan the crowd," I said.

Our truck is thirteen feet high. There's a camera on the roof that's mounted on a telescoping mast that extends another twenty-seven feet into the air. Brainard did a slow three-sixty of the people below. It was more than just a cursory sweep. The lens on the camera was powerful enough to zoom in on a license plate a city block away.

I studied the faces. Fans hoping to reach out and touch their favorite movie star, paparazzi hoping to get the one picture that the media would pay through the nose for, and cops, in uniform and plainclothes—nearly a hundred strong, working the crowd—New York's Finest doing what they do best.

I had no idea where or how or even if the killer would strike, but sitting behind that console, looking up that wall of monitors, I knew one thing for sure. We were damn ready for him.

Chapter 23

EXT. RADIO CITY MUSIC
HALL—NIGHT

The Chameleon understands the
power of a uniform. Dressed in
blue, badge pinned to his shirt, he
walks past the food carts doing a
brisk business on 51st Street and
works his way to the front of the
crowd on the west side of Sixth
Avenue.

He's twenty years older now,
with a fringe of gray hair sticking

out from under his cap and a neatly trimmed gray goatee. Thick horn-rimmed tortoiseshell glasses, with the lenses tinted amber, and a bulbous prosthetic nose are all he needs to make sure anyone who sees him on the front page of tomorrow's newspaper won't recognize him.

A bored cop, standing in front of the police barrier and wishing he could be home sucking down a beer, sees him. The Chameleon flashes his photo ID. The cop lifts the barrier and waves him through.

The Chameleon gives him a nod and heads for the thirty-foot-high TV camera tower across the avenue from the red carpet.

Let the fun begin.

THE SCENE DIDN'T go exactly as writ. It went better. There were two cops at the barricade, an older white guy and a young Latina woman.

"What's that mean on your ID," she said. "'Best Boy'? You don't look like no boy."

"It's a film term," The Chameleon said. "It means I'm the main assistant to the gaffer—you know, the head electrician."

"Funny," the second cop said. "I always see 'Best Boy' in the credits at the end of a movie. Never knew what it meant."

"Well, next time you see it, you can think of me," The Chameleon said.

"What happens if the main assistant is a woman," the female cop said.

The Chameleon gave her his most charming grin. "Then the head electrician does whatever she tells him."

Big laugh, and the two cops ushered him through the barrier.

The E! channel had set up three TV camera scaffolds—one on 50th Street, one on 51st, and this one on Sixth Avenue, directly across from the theater.

It was dark under the scaffold, and he turned on his flashlight. The ground was a hodgepodge of feeder cables snaking off in different directions, but the transformer where they all met was clearly labeled.

He found the two cables he was looking for and yanked them both.

He couldn't hear over the crowd, but he'd bet that thirty feet above him the TV cameraman was cursing up a storm.

The Chameleon climbed three quarters of the way up the scaffold.

"You having power problems?" he yelled up to the cameraman.

"Yeah. I got no picture. No audio to the booth. No nothing."

"Tranny problem," The Chameleon said. "I can fix it. But I need a third hand. Can I borrow one of yours?"

"Not my union, bucko."

"I just need you to hold the flashlight. I promise I won't report you to the gaffers' union."

"All right, all right," the cameraman said.

He followed The Chameleon down to the bottom of the scaffold.

"Can you get down there and shine the light directly at the fun box," The Chameleon said, pointing at the unit that picked up the power from the generator truck.

The cameraman grunted as he squatted. "Hurry up, I don't have the knees for this kind of sh—"

The blow to the temple was swift and accurate. The cameraman collapsed in a heap. He was out cold, but that wouldn't last long.

"What you need now is a little vitamin K," The Chameleon said, sticking a syringe into the man's right deltoid and injecting him with ketamine. "You have a nice nap. I'll go upstairs and operate the camera," he said, plugging the two cables back into the box and rebooting the audio and video feeds.

He climbed to the top of the scaffold and put on the headset that was dangling from the camera.

"Camera Three," the voice came from the production truck a block away. "Brian, you there?"

"I'm here," The Chameleon said.

"We lost you for a minute there. Everything okay?"

The Chameleon adjusted his E! channel cap and got comfortable behind the camera. "Everything's perfect," he said.

As writ.

Chapter 24

LEXI SAT CROSS-LEGGED on the sofa, el-
bows on knees, chin resting on her open
palms, eyes riveted to the TV screen, not
wanting to miss a single tidbit Ryan Seacrest
might unearth.

She was a full-fledged, card-carrying, dyed-
in-the-wool Celebrity Junkie, and she didn't
care who knew it. They were glamorous, they
were hideous, they were superstars, they
were flaming assholes—it didn't matter, she
couldn't get enough of them. Even the ones
she hated. Even the ones she wanted to kill.

The cheese platter was sitting on the coffee

table, the Saran Wrap still on. She had brought out the two champagne glasses and filled hers with Bud Light. The bubbly was definitely staying on ice till Gabe got home.

The cell phone between her legs vibrated, and she grabbed it.

The text made her giddy: **Greetings from Camera 3. DTB. Luv, G**

DTB. Don't text back. God knows she wanted to, but this was Gabe's biggest scene yet. Not fair to distract him.

She sipped her beer and watched Ryan joke around with all the celebs as their limos pulled up to the red carpet. It had to be the most awesome job in the world. Plus he got paid zillions.

"I'd do it for free, Ryan," she said to the screen. "Hell, I'd even pay you to let me do it."

She was born and raised in Indiana. Her family was still there. But she was a New Yorker now, so she really loved it when all the big stars said how fantastic it was to shoot movies and TV shows in New York City. That's what this whole Hollywood on the Hudson thing was about. So, yeah, maybe they got paid to say stuff like that, but as far as she was concerned, it wasn't hype. New York was the best.

"Look out, world," Seacrest said to his audience. "Here comes the most-talked-about, most-written-about, most-tweeted-about bad boy in all of Hollywood. You know who I'm talking about, don't you? It's Braaaaaaaaaaaad Schuck."

The picture cut away from Seacrest to a remote camera at street level. A stretch Hummer, blowing its horn, made its way slowly up Sixth Avenue. The moonroof was wide open, and standing on the backseat, half in, half out of the car, was Brad Schuck.

To toast the crowd, he raised a bottle of the vodka he was famous for hawking, tipped it to the sky, and guzzled down four long swallows. The fans howled.

The camera stayed on Schuck while Seacrest gave a running commentary. "I'll ask him when he gets here, but knowing Brad Schuck, I'm going to bet five bucks that wasn't water," he said. "Wait a minute, he's handing the bottle to someone in the limo."

Schuck lowered the vodka, ducked down,

and came up a second later with a two-foot-long tube.

"Oh, man!" Seacrest yelled off camera. "It's a bleacher reacher. Bad Brad has a T-shirt cannon, and since he's wearing one of his signature GET SCHUCKED T-shirts, I think we all know what he's going to be shooting into the crowd."

Whoomp. The first T-shirt launched into the air, and the people behind the barrier went berserk scrambling for the souvenir.

Then the Hummer made an S-turn from one side of the street to the other and Schuck fired again.

"The mayor invited everyone to shoot in New York," Seacrest said, laughing, "and crazy Brad is doing just that. Let's watch."

Lexi knew what was coming next. She was off the sofa now, jumping up and down, clapping her hands, her head spinning with excitement.

"Oh, God!" she screamed. "I heart New York."

Chapter 25

"I GUESS EVERYTHING they say about this Schuck character being a raving lunatic is true," Jerry Brainard said.

He had thrown the feed from the E! channel onto the large center monitor and, along with a few million other viewers, we watched Brad Schuck fire T-shirts at the adoring multitude.

"You going to arrest him?" Jerry asked.

"Arrest him? It's more likely the mayor will invite him to lunch at Gracie Mansion," I said. "The first thing you learn at NYPD Red is that there's a time and a place to crack down on celebrity bad-boy antics. Radio City in front of thousands of doting fans is not the place, and the week that the mayor is trying to encourage assholes like Schuck to shoot more movies in New York is definitely not the time. Besides, those T-shirt missiles are harmless enough. They're only made of cott—"

The back door of the Command Center flew open and a uniformed cop struggled up the steps, trying to hold up a dazed, incoherent civilian. Brainard helped them both in, and the cop lowered the civilian gently to the floor.

"I found this guy under the TV camera scaffold," he said. "I smelled his breath. He's not drunk. Judging by the bruise on the side of his head, I think somebody coldcocked him. I called for an ambulance."

The man on the ground had the E! channel logo on his blue shirt. The badge on his breast pocket had turned around, and I flipped it over.

"Oh shit," I said. "Jerry, get back to the board."

"You know him?" Brainard said, scrambling back to his chair.

"No. Never saw him before in my life. But he's with E! TV, and his badge says 'Cameraman.'"

"So?"

I've been playing chess since I was seven years old. Somewhere along the way I learned how to think three, four, five moves ahead. But I didn't have time to explain to Jerry where I was going.

"Just give me the mast camera, and zoom in on those E! channel camera scaffolds," I said.

Jerry panned over to the 50th Street scaffold and zoomed in on the camera at the top.

"Looks normal," I said. "Next one."

I turned to the cop in uniform. "Where did you find him? Under what scaffold?"

"Sixth Avenue."

Jerry was already panning over to the scaffold on 51st Street.

"Forget that one!" I yelled. "Give me the guy in the center. Sixth Avenue."

Jerry leaned on the toggle switch and the camera slowly started to creep back in the opposite direction. It was agonizing, like watching someone park a battleship.

"Zoom in on the cameraman," I said.

Jerry brought the man sharply into focus. For a few seconds it all looked perfectly normal, and I was starting to doubt my instincts. And then the cameraman stepped away from the camera.

"Pull back!" I yelled. "Track him, track him!"

The cameraman moved to the edge of the scaffold. He had something in his right hand. He pulled his arm back, like he was about to throw a Hail Mary pass.

"It's glass," Brainard said, zooming in on the man's hand. "A bottle, I think."

And then he let it fly. The camera tracked the bottle perfectly as it arced through the air over Sixth Avenue.

I didn't have to be a chess player to know what was going to happen next.

The Molotov cocktail hit the roof of Brad Schuck's Hummer and exploded on impact. The screen lit up bright orange, and Brainard pulled back to get a wider picture.

"This is Command," I said into the mic. "I need every available unit to the camera scaffold on Sixth Avenue between Five Zero and

Five One. There's a white male, fifty to sixty years old, wearing a blue E! channel uniform. He's our bomb thrower. Stop him. He's probably coming down the north side of the tower. I can't see him from here."

I stood up and watched what I could see. Brad Schuck, in flames, frantically crawling onto the roof of his scorched limo.

He rolled off the car onto the road, got up, and stumbled, screaming, toward the theater, globs of flaming napalm flying off his body.

Just before he could rush headlong into Ryan Seacrest and the horrified crowd under the marquee, Schuck blessedly lost consciousness and collapsed in a smoldering heap on the red carpet.

Chapter 26

ONE SECOND I was staring at the guy who torched Brad Schuck, and the next he was gone.

"We lost him," I said. "He knows where our camera is, and he's climbing down the back side of the scaffold."

I'd never worked with Jerry Brainard before, but the man was a total pro. Unflappable. Grace under fire.

"Of course he knows where *that* camera is. It's twenty-seven feet high and pointing right at him," Brainard said. "But I wonder if he knows about this one."

His fingers worked the console, the picture changed, and suddenly there was our bomber, climbing down the opposite side of the camera tower.

"Traffic cam," Brainard said. "I preset every one in a six-block radius before we started. Just in case."

Jerry was good, but the guy we were after wasn't stupid. He had to know we'd pick him up with another camera soon enough. As soon as his feet touched the ground, I understood why he needed to be off camera, even if for just a few seconds.

In one swift, almost invisible move his distinctive blue E! channel shirt was transformed into a red, orange, and gold tie-dyed T.

"Velcro," Brainard said. "Pretty slick."

I grabbed the mic. "Command to all units. Suspect is on the ground and on the run. He's removed the E! channel uniform and is now wearing jeans and a red, orange, and gold tie-dyed sixties-type T-shirt. He's in front of the Time-Life Building and headed for West Five One Street."

You might think that with more than a hundred cops blanketing the area we'd have no problem grabbing one man. But it wasn't that easy. Most of our guys had been stationed in front of the barricades, and they had to work their way back through the crowd.

Under normal circumstances, a bunch of New Yorkers might begrudgingly get out of the way if a cop yelled "Coming through, coming through!" But tonight, the circumstances were far from normal. As soon as the Molotov cocktail hit, people stampeded for safety. To make matters worse, they didn't all agree on which direction was safe. It was every man for himself, and they pushed, shoved, and elbowed frantically, not caring if the person they bowled over was a pregnant woman or a cop chasing a lunatic.

Several of our uniforms broke through the crowd and made their way toward 51st Street.

"He doesn't have a prayer," Brainard said.

Then our screen went purple.

"Shit—he tossed a smoke bomb," Brainard said.

The smoke screen wouldn't win any special effects awards, but it worked.

Brainard pulled back to a wide shot.

"There he is," I said.

Tie-Dye was heading for the maze of food carts that had taken over the south side of 51st Street.

"Sir, we've got a bird's-eye view, but our guys at street level can't see two feet in front of them."

"But they can look up," I said, keying the mic.

"Suspect is in the row of food carts on Five One," I said. "He's between a yellow-and-blue Sabrett hot dog umbrella and a red-and-white that says 'Falafel.'"

The smoke was settling quickly, and I could see several of our uniforms aggressively pushing their way through the mob toward the target umbrellas.

The cop in the lead was ten feet away when it happened.

A motorcycle came roaring out from between the two carts and headed east on 51st Street.

"Damn," Brainard said. "This guy is good."

"Not as good as we are. We got him now. Command to all units," I said into the mic. "I need a total lockdown on all vehicular traffic, Forty-second to Fifty-seventh Streets. Ninth Avenue to Third. Suspect is on a bright green Kawasaki Ninja rice rocket."

The man on the motorcycle made a rubber-burning right turn and headed the wrong way on Sixth Avenue. The Ninja was at full throttle and was making a beeline for the flaming limo.

"Look at that crazy bastard," Brainard said. "Where the hell is he going?"

"It doesn't matter," I said. "The entire grid is locked up tight. It's impossible for him to get away."

And then, right before my very eyes, the son of a bitch did the impossible.

Chapter 27

STANDING THERE ON the scaffold with the Molotov in his hand, Gabriel the director gave a last-minute pep talk to Gabriel the star.

"This is the money shot. You only get one take, but you can do it. You've done it a thousand times."

Gabriel the actor rolled his eyes. A thousand? He'd gotten it right only six times. Six out of thirty-two. Tossing a flaming bottle onto a moving car isn't as easy as people think. Lexi had rehearsed him, but without the fire. And instead of a car, they had used a shopping cart they took from the parking lot at Pathmark.

He thought he could use some more practice, but she said, "No, you never want to over-rehearse."

They had made the napalm at home. It was ridiculously easy. Just mix gasoline with Styrofoam and put it in a glass bottle.

Lexi, of course, had to complicate it.

"Add some vodka," she said.

"What'll that do?"

"Probably nothing. It's just a little cinematic symbolism. Brad Schuck—vodka—get it?"

What the hell. He added a shot of Stoli.

And now it was showtime. The Hummer came rolling up Sixth Avenue.

"And action," the director called out.

As soon as the bottle left his hand, he knew that the thirty-third time was the charm. Perfect throw, perfect arc, perfect landing.

The explosion was louder, brighter, and more spectacular than he expected. He only wished he had time to stay and enjoy Brad Schuck's final performance, but he'd see it all on video tonight.

Scrambling down the scaffold, The Chameleon morphed from bland blue to brightly colored tie-dye, and bolted for the Kawasaki.

The smoke bomb was Lexi's idea. They had argued about the color. He thought red smoke would stick it to the NYPD Red cops. But she reminded him that there's also NYPD blue.

"Red plus blue equals purple," she said. "Perfect way to stick it to them both."

Never argue Lexi logic. It didn't matter. He was just glad she came up with the idea, because as it turned out the smoke saved his ass.

The Chameleon knew all the great movie motorcycle scenes—Schwarzenegger on the Harley Fat Boy in *Terminator 2*, McQueen on the Triumph TR6 in *The Great Escape*, and now yours truly on the Kawasaki Ninja.

He jumped on the cow, pinned the throttle, and peeled out. Most of the cops had moved to the inside of the barricade to try to control the freaked-out civilians, so it was clear sailing as he tore down Sixth Avenue.

He didn't have much time. It was only a

matter of seconds before they locked up Midtown, river to river.

At 48th Street he stood up, took his weight off the front wheel, and headed for the one place they wouldn't think to seal off.

Underground.

He pointed the bike at the entrance to the D train and barreled down the stairs.

Most subway stations would be a dead end, but the Rockefeller family had been thoughtful enough to build a twenty-acre concourse underneath their vast complex of skyscrapers. Lined with shops, restaurants, and art galleries, it connected all the office buildings from Fifth Avenue to Sixth, from 48th Street to 51st.

It was a magnet for tourists, a year-round temperature-controlled transportation hub for commuters, and of course an ingenious escape route for a man on a motorcycle trying to outwit the police.

There were no cops down here. Just wide-eyed sightseers who smiled when they saw the Kawasaki cruising slowly along the marble corridors, and jaded New Yorkers who clearly didn't give a shit.

INT. UNDERGROUND CONCOURSE AT ROCKEFELLER CENTER—NIGHT

The Chameleon pulls the bike into a blind corner behind Value Drugs and covers it with a tarp. They'll find it eventually, but there's no way to trace it back to him. The plates are stolen, and the ID numbers have been acid-washed off.

Next stop: the men's room at Starbucks. He emerges two minutes later, a shaggy-haired college kid wearing Harry Potter glasses and a T-shirt that says SAVE THE PLANET. IT'S THE ONLY ONE WITH BEER.

He walks to the subway entrance, swipes his MetroCard, and steps out onto the platform just as a downtown D train pulls in. It's crowded and he squeezes in with the rest of the straphangers—just another New Yorker headed home after a busy day.

It all went smoothly except for the train. It wasn't pulling in when he got to the station. It never is. He walked casually toward the far end of the platform checking out his fellow travelers.

And then he saw her.

Hilary Swank.

Not the real Hilary. It was a poster for her latest film.

He walked up to it.

"Hey, Hilary," he said. "Remember me? The jerk at the bar? Not anymore, baby."

Not. Any. More.

Chapter 28

THE COMMAND CENTER was crammed to capacity, including Kylie, Cates, the commissioner, the mayor, and Irwin Diamond, the deputy mayor in charge of damage control.

"I invite half of Hollywood to visit the fine film production facilities of New York City," His Honor said, "and on Day One we've got two dead and another one circling the drain? How is that possible?"

Like Reitzfeld had said earlier at Silvercup, shit floats up. The commissioner fielded the question. "This guy is good, sir. He's a master of disguise, he knows how to blend in, he's planned every killing, including his exit strategy, and he's got balls the size of Brooklyn. We had a hundred cops looking for him, and he sweet-talked his way right into the middle of them, and rode out on a Kawasaki."

"And in case you missed it on the West Coast, it'll be on the news at eleven, and on YouTube forever." The mayor pounded his fist on the console. "What's his goddamn motive? Why is he doing this to us? To me?"

Kylie, never afraid to speak, spoke. "He works in the business, sir. He's obviously got some kind of a grudge."

"A *grudge?* No, Detective," the mayor said. "A grudge you take to the union. This guy is a madman, and his mission is to single-handedly put New York City out of the film business." He turned to his deputy mayor. "Where do you net out on this shitstorm, Irwin?"

Diamond was much older than his boss. In fact, he was the oldest of all the mayor's advisers. Those who knew him said he was also the wisest. And those who saw him in action said the calmest.

"Actually, Stan," Diamond said, "I think Detective MacDonald is right. Whoever is doing this does have a grudge. If you don't like the word 'grudge,' call it a 'major hard-on.' But he's not angry at New York. He's fed up with the entire *fakakta* Hollywood system. And there's nobody he can bitch to because nobody did anything wrong to him. All they did was ignore him. Reject him. And now he's getting revenge."

Heads nodded. It made sense.

The commissioner jumped in. "Irwin is right, sir. This guy is a loser who's been chewed up and spit out by the whole ugly LA film business. He's only using New York as his venue because we happened to conveniently gather a lot of primo targets in a small space in a short time. But this is all about Hollywood."

The mayor pressed his fingertips to his temples and weighed the input. "So our position with the press is that a madman followed these Hollywood people to New York? What's that supposed to mean? It's not our fault? It won't fly, Ben. People got killed on our watch."

The commissioner didn't respond. Diamond held up his hand. "Stan, people die in hospitals all the time. Is that the hospital's fault? Would they have survived if they stayed at home?"

"Don't get all Talmudic on me, Irwin," the mayor said. "No matter how you serve it up, NYPD is going to get skewered in the press—especially by the *LA Times* and all those Hollywood rags. Don't quote me, but the best thing that can happen is this lunatic follows them back to California, offs a few more of them, and by next week this time the LA cops are taking the heat."

"That's not going to happen, sir." It was Kylie.

"You're saying he's not going to bother following them back to LA?" the mayor said. "Why? Because he only likes killing people in New York?"

"No, sir," Kylie said. "He's not going to LA because we're going to catch him before he ever leaves town."

And just like that, my new partner, on her first day on the job, promised the mayor of New York that in less than seventy-two hours, we would track down and capture the worst serial killer to terrorize this city since the Son of Sam.

Irwin Diamond laughed warmly and gave Kylie a thumbs-up. "Talk about balls the size of Brooklyn," he said.

Chapter 29

FIRST THEY WATCHED the video, ate the pizza, and drank the champagne. All of it. Then they made love—gentle, sweet, innocent—more like teenagers exploring the mysteries of sex than a pair of cold-blooded serial killers.

When it was over, they lay naked in each other's arms and played their favorite game. Acting out the worst cliché-ridden movie scenes they could invent.

"Oh, Professor Cunningham," Lexi said in her thickest southern drawl. "Ours is a forbidden love. Whatever shall we do if we get caught?"

"We shan't get caught, my Fair One," Gabriel said with mock British earnestness. "Unless…"

"Unless what, my darling?" Lexi pleaded. "Unless what?"

"Unless I'm dumb enough to give you an A in Eighteenth-century Lit. People see that— they'll figure the old prof must be shagging young Pamela Ward."

They laughed their asses off, filled their champagne glasses with beer, unmuted the TV, and surfed the news channels.

"Holy shit," Gabriel said. "CBS, NBC, ABC, Fox, CNN—it's all us all the time. Let's see if we're on ESPN."

"Wait, wait, the mayor is coming on," Lexi said.

They were tuned to ABC *Eyewitness News,* and the director cut away from the anchor to a shot of the mayor standing at a podium in front of the NYPD command post. The police commissioner stood to his right.

"Who's that behind them?" Lexi said.

"Those are the two cops from Silvercup. He's Detective Jordan and she's Detective MacDonald. They're the ones who ignored me. I don't know the black chick in the uniform. I think she could be one of their bosses."

"Detective MacDonald looks like she's kind of a bitch, but Detective Jordan, he's kind of cute," Lexi said.

"Shh," he said. "You wanna hear the mayor or not?"

"A vicious and violent crime was committed on the streets of our city tonight," the mayor said, "and our hearts go out to Brad Schuck's family and fans. Mr. Schuck is in a coma at the Burn Center of New York Hospital, and I have no further news on his condition other than that it is critical."

"Mr. Mayor!" a reporter shouted.

"Let me finish," the mayor snapped. "NYPD has mounted its most elite task force to track down the person or persons responsible for this hideous crime, and we in New York are saddened not only by the injuries inflicted on Mr. Schuck, but because this has marred what should have been a celebratory event tonight here at Radio City, where New York has opened its heart and its doors to the Hollywood filmmaking industry."

"What a crock of shit," Gabe said.

"Let me assure our colleagues from Los Angeles," the mayor continued, "that while this may well be a hate crime targeted at the Hollywood community, it happened here on our watch, and the city of New York and the NYPD will not rest until the perpetrators are brought to justice. Thank you."

He started to walk off camera.

"Mr. Mayor, Mr. Mayor!" a chorus of reporters called out.

"Now is not the time for questions," the mayor said.

"Is this connected to this afternoon's shooting of Ian Stewart and the sudden suspicious death of producer Sid Roth this morning?"

The mayor stopped in his tracks, said something in private to the police commissioner, and returned to the podium. "NYPD is in the middle of a criminal investigation. We can't elaborate on what we've learned so far, and we can't speculate about whether any of the incidents you cited are in any way connected to the brutal attack on Mr. Schuck. But the commissioner has assured me that the department is working around the clock to prevent any further violence and to bring about a swift conclusion to this tragedy. Right now, I think that instead of speculating, we all should pray for Brad Schuck to recover from this horrible ordeal. No more questions. Thank you and good night."

This time, the mayor walked off and the entourage followed.

The station cut back to the anchorman, and Lexi muted the TV. "Shall we pray for Brad Schuck to recover from this horrible ordeal?" she said.

"I don't pray when I'm naked," Gabe said, rolling over on his back.

She straddled him, lowering herself gradually, and moaned as she felt him slide inside of her.

He thrust his pelvis upward, and she arched her back. The pace was slow at first, unhurried, but as they moved in perfect rhythm together, the passion built. She cried out his name, and he reached around and dug his fingers into her buttocks.

They were both seconds away from an explosive climax when the phone rang.

It jolted him to the core.

"Don't stop, don't stop," she said.

But he did stop.

The phone rang again.

It was after midnight. Nobody called them this late. The agency called when they had a job for him as an extra, but never after five or six in the evening.

The phone rang a third time, and he picked it up.

"Hello, who's this?"

"This is a fan of yours," the voice on the other end said. "I just watched the mayor's press conference. Congratulations."

"Congratulations on what?"

"Come on, Gabe. I know you're behind all this."

He sat up, the passion completely gone. Lexi flopped off of him and sat cross-legged on the bed trying to figure out what was happening.

"Behind all what?" he said.

"Cut the shit," the caller said. "If Roth and Ian Stewart didn't tip me off, the Molotov cocktail sure did."

The Chameleon could feel his chest constricting and panic welling up in his throat.

This was not in the script.

BOOK TWO

MAJOR REWRITE

Chapter 30

THE CHAMELEON CLOSED his eyes and tried to home in on the voice on the other end of the phone.

"Who is this?" he said.

A raspy laugh. "An old war buddy."

"This is a new number. None of my old crowd has it."

"We got friends in common, Gabriel. Some of them still work at Silvercup. Your name was on the call sheet for the Ian Stewart movie today. I guess you saw that terrible tragedy unfold before your very eyes." Another laugh, even raspier.

The neurons in The Chameleon's brain were going off like a string of cheap Chinese firecrackers, and one of them zeroed in on the grating laugh. "Mickey?" The Chameleon said. "Is that you?"

"I'm happy to say it is, but you, on the other hand, don't sound too overjoyed to hear from me."

"Mick," The Chameleon said. "It's after midnight. My girlfriend and I were just—"

"Just what? Watching TV? Catching up on the news of the day?"

"We were asleep. What do you want?"

"Nothing we can talk about over the phone," Mickey said.

"Last I heard you were on an extended vacation up in the Adirondacks. It's six hours away, but if you tell me when visiting hours are, maybe I can take a run up there."

"They gave me time off for being a model vacationer. I got back into town last week. Remember where my old loft was?"

"Yeah. Long Island City. Skillman Avenue. The scenic part."

Another annoying laugh. "Scenic. I like that. Why don't you come over and we can sit on the veranda, have coffee, and watch the sun rise over the freight yard."

"Screw the sunrise, Mickey," The Chameleon said. "I'll be there in an hour."

He hung up and started getting dressed.

Lexi didn't move from the bed. "What was that all about?" she asked.

"Production snag. It goes with the territory."

"Bullshit," she barked. "Listen—if you don't want me to show up on location at Radio City and watch the pyrotechnics, fine. I can live with that. But if you'd rather go to Long Island City in the middle of the night than fuck, you damn well better tell me why. I'm not the girl at the popcorn counter anymore, Gabe. We're either in this together, or you're in it by yourself."

He sat down on the bed. "Sorry, Lex. You're a worrier, and I was trying to spare you."

"Don't. Don't ever. Now tell me what's going on?"

"Did I ever tell you about Mickey Peltz?"

"No."

"He was one of the best special effects guys in the business—especially with explosives.

He was good at blowing things up, but he cut corners so he could siphon off some of the production budget and put it in his pocket. One day he's working on a bank heist movie and they needed to blow up an armored car. Mickey was in charge of the blast, and he decided to buy some bargain-basement crap that was cheap and volatile instead of expensive and stable. A bomb went off prematurely, a stuntman lost an arm, and Mickey pulled four years at the Adirondack Correctional Facility up in Ray Brook."

"And?"

"And it looks like he got out early, saw the Molotov on TV, and knew it was me."

"How is that possible?"

"The one I tossed was wickless," The Chameleon said. "Only a handful of guys in the business do it that way. It was one of Mickey's signature effects. He taught me how to make it, and I guess he put two and two together."

"So what does he want from you?" Lexi said. "A screen credit?"

"My guess? He wants a few bucks, and he'll promise to keep his theories to himself."

"Blackmail."

"He didn't use that word, but that's where my brain went."

"And it won't just be a few bucks, will it?" she said.

"Blackmailers have delusions, so I guess his starting price will be somewhere between ridiculous and out of his fucking mind."

"I have one more question," Lexi said.

"And I already have the answer. No, you can't go. But you knew that before you even asked."

She hopped off the bed and wrapped her arms around him. She was still naked. The fading scent of their lovemaking still hung in the air. He draped his arms over her shoulders and pressed her close.

"You're a glass-half-empty person," she said. "I'm a glass-half-full."

"Understatement," he said, planting a kiss on the back of her neck. "You're a glass-overflowing person. What's your point?"

"This is the best thing that could have happened to us," she said. "Your little trip to Mickey's loft could be an incredible scene. It's another twist. Even we didn't expect it, and we wrote the script."

As soon as she said it, he knew she was right.

"This is why I love you," he said. "I can't believe I didn't see it right away, but you nailed it. Let's go write the scene."

"You and me?" she said.

"Who else would I write it with?" he said, pressing her to his chest and kissing her hair, her nose, her lips. "We're a team, aren't we?"

Chapter 31

WE FINALLY HAD something solid to go on. Photos of our killer. We sent Ellen Dobrin and Jason Garza, two bilingual detectives, out to the Bronx to wake up Rafe, the waiter from the Regency Hotel.

They showed him the picture of the fake E! channel cameraman and asked if it reminded him at all of the busboy from that morning.

"This is an old white guy," Rafe said. "I told them other cops that the busboy was a young Latino."

"Yes, sir," Dobrin said. "But imagine that this is a disguise. Let's say the white hair is a wig. Now imagine that the busboy was also wearing a disguise. Do you see any similarities between the two of them—you know, like height, build, bone structure?"

Rafe took another look at the photo. "They's both dudes," he said, hoping to be helpful.

Dobrin sent me a text. **We got nada. Nuance no es Rafe's strong suit.**

Then Matt Smith, our techie, put the bomber's picture through facial recognition software. Even with a disguise, it's not easy for a person to change the distance between his eyes, the depth of his sockets, the shape of his cheekbones, or eighty other distinct facial landmarks.

We collected headshots of every extra and every crew member on the set of Ian Stewart's movie. We also had a second batch of pictures of random people lifted off the Internet that we used as a control group. The software then uses some magic algorithm and compares each face to our perp.

"If this were the third act of *CSI: Miami*, the computer would spit out the one guy who's a match," Kylie said.

But real police work is nothing like TV. The computer picked out twenty-three possibles. Eleven extras, including two women, three crew members, and nine from the control group, including Leonardo DiCaprio.

"This whole facial recognition thing isn't nearly as foolproof as people might think," Smith said.

"Even so," Kylie said, "let's go pay Leo a visit and see if he has an alibi."

I finally got to sleep at 2:00.

At 4:15, my cell phone rang. I hit the light and looked at the caller ID. It was Kylie.

"This better be good, K-Mac," I said.

"This isn't K-Mac," the voice on the other end said. "It's Spence. I guess with a name like Spence Harrington, I can't have a cool street name like K-Mac. Maybe Spenning-ton."

"Is Kylie okay?" I said.

"Yeah, she's exhausted and I hated to wake her. Me, I'm a night owl. This is when I do my best thinking. I found your number in her cell, so I figured I'd give you a ring while it's still fresh in my mind. Maybe kick it around. Just you and me, guy to guy."

I was half-awake now, but I still had no idea what he was talking about. "Okay, what is it?" I said.

"You know I'm not a cop, right?"

I grunted in the affirmative.

"But I make a damn good living producing cop shows on TV," he said, "and I have an idea I want to bounce off you."

"An idea for a TV show?"

"God, no, Zach. About these murders. You should have invited me into that powwow with the mayor. I might have come up with it earlier, but I was outside with the rest of the civilians."

"Spence, I'm sorry you had to stay outside, but—"

"Don't worry about it. Kylie explained. Anyway, you want to hear my theory?"

Did I have a choice?

"Sure," I said.

"Now, I'm just pitching," he said, "but listen to this. New York is trying to attract LA production money. They invite all these Hollywood wheeler-dealers to fly in, and suddenly they're being bumped off. Who benefits from these murders?"

I was working on two hours sleep. Even if there were an intelligent answer, I wouldn't have come up with it.

"I give up, Spence. Who benefits?"

"The City of Angels. Los freakin' Angeles, California."

"I'm not sure I follow," I said.

"Making movies and TV shows is LA's bread and butter," he said. "They don't want to lose a crumb of it to New York, so they're trying to prove that New York is not a safe town for moviemakers. And listen to this—it's working already. Shelley Trager is having a blowout party on his yacht Wednesday. It's the premiere screening of my new TV show, and let me tell you it's the must-have invite of the whole week. As of tonight, six people canceled. They said they had to fly back to LA. They're full of shit. They're afraid of New York, and they're running back home to Mama. I know it sounds far-fetched, but all great plots have these kinds of quirky hooks to them. Look at *Lost*—it was off-the-wall crazy, but it ran six seasons. Like I said, I'm just tossing out an idea here. What do you think?"

"Spence, I don't think a city—even one with a good motive—could be behind these killings," I said. "Some person has to be behind it all. Have you narrowed it down to a human suspect?"

"No. That's your job. You and K-Mac," he said. "The obvious places to start are the California Film Commission, the LA Chamber of Commerce—hell, it might go all the way up to city hall."

"That's an intriguing thought, Spence," I said. *For a TV show, maybe. But hard to believe in real life that the mayor of Los Angeles would put a contract out on three people in New York.*

I thanked him, promised I'd talk to Kylie about it in the morning, and hung up. Thirty minutes later, I was still wide awake. Maybe because I was running all the events of the past twenty-four hours through my shit sorter. Maybe because I was trying to make sense of Spennington's phone call.

Or maybe because I knew Cheryl Robinson was probably already at the diner on her second cup of coffee.

Chapter 32

ALT. SCENE:

INT. MICKEY PELTZ'S
LOFT—LONG ISLAND
CITY—NIGHT

The Chameleon enters. He seems genuinely happy to see MICKEY. They talk about the old days, about prison life, and finally Peltz gets to the point. He never says blackmail. He calls it "hush money"—a little something to help him get back on his feet. The Chameleon says he can pay part now and have the rest in a day. He reaches into his pocket for the money, pulls out a gun, and shoots Mickey between the eyes.

EXT. MICKEY PELTZ'S LOFT—LONG ISLAND CITY—NIGHT

The Chameleon is across the street from Mickey's building. Suddenly the dark, quiet street lights up as the explosion blows out the windows, destroying the loft, and cremating everything in it.

"ARE YOU SURE he'll have something you can use to blow the place up?" Lexi had asked when they finished.

Gabe shrugged. "He just got out of prison. He may not even have a quart of milk in the fridge."

"Maybe you should just shoot him the second he opens the door."

"No," Gabe said. "I have to make sure he didn't tell anyone. Mickey's a nonstop talker. That's how I met him. We were shooting some piece-of-crap terrorist-on-an-airplane movie. I was a passenger and Mickey had to blow off the cockpit doors. I asked if I could watch him set up, and before you know it, Mick is giving me a short course in special effects. I figured this guy is a gold mine of tech stuff I can use one day, and I struck up a friendship. By the time he went off to prison, I kind of liked the old guy. It'll be nice to catch up with him."

"Catch up. Find out what he knows. Then kill him," Lexi said.

"Looks like you've been reading the script."

Gabe took the number 7 train to Flushing, got off at 33rd Street, and walked to Skillman Avenue. He was glad he had a gun. A guy could get rolled in a neighborhood like this.

Nothing had changed since he had last been here. He wondered how Mickey managed to keep the place the whole time he was in jail. He'd have to ask him during the nice-to-see-you-again part of the conversation.

He rang the bell and identified himself over the intercom. Mickey buzzed him in.

The ground floor reeked of garbage and piss. He waited for Mickey to send the elevator down, then rode it up to the fifth floor, patting the compact Walther PPK tucked into the pocket of his windbreaker.

The door to the elevator opened directly into the loft, and Gabe walked in.

"Hey, I'm over here at my workbench," Mickey called out from the opposite end of the space, forty feet away.

Gabe crossed the length of the room. Peltz was sitting on a wooden stool. He had aged at least ten years in the past four. His shoulders were stooped, and his hair and skin were both ashy gray.

"One thing's for sure. You didn't get too much sun," Gabe said.

"Grab a seat," Mickey said. "This is cool. You really got to see this."

There was only one place to sit—a threadbare old armchair—and Gabe lowered himself into it and sat back. "What's so cool that I got to see?"

"This," Mickey said, holding up a chrome cylinder about the size of a penlight. "It's a pressure-release trigger. Watch what happens when I click it." He pressed the silver button at the top of the cylinder and held it in place with his thumb.

"Nothing," Gabe said. "Nothing happened."

"Exactly. But guess what happens when I lift my thumb off the button?"

Gabe didn't have to guess. He knew. He started to stand.

"Don't move," Mickey said. "The seat cushion is lined with C4. The instant I release this button, your ass will be blown to kingdom come."

Chapter 33

"MICK, ARE YOU serious?" Gabe said.

Mickey sat motionless. "Serious as a body bag."

"What the hell is going on? Why would you want to blow me up?"

"I don't *want* to blow you up," Peltz said. "I'd rather talk business."

"No problem," Gabe said. "Talk."

"First, get rid of the gun. Wherever it is, reach for it, and set it down on the floor. If you shoot me, you're dead a half second after I am."

"Okay, relax," Gabe said. "I mean, *don't*

relax. Just keep pressing hard on that button."

He reached inside his windbreaker pocket, took out the Walther, and slid it across the floor. Peltz picked it up and put it on top of his workbench.

"We good?" Gabe said.

"So far."

"Okay, so talk business."

"I didn't call you so I could blackmail you, Gabe. That's what you're thinking, but that's not my style."

The Chameleon just nodded.

"I got a memory like a steel trap," Peltz said. "Eight years ago we did a bunch of *Sopranos* episodes together. I remember we were on location in Jersey, just hanging out, and you told me you had an idea for a movie about a guy who starts killing off a bunch of assholes in the film business."

"Half the people who work in this business come up with that idea," Gabe said.

"I didn't get much sun in prison, Gabe, but I didn't get stupid. That day, you and me talked about a bunch of cool ways to kill people off. One of them was swapping blanks for real bullets in a prop gun. Funny that you should be on the set today when Ian Stewart gets killed exactly that way."

"It doesn't mean I had anything to do with it."

Peltz just grunted. "It's also funny that the Molotov that got tossed at Brad Schuck tonight was a wickless. The same one my father taught me to make. The same one I taught you. Now that I see you again in person, you look about the same size as the guy who tossed it."

"I'm average height, average weight, along with a million other guys."

"But I'll bet you're the one guy behind those three pricks getting offed today."

"I'm not, Mick. I swear."

"Then why were you so quick to come running over here in the middle of the night? And why'd you bring the gun? I told you—I didn't ask you over here so I could blackmail you."

"Then why did you ask me?"

"Because I want in," Peltz said. "Remember the ending I pitched for your movie idea? Get about a hundred of those dickwads all together in one place and blow them up. You loved it. You going to do it?"

"Even if I was the guy behind all these killings, I could never afford to put something like that together. You of all people ought to know, Mickey. Explosives cost an arm and a leg."

"An arm and a leg. *Ba-da-bump*. That's why I like you, Gabe. You got a bomb under your balls, and you're not afraid to crack wise with the guy who's got his finger on the button."

"Jokes aside, Mickey, C4 is cheap if you got a license to buy it legal. But once you're out there on the black market, it's hard to find, and even if you can, the prices are through the roof."

"Not if you know where to shop. Listen to me, Gabe; if you're looking for the big bang, I'm your powder monkey. I not only know where to get what you need, I know how to rig it, and where to put the charges for the best body count."

Sweat dripped down Gabe's face as he stared at the chrome cylinder in Peltz's hand. Mickey might kill him, but he didn't seem bent on blackmail.

"Why would you even want to get involved?" Gabe asked. "Why risk going back to jail?"

"Because I could buy shit cheap, mark it up, make a few bucks, and still save you a bundle. And because I've spent the past twelve hundred and eighty-three nights laying in a prison cell thinking how I could get even with the system that put me there. So either tell me what's on your wish list and I'll make it happen, or just go home. I'm not going to blow the whistle on you. I'll be glued to the TV rooting for you."

Gabe reached into his pocket, pulled out a folded piece of paper, and put it in Mickey's free hand.

Mickey scanned it for less than thirty seconds. "I'd make a few adjustments, but not bad for an amateur. I guess I taught you pretty good."

"How much would I need?"

"Sixty pounds of C4 should do it," Mickey said. "It's big enough to do the job and light enough to carry around in a backpack."

"Can you get it?" Gabe asked.

"Piece of cake."

"Fast?"

Mickey coughed up a raspy laugh. "You want cheap *and* fast? Maybe if it was a blow job outside the Lincoln Tunnel, but we're living in a post-9/11 world, Gabe. Speedy delivery jacks up the price."

"How much to get it by tomorrow?"

Mickey took a beat. "Twenty-five thousand plus another five for my connections and my expertise."

"Thirty total," Gabe said.

"If this were a film production doing it on the up-and-up, the sixty pounds along with my services would be double, maybe triple," Mickey said. "Thirty thousand is the friends-and-family price."

"Take another look at that diagram I gave you. Does it make sense? Are the charges in the best places to do the most damage?"

"Like I said, I'd have to finesse it, but that's why I tacked on the extra five thousand. I get paid for blowing shit up, not for blackmailing. It's thirty thousand, all in, and if you want the plastic by tomorrow, I need the cash today. Do you have it?"

"No," The Chameleon said. "But I know where to get it."

"Then go get it."

"It's a two-man job," The Chameleon said. "You interested?"

"It would have to be me and my parole officer. Son of a bitch is tracking me 24/7. Can't you find somebody else?"

"Probably."

"Then do it. I'll be right here waiting for you."

"I'm going to need my gun back," Gabe said.

"You going to shoot me with it?"

"Hell no, but I hate walking along Skillman Ave. without it."

Mickey picked up the Walther and passed it back to Gabe. "See how much I trust you?" he said.

"It probably doesn't hurt that you got your finger on the pressure-release trigger," Gabe said.

"You mean this?" Mickey said.

He lifted his thumb off the cylinder and the silver button popped up.

Gabriel leaped from the chair.

"Boom," Mickey said.

"You bastard," Gabe said. "It was all bull-shit."

"You call it bullshit," Mickey said, letting loose one of his signature croaky laughs. "I call it special effects."

Chapter 34

"I TEXTED YOU twenty times," Lexi said.

"I texted you back on the first one," Gabe said.

"God, Gabe—if I write *'what happened?'* you can't just text back *'we'll talk when I get home.'* It's not a real answer."

"Sometimes real answers don't translate to typing on a telephone."

"Whatever. Did he try to blackmail you?"

"Just the opposite. He wants to help."

"*Help?* What kind of *help?*"

"Remember the original ending I had for this movie?" Gabe said.

"Kaboom!" she yelled, flinging her arms into the air. "That ending?"

"Yeah, that one."

"It's the best. I loved it. But you said we didn't have that kind of money in the production budget, and I said how come Wile E. Coyote can afford to buy all that TNT from the Acme Dynamite Company, and we can't?"

"I got good news," Gabe said. "I found Mr. Coyote. It's Mickey Peltz. He can get us what we need. Cheap."

"How do you know we can trust him?"

"Lex, I know him. I've worked with him before. He's not going to screw us, and he can get his hands on everything we need. Think of him as part of the production team."

"How much does he want?"

"Around thirty thousand. But only five of it's for him. The rest is for the C4."

"I don't know why you're so excited," Lexi said. "It's still thirty thousand more than we've got."

"It's too good to pass up," he said. "I can get the money."

"What are you going to do? Stick up a bank?"

"No. A production company."

Lexi gave him the frowning-schoolmarm look that always cracked him up. Head down, lips tightly pursed, chin tucked to her chest, and her index finger drawn across the bridge of her nose so she could look at him over fake granny glasses.

"Oh, really, young man," she said in a high-pitched but stern voice that was a cross between Bea Arthur and Lisa Simpson. "Do you actually think you can walk into Paramount, or Fox, or MGM, point a gun at them, and single-handedly walk out with a bag full of money?"

"No, ma'am," he answered, laying on his Arkansas schoolboy accent. "'Twouldn't be none of them big-ass studios. It'd be much smaller. And 'twouldn't be just me by my lonesome neither. I got me a partner in crime."

Lexi's face changed, and she slipped out of character. She sat down on the edge of the bed, hurt, deflated. "You and Mickey?" she said, her eyes watery. "He's your partner now?"

"No, dummy," Gabe said. "I'm talking about me and you."

Chapter 35

LEXI JUMPED FROM the bed. "You and me? Really? Are you serious?"

"I told you that you'd be getting a scene to play. This is it."

"Give me the details. Tell me everything."

"Remember last week when I was an extra in that courtroom movie? I was Juror Number Seven. We shot it on location down on Chambers Street."

"I remember," she said.

"I got friendly with the line producer, Jimmy Fitzhugh. We hung out. Talked motorcycles. He's got a Zook—a brand-new Boulevard. Great wheels. I'm thinking, since

I had to get rid of the Kawasaki, maybe when this is over, I'll get me one too."

"Anyway . . . ," Lexi said.

"Anyway, they're shooting uptown this week at Fordham University, and the production trailer is parked on West Sixty-second. Every morning Jimmy gets on his bike early so he can cruise in from Rockaway and beat the traffic."

"Where's the money, Gabe?"

"He keeps it in the trailer."

She shook her head. "Not thirty thousand. They don't keep a shitload of cash around to pay the union guys on payday anymore. Now they write checks, and a check cashing service comes in with bags of money and a couple of armed guards."

"Don't you think I know that? I'm not still playing the dumb hillbilly schoolboy, Lexi. I'm not saying we should go up against a couple of trigger-happy rent-a-cops. Jimmy Fitzhugh has cash in his trailer, and it's not there to pay the union guys."

"Then what's it for?"

"Coke."

"Get out of here."

"Jimmy's boss has money up the wazoo,"

Gabe said. "He also likes to party hearty, and nose candy is always on the menu. But the boss man is too high-profile to risk getting caught doing a transaction, so if a line producer wants to work for him, part of his job is to score the dope. Jimmy told me he's been doing it three years now. Never a problem, and the big guy always gives him hazard pay."

"Pretty sweet setup. How do we get the money?"

"Jimmy shows up at the trailer. I stick a gun to his head. And I know for sure he won't put up a fight. It's not his money, and if it gets stolen, I bet the boss doesn't even report it to the cops, because they might figure out what he was using it for."

"What do I do?"

"It's your big break, kid," Gabe said. "You get a speaking part. Jimmy knows me, which means he could easily recognize my voice. So I can't say a word. You just tell him to hand over the money, then you play lookout while he fills up the bag. Once we have the cash, I pay Mickey, and I guess you know what happens after that."

Lexi grinned. "Yeah. Kaboom."

Chapter 36

I GOT TO GERRI'S DINER a few minutes after 5:00. Business was brisk, but they weren't so busy that I couldn't eyeball every booth, every table, and every counter stool. Cheryl wasn't in, at, or on any of them.

"You want some breakfast, Zach?"

It was Gerri Gomperts herself. Gerri is a Force of Nature—tiny enough to fit into a twenty-gallon soup pot and tough enough to single-handedly take on a junkie who was so strung out that he tried to rob a diner around the corner from a police precinct. Turned out Gerri didn't need a cop. She whacked him across the forehead with a hot spatula. The poor guy needed forty stitches before they could even book him.

"No thanks, Gerri," I said. "Just a large coffee to go."

"We're all out of coffee to go," she said. "We only have coffee you can drink here."

I looked at her. "You're kidding, right?"

"No, Zach. I'm meddling. It's what I do. Now go sit in that corner booth over there till that *gawjus* lady shrink comes out of the restroom. She just ordered breakfast."

I sat at the booth and two minutes later the restroom door opened and the shrink stepped out. I had to agree with Gerri. Cheryl was *gawjus*.

"You again," she said, sitting across from me. "I saw the mayor's press conference last night, so I'm not surprised you didn't get much sleep."

"It wasn't the mayor who woke me up at four in the morning," I said.

"Don't tell me your new partner is still keeping you awake."

"No," I said, "this time it's her husband."

I told her Spence's middle-of-the-night theory, sparing no detail. "And when I finally said to him that the actual city of Los freakin' Angeles can't be the criminal mastermind behind these murders, and I asked him if he's got a lead on a human suspect, guess what he says?"

She smiled. "I'm going to go with...'That's your job, Detective Jordan.'"

I pounded my hand on the tabletop and the silverware jumped. "That's exactly what he said. Damn, you're good."

"Thanks, but that was too easy. The way you set it up, there was only one answer."

"So what do you call that—you know, what Spence is doing?" I asked. "Is it passive-aggressive behavior?"

"I don't think so. He sounds pretty genuine. I think he really wants to help."

"I appreciate it," I said, "but there are four million people in LA. Why doesn't he call me once he's narrowed it down?"

"The mayor made the usual promises last night about working around the clock, blah, blah, blah, and bringing about a swift conclusion to this tragedy," she said. "Where are we really?"

"Somewhere between desperate and deep

shit. We don't even have enough on this guy to ask you to do a profile."

"I'm sure you've already figured out that he's someone on the periphery of show business who hates the business and everyone in the inner circle," she said. "Which narrows it down to every actor, writer, and waiter in the Tri-State Area."

"Unless Spence is right," I said, "and he's on loan from the LA Chamber of Commerce."

"Can I change the subject for a minute?" she said.

"Sure."

"How do you feel about opera?"

"Sounds like one of those trick shrink questions," I said. "If Zach is a cop, and he likes opera, then he's got as much chance of cracking this case as he has of finding a vegetarian pit bull."

You keep working at it, you get the million-dollar smile. I got it.

"A friend of mine had to go out of town and she gave me two tickets to see *La Traviata*," she said.

"And let me guess—you love opera, but none of your friends do."

"Actually, I hate opera...I take that back. I only went once, twelve years ago, and I walked out after three hours, and I think they still had another seventeen and a half hours to go. But I've got these tickets, and I'm trying to broaden my cultural horizons. Kind of a post-Fred renaissance."

"I appreciate the offer, but I have to be honest with you. I've never been. I know all the clichés like 'it ain't over till the fat lady sings,' but I'm a virgin."

"Perfect," she said. "I couldn't possibly ask someone who loves it. I'd be stuck there. But if you go, we can make a deal. If one of us hates it, we'll stay—at least for a while. If both of us hate it, we bail out, and go bowling, or find a tractor pull somewhere."

"In my case, a tractor pull would actually broaden my cultural horizons. When?"

"Saturday night."

"If I'm not still chasing maniacs, it's a date."

We sat and talked for another half hour. By the time I had to leave, I was sure of one thing—Cheryl Robinson was ready for her post-Fred renaissance. I just wasn't sure I was ready to be part of it.

Chapter 37

GABE WAS NERVOUS. The director always refers to a big important scene as the money shot. But this one really was the money shot. He couldn't afford to get it wrong—the ending of the movie was hanging on it.

The good news was that the production trailer was on a relatively quiet street, and it was only 6:00 in the morning, a solid hour before the foot traffic picked up.

The bad news was that he was right smack between Columbus Circle and Lincoln Center, an obvious target for terrorists. That meant there would be eyes—both human and electronic—all over the place. Add to that the fact that his getaway car was the D train, and his accomplice was a rank amateur, and he came to the conclusion that *a guy would have to be crazy to pull a stunt like this.*

Fortunately for me, he reminded himself, *I am crazy.*

There was no time for an elaborate disguise, so they decided to go commando. Ski masks.

The train stopped at Columbus Circle and they went upstairs and headed uptown on Broadway. When they got to 62nd, they walked west. They crossed Columbus Avenue, and there were the trailers—three of them—parked in a No Parking zone, blue film commission permits taped to their doors.

"Keep walking," Gabe said.

Jimmy's bike wasn't there yet.

They walked to the corner of Amsterdam and waited.

They didn't have to wait long. Jimmy Fitzhugh's Suzuki came up Amsterdam, turned right on 62nd, and stopped at the first trailer half a block away.

"Walk fast," Gabe said.

Jimmy chained his bike to the trailer hitch and headed for the steps.

"Masks," Gabe said.

The masks went on and they got to the trailer just as Fitzhugh was unlocking the door.

Gabe followed him up the three steps and shoved him inside. Lexi followed and slammed the door behind them.

They were in. He couldn't believe it, but they were in.

Gabe pointed the gun in Jimmy's face, and, as expected, there was zero resistance.

"I got about five hundred bucks in my pocket," Jimmy said. "It's all yours. No problem."

Silence.

Gabe kept the gun pointed at Jimmy, then reached around with his other hand and poked Lexi.

Even with her mask on, she appeared to be petrified. Frozen. This was her big scene, and she forgot to say her lines.

Chapter 38

FOR TEN SECONDS the three of them just stood there. A silent tableau. Gabe waiting for Lexi to say something. Lexi forgetting that she had something to say. And Jimmy Fitzhugh trying to put the pieces of the puzzle together. Finally, he made a stab at it.

"*Yo tengo dinero,*" Jimmy said. "*Cinco. Cinco* hundred dollars. *No habla español,* but I got five hundred bucks."

Gabe pointed his gun at Fitzhugh, then at a desk chair.

"You want me to sit down?" Fitzhugh said.

Gabe nodded, and Fitzhugh sat.

He was in his forties, but athletic—not one of those three-hundred-pound bikers you see riding on the Thruway. He was an aging jock and proud of it—a gym rat who played tennis, squash, and Broadway League softball. Gabe had no doubt that given the chance, Fitzhugh would pounce on him in a heartbeat and take him down.

With the Walther trained on Fitzhugh, Gabe backed up to where Lexi was standing and got as close to her ear as possible.

"Say your lines," he whispered.

"Oh, shit," she said. "I'm sorry."

She turned to Fitzhugh. "We want the money."

"You speak English?" Fitzhugh said.

"Of course I speak English," she said. "What kind of a stupid question is that? I repeat. We...want...the...money. Now."

"I've got five hundred in my wallet. It's all yours. Let me just reach into my pocket, and—"

"You think we came all the way up here to get your wallet?" Lexi said. "We want the drug money. Open the safe."

205

Gabe could feel his chest tightening. *Open the safe* was in the script. *We want the drug money* was not.

"Who the fuck are you?" Fitzhugh yelled. "Do you work for Monte? Did he send you?"

"We work for ourselves!" Lexi yelled back. "Now open the safe."

"I don't have the combination, and I don't know anything about drug money." He stood up. "And if you want to know what's good for you—"

Gabe slammed him across the face with the butt of the Walther. Fitzhugh fell back in the chair, both hands pressed hard to his bloody cheek.

"Open the safe now or die!" Gabe screamed, waving the gun at him and hoping that the pain and the fear would prevent Fitzhugh from recognizing his voice.

Fitzhugh was moaning. "Okay, okay. Please don't shoot. I got two kids."

He dropped to his knees and wiped his bloody hands across his shirt.

"Keep watch!" Gabe yelled at Lexi, hoping that two more words wouldn't make a difference.

Lexi went to the trailer window and parted the blinds with her fingers.

"There's people walking out there," she said. "Hurry."

Fitzhugh opened the safe and backed up. Gabe looked inside. No weapons. No nothing, except for a gray metal lockbox.

"The key is in my desk drawer," Fitzhugh said.

Gabe waved him toward the desk with the gun.

"Hurry!" Lexi yelled, stamping her feet. "I think someone's coming."

Fitzhugh opened the top desk drawer and took out a small key. Then he pulled the lockbox from the safe.

"There's enough in here for three separate buys," he said. "Let me give you a piece of advice. You take a bundle, and I guarantee you nobody will chase you. You take it all, and Monte will hunt you down, rape your girlfriend, slit her throat, and put her in a coffin. She'll be the lucky one, because you'll go in after her—still breathing. Then he'll bury the box and forget where he left you."

"Open it," Gabe growled, more concerned with getting out than being recognized.

Fitzhugh unlocked the box and flipped the top.

Three neat stacks of bills. Hundreds on top of each stack. Not very thick, but drug bundles didn't have to be thick. They'd all be hundreds.

"Trust me," Fitzhugh said. "You really don't want to take them all."

The Chameleon picked up one of the packets, then hesitated.

"I'm not kidding, Gabe—hurry up!" Lexi yelled frantically from her spot at the window. "I swear to God someone is really coming."

Fitzhugh stood up. "Gabe? The extra? The guy with the Kawasaki Ninja? Are you out of your mind? Do you really think you're going to get away with this?"

The Chameleon had no choice. He pointed the Walther at Fitzhugh's chest and squeezed the trigger.

"Shit, shit, shit, shit!" he bellowed as Fitzhugh fell backward onto the desk chair.

If Lexi had an ounce of composure left, it

was gone. "Are you crazy?" she screamed. "People outside heard that. He gave you the money. Why did you shoot him?"

"You told him my name!" Gabe screamed back.

"No I didn't. I swear."

Gabriel grabbed the other two stacks of bills and shoved all three into the pocket of his windbreaker.

Then he yanked Lexi by the arm and dragged her to the door.

"Mask," he shouted.

They each pulled off their ski masks and left the trailer.

They walked east toward Broadway. Ten minutes later they were sitting in the last car of the downtown D train.

"I'm sorry, Gabe. I'm sorry," Lexi said, tears running down her cheeks.

"Do me a favor," he said, barely parting his lips as he spoke. "Just shut the fuck up."

Chapter 39

THERE WAS A large coffee and a box of Krispy Kreme doughnuts sitting on my desk with a note taped to the top.

Sorry about Spence. He means well. Xxx, K-Mac

Kylie was sitting at her desk munching on the last few morsels of a glazed doughnut. "I took one," she said, washing it down with coffee. "The other eleven are all yours."

"I appreciate the gesture, but don't you think that's profiling? Cops and doughnuts?"

"For the record, I did not give Spence your number," she said. "He found it in my cell."

"Did he share his theory with you, or shall I?"

"He laid it on me this morning," she said. "The powers that be in Los Angeles come up with a devious plan to cripple film production in New York."

"Devious and dastardly," I said. "The kind of scenario where you definitely expect to see Lex Luthor."

"I know it's off-the-wall," she said, "but at least you have to give him points for creativity."

"Creativity? No wonder I can't crack this case. Like an idiot, I've been trying to connect the facts."

"That's the difference between police work and the television business," Kylie said. "As far as TV people are concerned, reality is highly overrated. They would never let it get in the way of their thinking."

"Yesterday was only our first day working together," I said. "But now that I have some insight into your husband, I'm wondering how many times a week you had to buy doughnuts for your former partners."

"Believe it or not, you're the first one Spence ever called."

"I'm flattered. Sleep-deprived, but flattered."

"You know Spence. He's always been fascinated with cops, and he loves that you get to combine cop stuff with show business. He told me last night that you have the coolest job, and he'd trade places with you if he could."

Spence Harrington wants to trade places with me? I didn't know how to begin to respond. I never got the chance.

"Zach! K-Mac!" Captain Cates was striding toward us, barking orders as she walked. "Robbery-homicide, West Sixty-two between Columbus and Amsterdam."

I knew the area well. It was a pretty quiet neighborhood. "What's there?" I said.

Cates stopped in front of us. She looked like she hadn't slept much last night either. "A film production trailer," she said. "And a line producer with a bullet in his chest."

Chapter 40

GABE AND LEXI crashed through the front door, knocking over the brass umbrella stand that she had picked up at a flea market for twelve bucks.

They hadn't spoken the entire subway ride home. They had walked in silence to the apartment building, him fuming, her sobbing.

When they got to the lobby, she just stood there waiting for the elevator, shoulders slumped, eyes red, spirit broken.

Finally she spoke. "You're never going to love me again, will you?"

She meant it. That's how her mind worked. *You fuck up; you get abandoned.* Her parents had done that to her.

"Don't be..." He swallowed the word *stupid.* "Don't say things like that," he said.

The elevator doors opened. She stepped in and stood in the corner, tears streaming down her cheeks, hands clenched at her sides.

"Lexi," he said, following her into the elevator, "what happened, happened, and I'm a little freaked about it, but I love you. I'll always love you."

If he thought that would cheer her up, he was wrong. Her body shook as she tried to hold back the anguish.

He had never seen her so despondent, and it cut him to the marrow.

He softened. "It's okay," he said, enfolding her gently in his arms. He kissed her forehead, her eyes, her salt-stained cheek, trying his best to comfort her.

She tilted her head up, and he gently touched his lips to hers. She sighed, parted her mouth, and he found her tongue. He reached down and clenched her butt, and she responded by arching her pelvis and forcing it against his.

He hardened.

The elevator door opened, and they stumbled down the hall, banging into their front
door till he finally fit the key in the lock.

She was peeling off her pants and panties
before the door had even shut behind them.
Then she grabbed his belt and expertly undid
the buttons on his jeans while he ripped off
his windbreaker and threw it on the floor.

The bedroom was too far, and she turned
away from him, leaning over a chair, hands
flat on the table. He grabbed her hips from
behind and entered her hard.

"I'm sorry, I'm sorry, I'm sorry," she whispered with every thrust.

"Shhh, shhh. It's okay. It's okay," he said.
"Don't talk."

It was powerful, raw; it was pure, primal,
postmurder adrenaline sex. It was what he
needed. What they both needed.

Lexi's orgasms had always had their own
sound track, and he held back until he heard
the first familiar muted moan. Her pitch
grew louder and more frenzied, and he

finally let go, stifling his own screams as he climaxed in waves.

Eyes glazed, she slumped into his arms, and he carried her to the bedroom. They stripped off the rest of their clothes and made love, slowly, gently, without apologies.

When it was over, Lexi clutched a pillow to her chest and curled up in a fetal position. Gabe wrapped his body around hers and pulled the sheet over them.

The money, he thought.

The wads of hundreds were still stuffed into the pocket of his windbreaker. He had no idea how much there was.

It could wait.

Chapter 41

"DRIVING LIKE A maniac isn't going to make our murder victim any less dead," Kylie said as I drove balls out through the Central Park–65th Street transverse.

"I know," I said, not slowing down. "I think it's like getting addicted to a bad soap opera. I want to know what happens in the next episode."

"So do I, but not enough to die in crosstown traffic. And for the record, 'bad soap opera' is redundant."

We made it to West 62nd in under five minutes. There was a squad car from the

20th Precinct parked alongside the production trailer. A uniformed cop, Frank Rankin, was waiting for us outside the trailer.

"My partner and I got here two minutes ago," he said. "The permit on the trailer says they're part of the movie company that's shooting at Fordham. The victim, according to the guy who called it in, is Jimmy Fitzhugh."

"Did you or your partner go inside the trailer?"

"I did, but not too far. I didn't want to contaminate the scene, but I wanted to make sure he was dead."

"And?"

"Gunshot wound to the chest at close range. The Crime Scene Unit isn't here yet to make the call, but I know dead, and this guy definitely is. There's also a safe in there—door wide open. I didn't check it out, but I figure if the door is open, whatever was in it is gone."

"Who called 911?" Kylie asked.

"His name is Michael Jackman. Said he's the assistant director. He didn't see or hear anything. He came over for a meeting with the victim and found the body. He's sitting in the back of our unit with my partner."

"Keep him there," I said. "We're going to take a look at the scene."

Fitzhugh was slumped in a desk chair, his gray T-shirt stained dark brown from the collar to the waist. There was a fresh bloody gash on his right cheek.

"Pistol-whipped," Kylie said.

I shined a light inside the open safe. "The uni called it on the safe. It's empty."

"Except for the movie connection, this doesn't feel like any of the other homicides," she said.

"I had the same gut reaction," I said. "The other three murders were planned out, artful almost. This just looks like a robbery gone bad. Vic working at his desk, perp walks in and says open the safe. Fitzhugh says no; perp gives him a convincer with the gun butt. Fitzhugh opens it, and the perp pockets the cash."

"That's a robbery gone good," Kylie said. "If the perp got the money, why did he shoot Fitzhugh? Why up the ante from robbery to murder?"

"Fitzhugh recognized him," I said.

"There's only one hiccup, Zach. The man we're looking for is a master of disguise. We have him on video, and we can't even ID him."

"So if it's impossible to recognize this guy," I said, "why'd he pop Fitzhugh?"

"That's the question I just asked you."

"In that case, it's unanimous," I said. "We're both clueless."

We backed out of the trailer and walked over to the squad car where Rankin's partner, Robin Gallagher, was waiting for us.

"Mike Jackman, the guy who found the body, is all shook up," she said. "He not only worked with the victim, he's his brother-in-law."

"Did he say anything worth repeating?" Kylie asked.

"'Who's going to tell my sister and the kids?'" Gallagher said. "Which you kind of expect. And one other thing which you wouldn't."

"What's that?" I said.

"'Fucking Levinson.' He said it maybe half a dozen times."

"Did he say who fucking Levinson is?"

"No, sir," she said.

"Ask Mr. Jackman to step out of the car, Officer. If he's up to it, we'd like to ask him a couple of questions."

The CSU wagon pulled up. I was hoping I'd get to see the enticing Maggie Arnold two days in a row.

No such luck. The driver's side door opened and out stepped the humorless Chuck Dryden.

"Hello again, Chuck," I said. "You remember my partner Kylie MacDonald, don't you?"

"Where's the body?" he said.

I pointed, and he lumbered toward the trailer.

"What a pill," Kylie said.

"Hey," I said, "you're lucky you didn't know him before the department sent him to charm school."

Chapter 42

THE CHAMELEON SLEPT for three hours.

When he woke up, Lexi was in the kitchen.

"What's for breakfast?" he called out.

"It's too late for breakfast!" she yelled back. "We're having brunch. Pancakes. The real kind, not the frozen crap. And I went out and bought fresh raspberries. We can afford them now."

He padded to the kitchen, still naked. "What do you mean 'we can afford them now'?"

"I counted the money. There was forty-five thousand dollars. Can you believe he was going to give it all to a drug dealer? I hate drugs. I don't understand why people do them."

"You sure it was forty-five thousand?" he asked.

"Three bundles of Benjamins worth fifteen thousand each. I counted it twice. Pancakes in five minutes."

He showered, slowly turning the water from warm to hot to excruciating. The remorse was overwhelming. He had killed two, maybe three people yesterday, and he would happily kill them all over again today without batting an eye.

But Jimmy Fitzhugh was different. Jimmy was one of the good guys.

Please don't shoot. I got two kids.

I know, I know. Tracy and Jim Jr. But what was I supposed to do once Lexi blurted out my name? I had no choice.

Bullshit, Gabe—she didn't pull the trigger. You did.

He edged the water up even hotter. The pain helped.

I'm sorry, Jimmy. Really sorry.

The pancakes were excellent—real butter, fresh fat raspberries, thick Vermont maple syrup—and so was the steaming hot coffee. If he had needed a domestic scene in his movie, this could have been it.

"You sure I yelled out your name?" she said. "I swear, if I did, I didn't even know it."

"You said, 'Gabe, hurry up.' That's all it took."

"Fitzhugh should have pretended not to hear me. If he'd ignored it, you'd have thought he didn't hear what I said, and you wouldn't have killed him. It's just as much his fault that he got shot as mine."

"No," Gabe said. "Bottom line, it's my fault. I'm the director, I'm the producer—I put too much pressure on you. It was too big a part. We didn't rehearse. I shouldn't have put you on the hook for such a big role."

"It'll never happen again," Lexi said. "I promise."

"Just to be on the safe side, I think you should stay behind the scenes for a while."

"I'm fired from the production?"

"No. No. Just the opposite. I really want you to be my coproducer. We've got a new scene or two to write. I need you now more than ever."

"What new scene?"

"I'm not sure yet, but we netted forty-five thousand, and we only need thirty, so I thought maybe we could come up with a couple of cool new scenes and buy some more of Mickey's pyrotechnics. We have fifteen thousand dollars to play with."

"Fourteen thousand, nine hundred and ninety-four," Lexi said. "The raspberries cost six bucks."

Chapter 43

MIKE JACKMAN WAS tall with broad shoulders, warm brown eyes, and an air of intelligence about him. On a good day he was probably just the kind of guy you'd want on your crew. But this was not a good day, and Mike looked like Bambi staring down the barrel of a shotgun.

"Did the lady cop tell you that Jimmy Fitzhugh is my brother-in-law?" he said.

"Yes, sir, and we're sorry for your family's loss. I'm Detective Jordan, and this is my partner, Detective MacDonald. With your help we can find the man who killed your brother-in-law. What can you tell us?"

"Nothing," Jackman said. "Fitz and I meet first thing every morning to go over production notes for the day. I'm the AD; he's the line producer. He always shows up before I do, so as soon as I got here, I went straight to his trailer. The safe was wide open. Fitz was dead in his chair. I called 911."

"What was in the safe?" Kylie asked.

"Not my job to know."

"Did you and Jimmy have a good relationship?" she asked.

"We were best friends. More like brothers than in-laws."

"So your best friend, the guy you sat down with over coffee every morning, never gave you a clue about what might be in the safe worth killing him for?"

"No."

"Maybe your sister knows. When we break the bad news to her that her husband is dead, we'll ask her."

"Don't. She has no idea..."

"Sounds like maybe *you* do," Kylie said.

"Mike," I said. "You seem like the kind of true friend who would hold back information because you think it will protect Jimmy. But the truth is, you're protecting his killer. Why don't you tell us what you know? We won't use it against Jimmy."

"Jimmy's dead. It's not him I'm worried about." Jackman shook his head. "Shit like this gets out, it's my sister and the kids who suffer."

"We're not here to trash Jimmy's reputation," Kylie said. "We're here to catch his killer. Please...help us."

Jackman sat staring into Kylie's eyes. He let out a long, slow breath. "Just make me a promise," he said. "Whatever I tell you, it never gets back to my sister."

"Promise," Kylie said.

He nodded. "Okay. Fitz was a...I don't know what the cops would call it," he said. "Like a mule."

"A drug mule?" Kylie said.

"Maybe that's the wrong term. He was the middleman between the buyer and the seller."

"Who was the seller and what was he selling?"

"Monte. That's all I know. Just Monte. He was selling coke."

"And who was the buyer?"

"Our boss, Bob Levinson."

"Is that the guy you were cursing out in the squad car?"

"He makes great movies, but he's the boss from hell. He's got a ton of money and a never-ending supply of blow buddies. He buys by the kilo, but he doesn't personally go near the supply chain. His line producers always act as the go-between."

"And if the line producer says 'no,' he finds himself on the unemployment line," Kylie said.

"Right," Jackman said. "Levinson always hires top-notch producers. They're always family men who need the job, and they're always clean—no past, no drug history, no rap sheet."

"How much do you think was in the safe?"

"Every month Levinson would give Jimmy four packets with fifteen thousand in each one. Monte showed up every Thursday with a key of cocaine, and Jimmy would give him one of the packets. Today is the ninth, so there were probably three packs still in the safe."

"Did anyone else working on this production know about the drug deals?"

"People talk. Rumors fly around. So yeah, but I have no idea who knew what about what."

"We need a list of every single person connected to this production. Grips, gaffers, catering truck drivers—everybody," said Kylie.

"Yes, ma'am. I'll get you a printout."

He started to leave, then turned back. "One question—are you going to arrest Levinson?"

"We would if we could," I said, "but we don't have anything we can charge him with."

"Maybe it's just as well. Keep Fitz's memory clean," he said, and walked off.

"You got a minute?"

We turned around and there was the humorless hulk of Chuck Dryden.

"You find something?" I said.

He gave me a look that basically said *Dumb question. There's only one reason I would ever interact with the detectives on the scene. Of course I found something.*

He gestured with a short jerk of his head, and we followed him back to the trailer.

"Look at this," he said, pointing to the window on the left side of the trailer. "Window Number One. Blinds down.

"Now this." He pointed to the window on the opposite side of the trailer. "Window Number Two. Blinds down. Except these two slats are turned so a person could stand here and look out onto the street."

"A short person," I said. "The opening in the slats is only about five feet high."

"But judging by the angle of the bullet in the victim, whoever pulled the trigger was a foot taller," Dryden said. "You're looking for two people. The shooter and a lookout."

"Two people," Kylie repeated. "We can't even find one."

Dryden shrugged. *Definitely not his problem.*

Chapter 44

THE WALTHER PPK was Gabe's gun of choice, the perfect little pocket pistol—the same one James Bond used. But right now his was too hot to carry. Still, he wasn't about to transport $45,000 on the subway unarmed.

He went to his closet and dug out the Glock 23. It was a .40-caliber, bigger than the PPK .380, so it was harder to conceal, but on the off chance that a cop stopped him, it wouldn't connect him to the robbery-homicide on West 62nd Street.

He took the number 6 local uptown, got off at Grand Central, and transferred to the number 7. The ride was uneventful—pleasant, actually. He couldn't stop thinking about Lexi. The girl was a genius. When he asked her to help him come up with a scenario for using the extra fifteen thousand, he was just trying to make her feel wanted. He didn't expect much.

And then she came up with an absolutely mind-blowing idea. It made the script a thousand times better.

"I want to supersize my order," he said to Mickey when he got to the loft.

"What kind of weapons of mass destruction did you have in mind?"

Gabe had sketched Lexi's idea out on a notepad. "I'm not sure of the exact layout, but best as I can tell, it's something like this. What do you think?"

"Whose place is this?" Mickey asked.

Gabe told him.

Mickey let out a slow whistle. "You got balls, Benoit," he said.

"It was my girlfriend's idea. Can we do it?"

"I can get as much plastic as you'll need," Mickey said. "What kind of detonators are we talking about?"

"I don't know yet, so mix it up—timers,

remotes, something I can set off with a trip wire. Just keep it simple and idiotproof. Remember, I'm not a pro."

"You got a budget for all this extra stuff?"

Gabe nodded. "I got a number in mind."

"How much?"

"What can I get for another fifteen grand?"

Mickey's eyes widened, and he coughed up a phlegmy chuckle. "My boy, for fifteen thousand dollars more you can get one hell of a lot of noise."

Gabriel took the three stacks of hundreds out of his backpack and set them down on the table. "This is forty-five thousand."

Mickey picked up a bundle, fanned the bills, and put it back. "I wondered how much Jimmy Fitzhugh had in his safe."

Gabriel stiffened. "Who said anything about Jimmy Fitzhugh?"

Mickey lit up a cigarette and blew the smoke up toward the ceiling. "Nobody *said* anything. It was all over the police scanner. Robbery-homicide over at one of Bob Levinson's production trailers on the West Side. Two perps involved. James Fitzhugh, producer, shot dead. What am I—stupid? You told me you knew where to get the money, but you needed a partner. I put one and one together. So, who did you team up with?"

"Your mother. And she sucked at it," Gabe said. "You need the work or are you more interested in meddling in my private life?"

Mickey held up a hand. "Easy there, Gaby baby. I'm not meddling. Not meddling is the first thing you learn when you're up there in Ray Brook. I was just making small talk. Forget I asked. Let's talk about delivery."

"Part of the deal was you said you could deliver tomorrow," Gabe said.

"No problem. I still can."

"Okay, but no later," Gabe said. "I got a crazy production schedule."

"Tomorrow, first thing. Right here. Forty-five thousand worth of boom."

"Actually, one of the packs is shy a hundred bucks," Gabe said. "My girlfriend used it for groceries."

"No problem. Tell the little woman the groceries are on me," Mickey said. "Deal?"

Gabe didn't hesitate. "Deal," he said.

And they sealed it in the time-honored old-school Hollywood tradition. With a handshake.

Chapter 45

"I THINK WE finally hit pay dirt," Kylie said.

We had two lists—the one Shelley Trager had given us with the names of everyone who had been on the set when Ian Stewart was shot, and Mike Jackman's printout of all the people connected to the Levinson production.

We cross-checked the names, more than four hundred in all. Twelve people were on both lists, eight of them men.

"We could get this done a lot faster if we split the list in half and gave four to another team," I said.

"We could get it done even faster if we got seven other teams to jump in and we all took one name," Kylie said.

"I'm guessing my quest for departmental efficiency does not sit well with you," I said.

"Absolutely not," Kylie said. "First of all, you and I were at both crime scenes and it would take us way too long to get another team up to speed. Second of all, I'm consumed with ruthless ambition, and I refuse to let another team steal the biggest case of my career right out from under me. Now, just tell me which one of those answers you're more likely to buy, and I'll do my best to ram it down your throat."

"No need to press any harder," I said. "I think 'consumed with ruthless ambition' sums it up nicely."

"Good. Make sure you put that in your report to Captain Cates. I don't think she'll hold it against me."

By midafternoon we had struck out five times. Two of the possibles had been on the Ian Stewart set since seven in the morning, which ruled them out for poisoning Sid Roth at the Regency. Two others had solid alibis for Monday night's bombing at Radio City.

The fifth guy was black. He laughed when he figured out why we were there to question him. "Didn't you guys watch the video of the guy who firebombed Brad Schuck's limo? That dude was white. You may want to adjust the color on your monitor."

We laughed along with him, apologized, and left.

"Where to next?" I asked Kylie.

"Middle Village, Queens. Furmanville Avenue off Seventy-ninth Street. I've got a street address, and next to that in parentheses it says 'Paradise Garden.'"

"Sounds like a Chinese restaurant." I said.

"Or a massage parlor. Give me a sec. Let me Google it."

She poked at her iPhone.

"Holy shit," she said. "This is encouraging. It's a mental health facility."

"That's the funny thing about trying to hunt down a homicidal maniac," I said. "The last place you'd ever think of looking for him is in a loony bin."

She gave me the exact address. We were

twenty minutes away, and I headed for the Long Island Expressway.

"What do we have on this guy?" I said.

"He was an extra on the set of the Ian Stewart movie yesterday, which means one of our guys would have questioned him. Then last week he worked for three days as an extra in the Levinson production, so he could have found out about the drug money Fitzhugh had stashed in the trailer."

"What's his name?" I said.

"Benoit. Gabriel Benoit."

Chapter 46

THAT SECTION OF Furmanville Avenue in Queens was a quiet working-class neighborhood lined with small two-story homes, even smaller front yards, and a schizophrenic mix of Japanese compacts and oversized gas-guzzling SUVs. In the middle of it all was a serviceable 1960s white-brick, four-story building that strived for nondescript, but landed on ugly.

The maroon canopy in front said PARADISE GARDEN.

"It's nice to see that the zoning laws in New York City are flexible enough to allow someone to build a funny farm right in the middle of a neighborhood filled with impressionable youth," Kylie said.

"Don't jump to conclusions, Detective," I said. "Maybe the nut jobs were here first, and the happy little neighborhood just sprang up around them."

"I've been to places like this before," Kylie said. "Private clinics, nursing homes, psych hospitals. You try to ask them a few questions and they're more defensive than a mob lawyer. Usually there's some smarmy little weasel who *really wishes he could help,* then falls back on doctor-patient confidentiality and won't tell you squat without a subpoena."

"Maybe we could threaten to bust the smarmy little weasel for false advertising," I said. "The sidewalk is cracked, the grass is brown, and the building is an eyesore. Paradise Garden, my ass."

The lobby was warm and humid. If the inmates were paying for air-conditioning, they weren't getting their money's worth.

The receptionist was a middle-aged woman who obviously bought her red hair coloring by the gallon. She looked up and gave us a welcoming smile. We were off to an excellent start.

"Gud aftanoon. Kin I help ya?" she said in an accent that branded her as born, raised, and educated in Queens.

"NYPD," I said, flashing my badge. "We're looking for Gabriel Benoit."

"Who?"

I pronounced the name slowly. *Ben-oyt.* B-E-N-O-I-T.

"Oh. *Ben-wah,*" she said, shaking her head at my lousy diction. "He's no lawnga a resident."

"Where can we find him?" I said.

"You'd hafta tawk to our directah, Dr. Ben-David," she said. "Have a seat."

The waiting area was filled with over-stuffed furniture that might have been considered gracious during the Truman administration. At this point in its life cycle, the grace had turned to gloom.

We sat. "Bet you five bucks he's a die-hard Mets fan," Kylie said.

I was about to turn down the chump bet when we heard a piercing scream. People who live in psych wards scream day and night. But this was different. This was someone in agony. I knew it, Kylie knew it, and the receptionist knew it.

"Oh my Gawd," the receptionist said and started running down the hall. "It's Dr. Ben-David."

Chapter 47

KYLIE AND I followed the receptionist down a wide hallway that might once have been painted a cheery yellow, but was now a sorry shade of jaundice.

The door to Dr. Ben-David's office was open, and the three of us stormed in. The director was not at all what we had expected.

Laura Ben-David was in her midthirties, strikingly attractive, and lying there, sprawled out on a sofa, strikingly pregnant.

"Dr. Ben-David," the receptionist said. "You awl right?"

Ben-David sat up. "I'm fine, Doris. I'm so sorry about that scream, but this little bugger seems to want to get out two weeks ahead of schedule," she said, putting both hands on her belly. "He just gave me a doozy of a contraction."

"You're in labor?" Kylie said.

"Full blown."

"We're with NYPD. Can we drive you to the hospital?"

"No, thanks. I called my husband. He'll be here in a few minutes."

"They were asking for Gabriel Benoit," Doris said.

"I've been worried about him," Ben-David said. "Is he okay?"

"We don't know," Kylie said. "I'm Detective MacDonald, and this is my partner, Detective Jordan. Are you up to answering a few questions?"

"I can probably handle a couple of true or false. But I'm not sure this kid is going to stay put long enough for me to answer the essay questions." She winced. "Doris, go back to the front desk, and send Lawrence back as soon as he gets here."

Doris left and Kylie sat down next to the doc.

"Your receptionist said Mr. Benoit is no longer a resident," Kylie said. "What was he in here for?"

"You know I can't answer that."

"Can you tell us when he left?"

"A few months ago."

"And could you give us the name of the doctor who checked him out?"

"He checked himself out," Ben-David said.

"These people can just walk out on their own?" Kylie said.

"*These people?*" Ben-David said. "Most of them can't, but Gabriel came in voluntarily, so he could discharge himself at any time."

"Did he leave a forwarding address?"

Ben-David laughed. "Ouch," she said, grabbing her belly again. "Don't make me laugh. People in Gabriel Benoit's mental state never leave forwarding addresses. They're always afraid somebody is out to get them."

"In his case," Kylie said, "he'd be right."

A man opened the door without knocking and knelt down beside the doc.

"Laura, you all right?" he said.

As if on cue, she let out a yelp, not nearly as loud as the scream we'd heard a few minutes before, and dug her fingers into his back as she powered through a thirty-second contraction.

"I'm fine," she said, coming out of it. "Detectives, this is my husband, Lawrence."

"Honey, whatever this is, it can wait. The car's outside. Let's go." He helped her off the sofa.

Our best link to Benoit was about to rush off to a maternity ward. We needed a Hail Mary.

"Dr. Ben-David," Kylie said. "Gabriel Benoit is a suspect in a string of violent homicides."

Ben-David stopped in her tracks.

"Homicides," she said. "Oh, my Lord. That's terrible."

"We know about HIPAA, we know about doctor-patient confidentiality, but more people—a lot of innocent people—are at risk," Kylie said. "Is there anything—*anything*— you can say that will help us?"

Ben-David turned to her husband. "Lawrence, give me a minute. Please. Wait outside. I'll be right there."

"Laura, are you...? All right. You got one

minute and then I'm coming back in and dragging you to the hospital."

He walked out and shut the door behind him.

"Detective MacDonald," Ben-David said. "I am bound by law not to divulge any patient information without a court order."

"That's not helping," Kylie said.

"You're not listening. Let me finish. *I—repeat, I—*am bound by law not to divulge any patient information without a court order. *My staff* is bound by the same law. Our job is not to help you catch a murderer. Our job is to take care of the one hundred and eighteen other people who live in this facility who *are not—repeat, are not—*bound by any such law. Are you with me so far?"

Kylie nodded.

"Most of our residents are very inquisitive," Ben-David said. "In fact, a lot of them are downright nosy. And they're talkative. Especially J.J. But they are also fragile, delicate, and easily frightened. *Do not—repeat, do not—*scare them. Are we clear?"

"Yes, ma'am," Kylie said. "Thank you."

"It's the least I could do," Ben-David said. "Unfortunately, it's also the most I could do."

Kylie hugged her gently. "Have a wonderful baby."

I opened the door, and Lawrence led her down the hall.

"Nice lady," I said to my partner. "Hardly the smarmy little weasel I was told to expect."

Chapter 48

DORIS WAS BACK at the front desk.

"Thanks for your help," I said. "Dr. Ben-David said she wouldn't mind if we took a quick look around."

"Then you may want to look for the man in the Freud T-shirt," she said, barely making eye contact with us. "The dayroom is over there." She cocked her head to the right.

Doris was obviously in the loop.

Nothing says *"I'm glad I'm not locked up in here"* like a large communal room in a mental institution.

There were a few dozen men and women

scattered about, both alone and in groups, some watching TV, some staring into space, some talking to one another, some sitting off to the side quietly tapping away at a laptop or a video game.

It's the same kind of tableau you might see in an airport lounge. Except it was obvious that these people had no place to go. You could see it in their eyes.

"Sigmund Freud T-shirt at eleven o'clock," Kylie said.

The man was my age, with a long, lean body, thinning blond hair, and round wire glasses. He was looking out a window, holding two unlit cigarettes in his left hand.

"Don't forget what the doc said," I reminded Kylie.

"He's nosy and likes to talk."

"I mean the part about him being fragile. Be gentle."

"You know me, Six. I'm as gentle as a kitten."

She didn't mean it to be any kind of a sexual reference, but the male brain doesn't need innuendo to get it thinking about sex. My mind flashed to our first month in the police academy. Before Spence came back into the picture. Kylie MacDonald was more tigress than kitten.

"You probably have a problem preying on the mentally ill," she said. "I don't. Follow my lead."

She eased toward Freud, then stopped a few feet away, within earshot.

"I thought Gabriel would be here," she said to me.

"Gabriel who?" I said.

"The film director," she said. "Are you new here? I thought everyone knew him."

Freud turned away from the window. "Excuse me," he said. "You looking for Gabriel?"

Kylie smiled, perky and happy to find a helpful soul.

"Yeah. Hi. I'm Kylie."

"I'm J.J.," he said. "What are you looking for Gabriel for?"

"I'm an actress. He's a director. Duh."

J.J. laughed. Crazy or not, he was as susceptible to Kylie's charm as the rest of hetero mankind. "I know him," J.J. said. "Are you in one of his movies?"

"I wish," Kylie said. "I'm auditioning. Is

there anything you can tell me that would help me nail the part?"

"Let's sit on the porch," he said. "We can smoke out there."

The two of them stepped through a pair of French doors onto a narrow porch with outdoor furniture as run-down as the indoor stuff.

J.J. sat on a wicker rocker and Kylie sat on a bench across from him. I hovered in the background.

J.J. shifted the two cigarettes to his right hand, but made no move to light them. "Gabriel is a difficult director," he said. "When you audition, never ad-lib. I'm serious. Always do the script as writ. He hates it when somebody tries to rewrite him. Like one night at dinner, we were supposed to have meat loaf, but they gave us fried chicken. He went ballistic, screaming, 'Who rewrote this scene?'"

"He sounds dedicated."

"No, Kylie. Scorsese is dedicated. Gabriel is just crazy."

"I still want to audition," Kylie said. "Where is he?"

"Gone. Vanished. Poof—just disappeared into thin air. One night he walks into the dayroom—some of us were watching that show with the Japanese robots—do you watch that?"

"No. Is it good?"

"If you like robots, yeah. Anyway, Gabriel, he just walks in and announces that he's finished shooting all the wacko-people shit in his script. He says we're all stars, but he can't promise who's going to be in the final cut until he edits it. The next morning he was out of here."

"Did you ever see the script?"

"No. The only ones who were ever allowed to see it were Gabriel and Lexi."

"Who's Lexi?"

"His girlfriend."

"Do you know her last name?"

J.J. shook his head. "No. It's just the one name, like she's so famous that she doesn't need a last name. Like Oprah. Except most people know it's Winfrey."

"Is Lexi still here?"

"No. She never lived here. But I bet he's with her. They go everywhere together. You know what I think?" he said, gesturing with the cigarette hand.

"Tell me."

"I think Gabriel doesn't have to be locked up in a place like this. I think he only came here to shoot scenes for his movie."

"I'm surprised they let him bring a camera in here," Kylie said.

J.J. looked at her like she was nuts. "There's no camera," he said. "It's all in here." He tapped his forehead.

"The movie..." Kylie took a second to re-process the information. "The movie is *in his head?*"

J.J. shrugged. "Hey, I told you—the guy is crazy."

Chapter 49

LEXI HAD FOUND his hiding place months ago. It was in the desk. His desk—the one piece of furniture he had brought to her apartment.

She had been looking for the stapler, opened the bottom drawer too fast, and pulled it out completely. The drawer was half the length of the others. It had a false back.

And there they were, stashed in his secret space. Letters. Lots of them.

Obviously they had to be from other women. Gabe had girlfriends before he met her. Still, it pissed her off that he had saved them, and worse yet, hid them from her.

She put the drawer back. The letters were none of her business. She made a vow never to read them. That lasted about ten minutes. She came up with a compromise. She'd read two or three just to get the flavor of the other girls. Maybe see how she stacked up. That would be enough. Unless any of them were written after she and Gabe were a couple. Then there would be hell to pay.

She pulled out the drawer and grabbed a handful of envelopes. They weren't from women. They were business letters. From movie studios, television networks, production companies, directors, actors. She read a half dozen.

Dear Mr. Benoit,

Thank you for your recent submission. However, at this time we are sorry to say...

Unfortunately, your story is not one we would like to pursue at this...

Regretfully, our production schedule for next season has already been...

They were all the same—thanks but no thanks. Rejection letters. Hundreds of them, some more than ten years old. How sad.

In the months that had passed, she hadn't said a word. She wished she could talk to him about the letters, maybe make him feel better about himself, but that would mean admitting she had read them.

And now, she had made his life even more miserable. She bungled the robbery scene. She so much wanted to be a part of his movie, and as soon as he said yes, she screwed up.

She had to make it up to him. She *would* make it up to him. And then, sitting at her computer, surfing the best sites for the latest Hollywood dirt, it hit her. Inspiration. Brilliant actually, because this would completely tie in to the rest of the movie.

She clicked on Microsoft Word, opened a new document, and began typing.

ALT. SCENE:

Chapter 50

CAPTAIN DELIA CATES sat in silent meditation with her right elbow digging into the arm of her desk chair, her mouth and chin resting on the knuckles of her right hand. It's the classic pose of Rodin's statue *The Thinker*, which also happens to be the squad's favorite nickname for her.

And when the boss lady is in statue mode, everyone else in the room shuts up and gives her time to think. Which is exactly what Kylie and I were doing.

"He's making a movie," Cates said for the third time. "Without any camera equipment."

"He's making it in his head," I said, also for the third time.

"That's the part I've been wrestling with. It doesn't make sense."

"The man is crazy, boss," I said. "We can't expect sense from a guy whose last known address is a loony bin."

"What about the Ian Stewart murder and the Brad Schuck bombing?" Cates said. "That's not in his head. Both of those are on film."

"Yeah, but for the most part he's acting everything out live."

"That's called a play, Zach, not a movie."

"We will happily point out the difference to Mr. Benoit when we arrest him."

"And when will that be?" Cates said. "You've got his name, you've got his photo, you've got a lead on his girlfriend—how long before you nail this maniac?"

"Captain, we're working on it around the clock, but he's smart."

"No, Detective, you were right the first time. He's crazy. Talk to Cheryl Robinson and see if she can help us figure out what's going on inside his head. Where would he hide, where could he strike next? Run it all past her."

"I've already left messages at her office and on her cell," I said. "If she doesn't get back to me tonight, I'll catch up with her first thing in the morning."

Cates turned to Kylie. "You're in the biz. What do you make of all this?"

"I'm not 'in the biz.' That's my husband," Kylie said. "But I've met hundreds of people who are totally immersed in it, and most of them are riddled with insecurity. They walk around as if they're always being judged. And you know what, Captain—they are."

"We're all being judged," Cates said.

"Not like this," Kylie said. "Let's say you sell cars for a living. Someone takes a test-drive, and when it's over, they look you in the eye and say, 'This car sucks. I'm not buying it.' That doesn't mean they hate you. They just don't like your product. But in show business, the product most people are selling is themselves."

"So they take every rejection personally," Cates said.

"Exactly. And Gabriel Benoit has been

kicking around the fringes of this business for years—overlooked, undervalued, ignored, rejected, tossed aside. He keeps on trying, but he's never broken through."

"Well, he sure as shit is making up for it now," Cates said. "Find him."

Kylie and I know an exit cue when we hear one. We both stood up. But Cates held up her hand and waved us back down in our chairs.

"I've been thinking," The Thinker said. "Maybe Mr. Benoit isn't so crazy after all. Maybe he *is* shooting a movie." Cates paused. "Okay, maybe not *shooting* it, but laying it all out. Writing the script for it. Right now, millions of people are caught up in his story. It's got action, drama, suspense, and everyone is on the edge of their seat waiting to see how it ends. Overnight, this overlooked, undervalued *extra* person has gone from show business loser to world-famous serial killer."

"But he's the only one who gets to see himself in the movie," Kylie said.

"For now," Cates said. "But by the time we get to the final act, don't you think that every studio on both coasts will be offering up millions to buy the rights?"

"Captain, he would never see a penny of it. It's the Son of Sam law. A criminal can't profit from—" Kylie stopped short. "Oh shit! How did we not think of that?"

Cates smiled. "It looks like Detective MacDonald just had a come-to-Jesus moment."

"And I'm about three seconds behind her," I said. "Benoit doesn't care about the money. He doesn't need any camera equipment. He's writing a script. Somebody else will make the movie."

"His movie," Cates said. "Starring Brad Pitt or Johnny Depp or George Clooney as Gabriel Benoit. And from the looks of things, he's well on his way to getting it made."

"Captain," Kylie said, "if you're right, then we're just in the middle of Act Two, and I'm willing to bet he's got a hell of a blockbuster finale planned out for Act Three."

Nobody took the bet.

Chapter 51

KYLIE AND I holed up in the office and started digging into all things Gabriel Benoit. We were eating sandwiches from Gerri's Diner when we got word that Brad Schuck died without ever coming out of his coma.

It didn't change anything. I updated his file and went back to work. It was after 9:00 p.m. when Cheryl Robinson finally returned my call.

"Zach, I just got your message," she said talking loudly. The background was noisy. Happy noisy. "I'm out to dinner, my phone was buried in my purse—sorry. What's going on?"

"We've got a suspect, and Captain Cates would like you to jump in and try to get inside this guy's head."

"Give me a top line."

"Gabriel Benoit, thirty-four, only child, born in Stuttgart, Germany, father was an officer in army intelligence. Family bounced around—South Korea, Alabama, Georgia—and eventually Dad wound up at the Pentagon. Gabriel went to high school in northern Virginia, where he was a B student with a keen interest in film studies. Dropped out of college in his freshman year. After that, it's spotty till he moves to New York, where he's in hundreds of movie and TV productions, using his real name and Social Security number. Two years ago, his mailing address changed from an apartment to a PO box, and finally to a mental health facility, which is where we tracked him, but he vacated a few months ago."

"Two years ago he either became so paranoid he didn't want anyone to find him, or that's when he started planning these murders," Cheryl said.

"Or both," I said.

"Email me whatever you have on him. I'll try to make sense of it when I get home tonight and I'll meet you at the diner in the morning. Is five too early?"

"Not for this case. Thanks, Doc. Sorry to interrupt your dinner."

"Don't apologize," she said. "He totally understands. He's a cop too."

She hung up.

He? She was having dinner with a guy? And he's a cop? It sure as hell didn't take her long to replace Fred. I wondered how this guy felt about opera.

Kylie and I worked another two hours, and I crawled into bed at midnight. Four hours later, my cell phone rang. Caller ID said it was Kylie, but I knew better.

"Hello, Spence," I said.

"This is not Spence," Kylie said. "I read him the riot act yesterday. 'If you have any bright ideas in the middle of the night, don't wake Zach, wake me.'"

"Well, tell Spence thanks for not waking me," I said.

"Listen up, I'm serious," she said. "I brought home a copy of the video of Benoit tossing the Molotov. I've watched it a dozen times. Sometimes Spence is in the room, sometimes he's not. Tonight he wakes me and says, 'I just figured it out.'"

"Colonel Mustard in the conservatory with the candlestick?"

"Zach, I know you think Spence is...I don't know...creative. But this time I think he has something."

"Sorry. I'm listening."

"I don't know about you, but when I watch that tape, I tend to zero in on Benoit. Spence did a freeze-frame on the Molotov cocktail. There's no wick on it. No oily rag. No flame."

"So?"

"So according to Spence, that's one of the tricks of the trade. If the bottle is flaming, you can't hand it to some megastar actor who's insured for millions. Rather than have a stuntman stand in for the shot, they go wickless. We know Benoit had an accomplice in the robbery, so maybe his partner is a special effects guy."

"I don't mean to shoot down another one of Spence's middle-of-the-night epiphanies, but any kid with a chemistry set and a mean streak can make a basic incendiary device—with or without a tampon for a wick. The simplest way is to take brake fluid, Drano—"

"A kid didn't make this, Zach. Spence said it looks very professional, and whatever else you think about him, give him some credit for knowing the film business."

"Kylie, let's not argue. We're both exhausted. Tell Spence I appreciate the input."

"He gave me a list of special effects guys he thinks fit the specs. There are only six of them, and even if they're all clean, one of them may see something in the video that points us to the guy who built it. I know it's grasping at straws, but what other clues do we have?"

"Okay, I'm meeting with Cheryl Robinson in about an hour," I said. "After that we can track down these special effects guys and talk to them."

"You didn't tell me you were meeting with the profiler," Kylie said.

"I'm meeting her at five in the morning. I thought you might want to get some sleep."

"Hell no. Besides, I'm awake now anyway. Where are you guys meeting?"

"Gerri's Diner on Lex around the corner from the precinct."

"Great. I'll see you there. Order me some coffee and a toasted English." She hung up.

And just like that, I had plans for breakfast. Just me, the beautiful old girlfriend I was trying to get over, and the beautiful new woman who, the more I thought about it, might be just what I needed to help me get over the old one.

I got down on the floor and unrolled my yoga mat.

Chapter 52

I DECIDED I'D show up ten minutes late. I figured it would give Cheryl and Kylie a chance to get to know each other. I also thought that if I got there last, it might be less awkward—even though I was the only one who saw this little threesome *as* awkward.

I was wrong. As soon as I walked in the door, Gerri Gomperts came out from behind the counter and cornered me.

"What's going on?" she said, wiping her hands on an apron that already showed the signs of a hectic morning behind the grill.

"The lady shrink was waiting for you, and that other one plops down right next to her."

"That's *Detective* Other One to you," I said. "She's my new partner."

"I don't care who she is," Gerri said. "Pick one."

"Tough call," I said. "They're both smart, beautiful, and fun to be with."

"Trust me, kid," Gerri said. "Go for the one without the wedding ring."

I ordered coffee and a bagel and sat down at the booth. Kylie and Cheryl were in the middle of an animated conversation. I don't know what it is about women. They barely knew each other, and they were already bonding.

"I just let Cheryl in on Captain Cates's theory," Kylie said.

"And it's frighteningly plausible," Cheryl said.

"Did you get a chance to look at the backgrounder on Benoit?" I said.

"I went through it twice. The army officer father is always a red flag. I hate to stereotype, but that's what profilers do. Military fathers can be hard on their sons. Gabriel probably had very little control over the events in his life, especially if Dad was abusive or controlled him to the extreme. He would develop significant rage, which he had to suppress in order to survive. So he created a world he could control—a world of fantasy."

"I thought all kids had fantasies," I said.

"We all had imaginary friends, but in Benoit's case the movies he played out in his head became more reality than fantasy. He was the writer and the director. He controlled everything. The problem probably began when he started working in the real-world movie business."

"Where he controlled nothing," Kylie said.

"Exactly. He's an extra, practically superfluous. It's not his fault that he's not a star. He blames those Hollywood people—especially the ones at the top. They're the oppressive force preventing him from succeeding."

"Let's face it," Kylie said. "In real life, those goons prevent a lot of people from succeeding."

"And in real life they get away with it, but in Benoit's script, he gets to kill them off."

"Do you have any guess where he'll hit next?" I said.

"Cates's theory makes a lot of sense, and if she's right, his next scenario will be huge. He started with a quiet little poisoning, escalated to a shooting, then ratcheted up to a firebomb with color commentary by Ryan Seacrest. Our boy is not going to go back to spiking someone's tomato juice. He's playing this out for his audience, and the murders will get more dramatic, more cinematic, and probably have a higher body count as he moves along. If I were talking to my fellow psychologists, I'd probably say he's suffering from psychogenic paranoid psychosis. But cop to cop, he's a sicko killer with a vendetta. And he's about to do something really nasty, so get him off the streets fast."

"Get him fast," I repeated. "You're starting to sound like our boss."

Kylie's cell rang.

"It's Karen Porcelli from Central Records," she said.

"At this hour?" I said.

"Right after you and I spoke, I left a message for Sergeant Porcelli to call me as soon as she got in. I want her to do background checks on the special effects guys Spence gave us. I'll be right back."

She stepped outside to take the call.

"She's one dedicated cop," Cheryl said. "And a terrific person to boot."

"You're not so bad yourself, Doc. Thanks for the insight. Sorry to sandbag you with all this crap so late last night."

"Don't apologize. In my job, I live for sociopaths. Of course lovesick cops are my bread and butter," she said playfully. "You and MacDonald will make a great team. If there's anything I can do to help you get rid of that old baggage you're hanging on to, just give me a buzz."

"I'll do that," I said. "Maybe we can start with a little opera therapy."

Chapter 53

GABRIEL FONDLED THE Walther. He now realized it was too hot to ever use again, but it was like an ancient hound dog. Too old to hunt, but he loved it too much to get rid of it. He put it back in his closet, then tucked the Glock into his backpack.

"Where you going?" Lexi said. She was still in bed.

"Out."

"You need a partner in crime?"

"I thought we had a deal," Gabriel said. "Coproducers work on the script, supervise wardrobe and makeup..."

"Sleep with the director," she said. "I thought maybe because the sex has been so good, you'd change your mind."

He sat down on the bed, rested one palm on her breast, and kissed her lips softly. "The sex was so incredible, I just want to think of you lying here naked while I'm out," he said.

"You're full of shit," she said, "but I love you for it. When will you be back?"

"A couple of hours."

Excellent, she thought. *The longer you're gone, the better.*

He left, locking the door behind him. She listened as the elevator arrived at their floor, the doors closed, and she could hear the whir of the motor as it descended to the lobby. Then she tiptoed to the window and watched him walk out the front door and down the street toward the subway.

She knew there was no way he'd let her go to Mickey's with him, but she had to ask. If she didn't ask, he'd get suspicious. That was her character. Now that he was gone, she was ready to become her new character.

She hadn't been able to decide whether to call herself Pandemonia or Passionata, so she opted for both. She was Pandemonia Passionata, Satan's beautiful lover.

She had found the perfect outfit in a thrift shop on Mulberry Street—a dull-looking gauzy black silk dress, trimmed with lace and velvet ribbon. It was at least fifty years old, and cost all of eighteen bucks. For another twelve she bought some jet-black beads and a little black ostrich feather hat with a black veil. She pinned her hair up, then carefully put on her makeup. The final touch was the lipstick—the brightest red she could find. Without that, she thought, the whole scene could have been shot in black and white.

She checked her watch. She still had plenty of time to get uptown and find a good spot.

She looked in the mirror.

Perfect. All she needed now was one last prop.

She went to Gabriel's closet and took down the Walther.

Chapter 54

KYLIE AND I went to the office and tried to figure out where Benoit might strike next.

It was only Day Three of Hollywood on the Hudson week, which meant the city would be chock-full of potential victims between now and the time they all headed west on Friday.

We called Mandy Sowter, the public information officer, at home and told her to fax us a list of everyone who was invited, and to flag the targets with the highest profiles. We also asked for the schedule of events.

"You realize that the PI office will only have access to the official schedule they get from the film commission," I said. "There's probably going to be fifty more private meetings, lunches, and cocktail parties that aren't on her list."

"And Shelley Trager will know about every one of them," Kylie said. Without missing a beat, she speed-dialed Spence and asked him to get us the names, times, and venues of every event, big or small, that Trager was aware of.

Ten minutes later, Spence phoned back. I could hear only Kylie's end of the conversation. "Okay, okay, tell him we'll be there."

"What was that all about?" I asked.

"Spence called Shelley. He's happy to help, but he also told Spence to remind us that the memorial service for Ian Stewart is this morning, and he expects to have police presence there."

"That actually sounds like a good idea," I said.

"Glad you agree, because even if you didn't, I'd have to go as Mrs. Spence Harrington," Kylie said.

Ten minutes later, Karen Porcelli called from Records. Kylie put her on speaker.

Anybody who handles explosives has to

register with NYPD, so Porcelli had no trouble tracking down all six men on the list.

"You're going to love this," Porcelli said. "One of them was just released from the Adirondack Correctional Facility in Ray Brook. His name is Mickey Peltz."

"What was he in for?" Kylie asked.

"He siphoned off some of the studio's money earmarked for explosives, bought cheap crap, and blew off somebody's arm. They had him on grand larceny and assault one, but he pled it down to assault two and took four years."

"Any connection to Benoit?" Kylie asked.

"They've worked on at least half a dozen different productions together. No record of Benoit visiting him in prison."

"Where do we find Mr. Peltz?"

"I checked with Corrections. They have him at 33-87 Skillman Avenue in Long Island City. Fifth floor. I'll email you his PO's contact info along with last known addresses on the other five special effects guys, but based on Peltz's prior, I'd put him at the top of your list."

"Thanks, Karen. I owe you one," Kylie said and hung up.

"And I guess I owe Spence one," I said. "We'll pick up Peltz on our way back from the memorial service."

Cates didn't arrive till after eight. Even on an easy day, she's there by six.

"Sorry I'm late," she said, "but I really needed to treat myself to a mani-pedi this morning."

Bullshit. She must have spent the morning being chewed out by the mayor, the commissioner, or both.

"What did Cheryl Robinson think?" Cates said.

"She thinks Benoit is crazy and you're smart," I said.

"It's nice to know somebody thinks I'm smart. Did she happen to mention why?"

"She likes your he's-writing-a-script theory, and she agrees that he's probably planning something bigger than anything we've seen," I said. "We have a list of possible targets and venues."

"We also have a lead on someone who might have helped Benoit build that Molotov cocktail," Kylie said.

We told her about Mickey Peltz.

"Zach and I are just leaving for the memorial service for Ian Stewart," Kylie said. "Once it's over we'll swing around to Long Island City and bring Peltz in for questioning."

"I'd rather telescope the time," Cates said. "I'll send some uniforms to pick up Mr. Peltz."

"That's okay," Kylie said. "We can get him. It won't take that long."

"Relax, Detective MacDonald," Cates said. "I'll just have the uniforms bring him in and put him in an interrogation room. I'm not going to ask another team to question him. I'll keep him on ice until you two get back."

Kylie gave the boss a half smile. "Sorry," she said. "Was it that obvious that I'm obsessed with this case and hate to let go of anything connected to it?"

"Yes, but given a choice between having a cop who is crazy possessive and one who doesn't give a shit," Cates said, "I'll take the crazy one every time."

"In that case, Captain, I have good news," I said. "Detective MacDonald is as crazy as they come."

Chapter 55

GABRIEL WAS BACK on the number 7 train. His backpack was empty except for the Glock, which was loaded. Maybe he should have taken a cab, but the odds of a cop stopping a blue-eyed, sandy-haired white boy to search his backpack were slim.

Plus, he liked the rattle and the rhythm of New York's underground. He lowered his eyes to half-mast, but did not completely shut them.

I'd like to thank the members of the Academy. Best screenplay, best actor, best director—and now best picture. I'd also like to thank my amazing girlfriend, who believed in me when nobody else did. I'd tell you her name, but then I'd have to kill you.

Gabriel laughed out loud and peered through narrow slits at his fellow passengers. None of them cared or dared to look at the laughing weirdo. New Yorkers know better.

"Man, you look like shit," he said when Mickey opened the door. The old man's long, lanky body was stooped, his face wan, and a few wispy hairs hung from his protruding chin. "Kind of like Shaggy from Scooby-Doo, only about eighty years from now."

"Thanks. I've been up all night putting your stuff together," Mickey said.

"You got the goods?"

"Mickey Peltz never disappoints."

Mickey led Gabriel to his workbench, where the blocks of C4 were neatly stacked. There were also spools of wire, two boxes of blasting caps, four digital timers, and four remotes.

"This is all you need and more," Mickey said.

"I'm going to need a crash course in demolition," Gabe said.

"Easy peasy." Mickey picked up a block of C4 and smashed it down hard on the workbench. Gabriel jumped.

"First rule. Don't be afraid of this stuff," he said, handing Gabriel the block of plastic. "It won't go off by accident. You can mold it, cut it, even fire a bullet into it, and it won't detonate. It takes a combination of extreme heat and a shock wave, which is what your blasting caps are for. You with me?"

Gabriel slammed the C4 against the top of the workbench. "With you."

Peltz was a good teacher, and for the next forty minutes he gave Gabriel a tutorial in the art of blowing things up.

"Not as easy peasy as you think," Gabriel said. "There's a lot to keep track of."

"I have a solution," Mickey said. "Take me along with you. I'll work dirt cheap."

"No."

"Why not?"

"I'm just playing it safe, Mick. You're on parole. Your PO can walk in here anytime and turn this place inside out without a warrant. You get seen carrying a duffel bag, and any cop can do a stop and search. I don't want my go-to pyrotechnician to spend the next twenty years in prison."

"I don't have twenty years," Mickey said. "I might not even have twenty months. I'll bite down on a blasting cap before I ever go back."

"Then why risk it?"

"Because this is what I do, and I lost my license to do it legally. I swear to God in heaven, Gabriel, these past two days have been the most fun I've had in years. I'm back doing what I love, and I just want to keep on doing it."

"I can't," Gabriel said. "I'm sorry."

Mickey closed his eyes and took a deep breath. "Yeah, me too." He opened a drawer and took out a three-ring binder.

"What's that?"

"I was afraid you'd turn me down, but I figured even if I couldn't be there with you, at least I could do something. So I put this together for you—no extra charge."

He handed Gabriel the binder. The cover page said *The Art of Blowing Shit Up.*

Inside it was filled with hand-drawn diagrams on graph paper. Alongside each illustration, Mickey had neatly hand-lettered simple instructions. "What to Do" was in black. "What Not to Do" was in red. It was a step-by-step recap of his tutorial. At the end was an appendix—more than a hundred pages of detailed information on explosives pulled together from scientific journals, *The Special Forces Demolition Training Handbook*, how-to websites, blogs, and of course that must-read for every wannabe revolutionary, *The Anarchist Cookbook.*

"This is incredible," Gabe said. "You did this for me?"

"No, I bought it at Bombs and Noble." Mickey hawked up a laugh. "That's funny, right? You can use that line in your movie. Of course I did it for you, asshole. I told you Mickey Peltz never disappoints."

"Thanks. Let's pack this stuff up."

"You got about a hundred pounds here," Mickey said. "Can you carry it?"

Gabriel pulled a retractable handle from his backpack, then rolled the bag on its in-line skate wheels. "I can pull it."

Five minutes later, he stepped out of the lobby, leaned the bag against the side of the building, and took out his cell phone.

And then he saw it.

It turned the corner onto Skillman. *Cop car.*

Gabe held his cell phone to his ear and pretended to talk while he watched the car.

It's just cruising. Looking for bad guys.

Sure enough, it drove past him, and he took a deep breath. *If you only knew what's in this bag.*

Ten yards past the building, the driver hit the brake. Gabriel watched as the reverse lights came on and the cops backed up. The driver rolled down the window.

"Hey, buddy!" the cop yelled. "Stay right there."

Gabriel froze.

Chapter 56

TWO COPS GOT out of the car.

Gabe looked them over. One was male, young, and big. The other was male, young, and bigger.

Officer Bigger walked up to him. The other cop went inside.

"Is this 33-87 Skillman or 33-97? The building address is rubbed off."

"I'm not really sure," Gabe said. "I don't live here."

The other cop came back out.

"Danny, this is the place. The guy's name is on the bell. Fifth floor."

"Looks like my partner solved it," Bigger said. "Have a good day, sir."

"You too, officer," Gabe said.

He watched them take the elevator, and then casually sauntered over to the patrol car. And there it was, painted in blue and white on the rear fender: 19 PCT.

No wonder these guys had trouble finding this building. They're from the 19th Precinct—the one Jordan and MacDonald work out of. This is no random parole check. They're not just here to rattle Mickey's cage. They're trying to connect him to me.

Bag full of C4 or not, there was no going home now.

He walked to the corner, crossed Skillman Avenue, and leaned against a traffic light, where he could watch Mickey's building and still stay out of sight.

Lexi was waiting for him at home. He called her. No answer. He tried her cell. Again no answer. He texted. Nothing.

Dammit. First she kills Fitzhugh, now she's off the grid, and to top it all off, the cops have come for Mickey.

His heart was thumping. He dialed Lexi again. This time he waited for her voice mail to pick up. As usual, the outgoing message sounded chipper, perky, and happy.

"Hi, this is Lexi. I'm making some changes in my life right now. If I don't return your call, then you're one of the changes. Bye."

"Lexi, it's me. Things are turning to shit. I'm outside Mickey's building, and the cops showed up. I'm pretty sure they're going to pick up Mickey. I got forty-five thousand dollars' worth of C4 in my bag, and there's not a damn thing I can do to stop them. That's all. Oh yeah, one more thing. *Where the fuck are you?*" he screamed.

Ten minutes later, the cops came out. Mickey was with them. No cuffs.

He's not under arrest. They're just bringing him in for questioning. I know Mickey. He'll play dumb—won't say a word.

But then his parole officer will show up and give him an ultimatum. Tell me what you know, and I won't charge you with violating your parole. But if you clam up and I find out you were with Benoit, you'll be back in Ray Brook in time for dinner.

Mickey would panic. He'd rather die than go back, and if the PO pushes him to the wall, he'll give me up in a heartbeat.

Chapter 57

ALT. SCENE:

EXT. FRANK E. CAMPBELL FUNERAL CHAPEL, MADISON AVENUE AND 81ST STREET—DAY

PANDEMONIA PASSIONATA looks so pretty in her little black mourning dress as she waits patiently behind the police barricade at Ian Stewart's memorial service. The mourners file slowly out of the chapel, but she ignores the little fish. She's here for the Big One. This is Pandemonia's moment. Redemption time.

LEXI WANTED TO scream.

Her calves were on fire, her toes were crushed, and every muscle in her lower back was in knots.

She hadn't worn heels in years, and these four-inch, half-a-size-too-small black thrift-shop pumps were killing her. But she had no choice. Not only did they complete her disguise as a soulful Upper East Side mourner, but they gave her the added height that she needed to see the front of the funeral chapel.

As it turned out, her line of vision was perfect. The police had set up metal crowd-control barricades on the sidewalk just to the right of the funeral home entrance. And the crowd was much thinner than she expected—fewer than thirty fans—so she found a spot right in front.

She'd been standing there for ninety minutes, and she couldn't even begin to count how many times Gabe had called or texted. She was dying to answer, but she couldn't. She'd have to wait till the scene was over. Too bad he wasn't open-minded enough to log onto TMZ so he could find out about these things right away. But just as well. She'd rather tell him herself over a couple of beers and maybe a nice foot massage. He'd be so crazy happy, he'd forget that whole stupid mess that happened in Jimmy Fitzhugh's trailer.

The double doors to the funeral parlor swung open, and the uniformed doorman hooked them into place. The funeral director came out first, walking backward, hands gently guiding the highly polished mahogany coffin.

Lexi tensed. Almost on cue, her cell phone vibrated and she flinched. It was Gabriel trying to reach her for the trillionth time. No way she could pick up. She opened her purse, took out a tissue, and dabbed her eyes. She left the purse open and stood in solemn tearful tribute to the departed as he rolled toward the waiting hearse.

A few mourners exited the chapel behind

the coffin. But they were nobodies. Like it said in the script—little fish.

And then the old Jewish guy stepped out. Shelley Trager. Edie Coburn was to his left, dressed to the eyeballs in her designer grieving widow's finery. Bullshit. She hated Ian Stewart as much as anybody did. To Trager's right was the young director, Muhlenberg. Lexi had seen his early indie work and thought, *Damn, this guy is good,* but he'd been making crap ever since he stepped up to the big leagues.

The trio stopped in the doorway, just out of line with the angle she needed for the perfect shot.

She reached into her purse, put her hand on the grip of Gabriel's gun, and waited.

And then the cop showed up. The pretty one she had seen on TV. MacDonald. Right behind her was her husband, the TV producer. She knew them both on sight. Google images had hundreds of pictures of the happy couple.

She had planned on shooting only Trager. But now there were five of them. *Oh my God, can you imagine if I killed them all? Gabriel would be over the moon. That would more than make up for screwing up the robbery.*

The lady cop and her husband caught up with Trager in the doorway. Lexi had no idea what they were talking about. Logistics, maybe. Like who's going in which car.

The conversation lasted only a few seconds, and then Trager stepped out onto Madison Avenue. The others followed. Five of them, side by side, headed her way. She didn't even know how many bullets were in the gun, but she'd bet there had to be at least five.

And action, she said to herself.

Pandemonia Passionata pulled the Walther PPK out of her purse and opened fire.

Chapter 58

THE SUBWAY WAS out of the question. Not with a bag full of C4. The bomb-sniffing dogs would have him for lunch.

And now that the cops had seen him, even a taxi was risky. Every yellow cab in the city had a decal posted on its rear window: THIS VEHICLE IS EQUIPPED WITH CAMERA SECURITY. YOU WILL BE PHOTOGRAPHED.

The hell I will, Gabriel decided.

It took him ten minutes to flag down a gypsy cab.

There was no meter, and the driver quoted a price back into lower Manhattan. "Fifty bucks."

Gabe opened the door, shoved his back-pack in, and flopped onto the grease-stained, duct-taped rear seat.

Any other time and he would have haggled with the guy. *Fifty bucks? For what? To ride in a hot, filthy death trap that stinks of pine freshener and whatever disgusting Middle Eastern camel shit you're chewing on? Fifty bucks so I can listen to you rant nonstop on your cell phone with the rest of your goddamn terrorist network? I'll give you thirty-five, and you're lucky I'm not a suicide bomber, or I'd blow your ass to Mecca and back.*

It could have been a good scene. But not today. Today he had more important things to do.

He gave up on leaving messages for Lexi. Wherever she was, she obviously didn't want him to know. He'd deal with her later. First he had to deal with Mickey Peltz. He dialed Mickey's cell.

"Hello."

He couldn't believe it. Mickey picked up.

"Mick, where are you?"

"Manhattan. Cops picked me up and brought me to the 19th, put me in an interrogation room, and told me to wait for these two detectives."

"Jordan and MacDonald?"

Mickey let out a low whistle. "Man, you're good."

"It was easy. Those are the same two who are looking for me."

"Well, don't worry about me saying anything. I'm not under arrest. They just want to talk to me, and trust me, I'm not talking."

"Did they call your parole officer yet?"

"They made me call him from the loft. That's the deal. He's supposed to be in the room when they question me, but he's in Sing Sing at a hearing till one o'clock. So now I'm just sitting here with my thumb up my ass till he shows up."

"Mickey, I can't hear you," Gabe said. "Bad cell connection."

"I said I'm just sitting here waiting for my parole—"

Gabe hung up.

Mickey was an idiot. He'd be oh so cool and cavalier with the cops, but the PO would crush him in no time. Gabe was already writing the scene in his head.

INT. 19TH PRECINCT—NEW
YORK CITY—DAY

Mickey Peltz is sitting in the
interrogation room with
DETECTIVES JORDAN and
MACDONALD. His PO walks
in.

PO

Hello, Mickey. You ready to play
ball with me?

MICKEY

Sure, coach. Always.

PO

Football or baseball?

MICKEY

What do you mean?

PO

With football, you're going back
to prison for six to twelve. With
baseball, it'll be two to four.

MICKEY

Go back? Why? I didn't do nothing.

PO

I hear you've been associating
with a wanted criminal. A mass
murderer. Gabriel Benoit.

MICKEY

I told these cops I haven't seen or
heard from Gabe in years.

PO

In that case, when I go back and
search your loft, his DNA won't
be there.

MICKEY

So what if his DNA is there? He used to visit me back in the old days. Or maybe he broke in when I was out. That's no proof that I met with him.

PO

Cops need proof, Mickey. I don't. All I need is reasonable cause to believe you lapsed into your old criminal ways and you've violated the conditions of your parole. Now, listen carefully, because I'm only going to say this once. Tell me what Gabriel Benoit is planning next, and I'll be too busy to look for his DNA at your loft. But I want every detail and I want it on a gold platter, because the silver platter is already off the table.

And that would be that. Mickey would open up like a three-dollar hooker at a lumberjack convention.

Gabriel's cell rang.

Lexi. Please let it be Lexi.

He checked the caller ID. Mickey.

He didn't answer. Talking to Mickey was a waste of time. What he had to do now was shut the bastard up.

He had till 1:00.

Chapter 59

BY THE TIME he got back to the apartment, Gabriel's clothes were sweat-soaked all the way through. He wheeled the explosives into the bedroom, stripped down, took a quick shower, and tried to figure out what to wear for the next scene.

Lexi would know, but she wasn't here. He rummaged through their wardrobe supply and did the best he could.

It was 10:30. He had time before Mickey's parole officer showed up, but first he needed a drink. He grabbed one of Lexi's champagne glasses from the dish rack and poured a shot of vodka. Not enough to get him buzzed. Just a little something to take the edge off.

He sat down at Lexi's computer, booted up, opened Firefox, and checked her recent browser history to see what sites she'd been visiting. It was the usual crap—Perez Hilton, TMZ, Astrology Connection.

He checked her email. Maybe she sent him something and he didn't get it on his cell. But there was nothing.

He opened her recent document folder. And there it was at the top of the list— AltScene.doc with yesterday's date.

Alt. Scene? Lexi, what are you thinking?

He double-clicked and the document filled the screen.

ALT. SCENE:

EXT. FRANK E. CAMPBELL FUNERAL CHAPEL, MADISON AVENUE AND 81ST STREET— DAY

PANDEMONIA PASSIONATA looks so pretty in her little black

mourning dress as she waits patiently behind the police barricade at Ian Stewart's memorial
service. The mourners file slowly
out of the chapel, but she ignores
the little fish. She's here for the
Big One. This is Pandemonia's
moment. Redemption time.

Who the hell is Pandemonia Passionata?
He kept reading. Halfway through the
scene, he stood up, and stormed off to his
closet.

The Walther wasn't there.

He flung the champagne glass against the
wall.

"Shit, shit, shit, shit, shit!" he screamed,
pounding his fist against the closet door.

It wasn't anger. It was agony.

Chapter 60

THERE WERE AT least thirty cops on the scene and none of us saw the gun. But as soon as I heard the first shot, I had no doubt what we had on our hands. *Active shooter—an individual actively engaged in killing or attempting to kill people in a confined and populated area.*

Our Counterterrorism Bureau issued a book on the subject. I've read it three times, and what stands out for me is this: *Active-shooter attacks are dynamic events. Police response depends on the unique circumstances of the incident.*

In other words, when the bullets start flying, we can't tell you what's going to happen. You're on your own.

The first shot hit Shelley Trager. He stopped abruptly, his hands to his chest. A potted plant, one of two that stood in solemn repose on either side of the front door, broke his fall, and he slid to the ground, his face contorted in pain.

The crowd hemorrhaged in every direction, and that's when I got my first look at the shooter. A woman in black. She was standing directly behind the metal barricade, right arm outstretched, gun pointed at the people caught in the front doorway of the funeral home.

Her? Ninety-six out of every hundred active shooters are men. Our heads had been wrapped around looking for a man.

My gun was out, and I bolted across Madison as she pulled the trigger a second time. She was not a pro. Her one-armed shooting stance was all wrong, and her hand kicked back when she took the shot. I have no idea who she was aiming at, but I watched as the bullet drilled through Henry Muhlenberg's skull, exiting in a trail of blood, bones, and brains.

The crowd was in chaos. With the barricade trapping them on one side, and the funeral home on another, a handful of people ran north toward 82nd Street, but the bulk of them came running straight at me, heading for the opposite side of Madison. The shooter, who was less than ten feet from Spence and Kylie, turned her gun toward them.

I stopped, trying to line up a clean shot.

And then I went down hard.

A large man in a purple sweatshirt had broadsided me, kicked the gun out of my hand when I hit the ground, fell on top of me, and screamed, "I got him, I got him!"

I heard another shot, then another, then a third, as more wannabe-hero civilians piled on top of me.

I had counted five shots in all. And then nothing. Five seconds passed. Seven. Ten. The gunfire had stopped.

The Counterterrorism Bureau was right. Every active-shooter event is different. I had no idea what was going to happen, and now with my face pressed to the oil-streaked pavement, I had no idea how this one had ended.

Chapter 61

I COULD HEAR NYPD coming to my rescue. "Let him up, let him up. He's a cop."

"He has a gun," the fat guy directly on top of me yelled back in a thick southern drawl.

"He's a *cop,* you idiot. We all have guns. Now get off him."

And then, from ten feet away, another voice—loud, official, conclusive. "She's dead."

Who's dead?

I was at the bottom of a dogpile that must have been four or five guys high. I could feel the load getting lighter as the uniforms dragged them off one by one.

Finally, the 250-pound guy who brought me down, who turned out to be a high school football coach from Batesville, Mississippi, got up and reached out to help me.

"I'm sorry, Officer. It's just that I saw you running toward a bunch of people with a gun..."

Who's dead? WHO'S DEAD???

I stood up, got my bearings, and pushed my way to the front of the funeral home.

"You laying down on the job again?"

It was my partner, service pistol still in her hand, the hint of an inappropriate smile on her face, and, most important, not dead.

"You all right?" I said.

"No. But I'm better off than she is."

The woman in black was lying on the sidewalk, face up, two bullet holes in her chest, one in her forehead.

"You do that?" I said.

Kylie nodded.

Perfect shot group.

"I saw Trager and Muhlenberg go down," I said.

"Muhlenberg was dead before he hit the

ground," Kylie said. "Shelley has a few broken ribs, but he'll be fine."

"A few broken…how is that possible? I saw him take a direct hit to the chest."

"The son of a bitch was wearing a vest."

Trager was lying on Madison, a jacket propping his head up. I knelt down beside him.

He smiled up at me. He still had the crooked teeth of a kid who had grown up in poverty. At this point, he had enough money to straighten them a thousand times over, but he kept them as they were—a daily reminder of his roots.

I smiled back. "You were wearing a vest?" I said.

"My wife bought it for me. I think Bloomingdale's was having their annual Kevlar sale."

"Your wife bought you a bulletproof vest?" I said. "Really?"

"She said I'm high enough on the food chain that if some *meshuggener* is out there killing people, odds are I'm on his list. I hate it when she's right, but in this case I'm willing to make an exception."

I stood up. "You're a lucky man, Shelley."

"I know, I know." He sighed. "And she'll never let me hear the end of it."

"Zach. Over here."

Spence Harrington was sitting on the front step of the funeral home. "You see that?" he said, pointing to a chunk of the building's brownstone façade that had obviously taken a bullet. "Another half a second, and that would've been my head. Kylie shoved me out of the way. Saved my life."

"I think she saved a lot of lives," I said.

"You've got one hell of a partner," he said.

"So do you."

Kylie came over holding the shooter's purse. "Her name is Alexis Carter, twenty-eight years old."

"Alexis," I said. "Lexi. The girlfriend J.J. told us about. What's her address? He may still be there."

"She has an Indiana driver's license. There's nothing in here that connects her to a New York City address. Damn it, Zach, I never thought about looking for the girlfriend. I was totally focused on looking for a man."

"We were all looking for a man," I said. "Gabriel Benoit."

"And we're still looking for him," she said. "Let's make sure this whole scene is locked down. Have the uniforms get statements from everyone in the crowd. I don't care if it takes all—Zach...her cell phone. It's vibrating."

"Answer it."

She scrambled to pull the shooter's cell phone out of the purse. "The ID says 'Gabe.' It's him."

"Put him on speaker."

She pushed the answer button. "Hello," she said.

"Who is this?" the voice on the other end demanded.

"This is Detective Kylie MacDonald, New York City Police Department."

"Where's Lexi? Where is she?"

"I have a better question," Kylie said. "Where are you?"

The line went dead.

BOOK THREE

THE SHOW MUST GO ON

Chapter 62

THE BIGGER THE crime, the more likely it is that someone important will show up to keep the cops from solving it. In our case, it was a close personal friend of Shelley Trager, who just happened to be the mayor of the city of New York.

Trager was on an EMS stretcher, about to be transported to Lenox Hill Hospital, when the mayor and the rest of his entourage arrived at the crime scene. After congratulating his friend on being smart enough to wear a bulletproof vest, His Honor turned on Kylie.

"Detective MacDonald," he said. "Aren't

you the one who told me you were going to catch this maniac before he left town? The way you keep promises, you have a bright future ahead of you. As a politician."

"Stan!" Trager yelled from the stretcher. "If it hadn't been for MacDonald, there'd be more bodies piled up outside this funeral home than there are inside. The same goes for Detective Jordan. You got good cops here. Don't be a schmuck. Let them do their job."

"Fine," the mayor huffed. "And I'll do mine. I'm going to pull the plug on Hollywood on the Hudson week."

Trager winced in pain as he propped himself up on one elbow. "Hop in the ambulance, Stan, and I'll drop you off at Bellevue, because you're out of your fucking mind. What message do you want to send to Hollywood? If the shit hits the fan, New Yorkers run from a fight? Or that we've got the fastest, smartest, bravest police force in the world, and nobody—anywhere—backs up the film industry like NYPD Red?"

"So what are you saying, Shelley? If we quit now, the terrorists win?"

"I don't know who would win," Trager

said, "but I can damn well tell you who would lose. You bail out now, and next November you'll be lucky to get half a dozen votes on Staten Island. Grow a pair, Stanley."

"All right. I'll give it one more day." He turned to Kylie. Anyone who thought he might apologize for jumping down her throat, or at least congratulate her for bringing down an active shooter, didn't know him very well. "Who's the dead girl?" he said.

She told him.

"Now what?" he asked.

"We're going through her text messages and her voice mails," Kylie said. "She's only one degree of separation from Gabriel Benoit, the guy we're looking for. We're closing in on him."

"I'll ask you one more time," the mayor said to Kylie. "You still think you're going to catch this guy?"

"Yes, sir," she said without missing a beat. "Absolutely."

I didn't think it was possible, but Kylie actually sounded more confident than she did when she answered the same question two nights and four dead bodies ago.

Chapter 63

DELIA CATES IS not the kind of cop who shows up at a crime scene just because the mayor is there. She's smart enough to give her team enough time to pull together some information. When she got there, twenty minutes after the mayor left, we had plenty. Some of it downright scary.

"Give me what you've got," she said.

"The shooter was Benoit's girlfriend, Alexis Carter, a.k.a. Lexi. Her cell phone is a treasure trove. Nothing is password-protected," I said. "From what we can put together from the texts between her and Benoit, she knew what he was up to, but she didn't go with him when he killed Roth, Stewart, or Schuck."

"She definitely made up for it this time around."

"All of it behind her boyfriend's back. Benoit had no idea she was going to pull this. In his last few messages he was looking for her frantically. And you were right. They're plotting out a movie. We found the script for this scene in her purse. It had two endings."

"One where she gets away, and one where she dies tragically?" Cates said.

"No. One where she gets away, and one where she gets caught by NYPD Red, and she stands up to us, protecting her man."

"With Tammy Wynette on the sound track?" Cates said.

"She even uses my name and Zach's in the script," Kylie said, unfolding one of the pages we found in Lexi's purse. "Her character is called Pandemonia Passionata. I'll give you some of the dialogue."

DETECTIVE JORDAN

Where is your partner? What does he have planned?

PANDEMONIA

Save your breath, pretty boy. You'll get nothing out of me.

DETECTIVE MACDONALD

You have no idea how much trouble you're in.

PANDEMONIA

And you have no idea how much trouble *you're* in.

"That's the way she saw this going down?" Cates said. "We either catch her, or she gets away? Did she ever write the ending the way it happened?"

Kylie shook her head. "No. She was blissfully delusional to the very end."

"We need the rest of the script," Cates said. "Do you have any idea where it is?"

"It may be in her computer, but she has an out-of-state license and all her last known addresses in New York are dead ends," I said. "But we do have something. Remember Cheryl Robinson predicted that Benoit is about to do something big—much bigger than the previous murders? Listen to this."

I pushed the message retrieval button on Lexi's cell phone.

"Lexi, it's me. Things are turning to shit. I'm outside Mickey's building, and the cops showed up. I'm pretty sure they're going to pick up Mickey. I got forty-five thousand dollars' worth of C4 in my bag, and there's not a damn thing I can do to stop them. That's all. Oh yeah, one more thing. Where the fuck are you?"

"Forty-five thousand?" Cates said. "That's a lot of C4."

"It's enough to call in Homeland and anybody else we need to help us track him down," I said.

"I don't want to track him. I want to be three steps ahead of him."

"Zach and I have a list of all the events happening connected to Hollywood on the Hudson. But they're spread all over town—hotels, theaters, restaurants, private parties. I don't think we can find enough bomb-sniffing dogs to handle it all."

"Can Benoit do this on his own?" Cates said. "It's one thing to rig a Molotov cocktail, but that's a lot of plastic for him to be handling without his resident bomb guy. We've got Peltz in custody. We can hold him for seventy-two hours."

"That might slow him down, but I don't know if it will stop him," I said. "Benoit is smart. He had to figure we'd be paying a visit to a bomb expert who just got out of prison. That's why he didn't leave the explosives at Peltz's place. More likely he used Peltz to score the fireworks and give him a short course in how to use them. C4 is not all that complicated."

"Well, if Peltz taught Benoit how to use that plastic, then Peltz would have to know what the targets are," Cates said. "Get back to the station as soon as you can wrap it up here and put the fear of God into Mr. Peltz."

"Are we still waiting for his PO to show up?" Kylie asked.

"That's the rule, isn't it?" Cates said. "Don't question the parolee without his parole officer present."

"Yes, ma'am," Kylie said. "That's the rule."

"And you of all people ought to know, Detective MacDonald...some rules are meant to be broken."

Chapter 64

IT WAS A half hour before shift change when we finally got back to the station house, and a steady stream of people were either coming, going, or waiting to speak to the desk sergeant.

The One Nine is one of the busiest precincts in the city, and it takes an old pro like Bob McGrath to man the front desk.

When we got there, he was dealing with two women in their early twenties—one of them an amazingly beautiful Latina. Four more civilians were stacked up in a holding pattern.

Kylie and I went to the front of the line.

"Sorry to interrupt, Sarge," I said, "but Captain Cates sent a patrol car to pick up this guy Mickey Peltz in Queens. Did they?"

"Yeah, Detective, hold on, I got his intake sheet here somewhere," McGrath said. "Either of you two guys *habla español?*"

"I can *habla un poco,*" Kylie said.

"No good," McGrath said. "All cops can *habla un poco.* This lady here is from Colombia. She speaks zero English, and her friend speaks no Spanish."

"I'm not really her friend," the woman said. "She was staying in the apartment next door, and I just brought her here. I was only trying to be a Good Samaritan. Somebody stole her passport and—"

"Lady, stop," McGrath said. "I got the English part down. Give me two seconds to rustle up a cop who speaks Spanish."

"Can I get through, Sergeant?"

It was the Pepsi deliveryman pushing a dolly stacked high with cases of soda for the vending machines.

"Your truck better not be blocking any of my squad cars out there, Vernon," McGrath said as he waved him through with one hand.

"And your cops better not be putting any more slugs in my soda machine," the Pepsi man said, laughing.

McGrath turned the wave into a single finger and used the other hand to rummage through the pile of paper on top of his desk, looking for the one on Peltz.

"Excuse me, but I have to pick up my son from school in a half hour," the Good Samaritan lady said.

"I understand, ma'am," McGrath said. Looking over his shoulder, he yelled, "Donna, did you give a shout out for Rodriguez or Morales? I still need a Spanish translator over here."

A civilian in the glass-walled office behind him rolled her chair to the door so she could yell back. "They're both busy, Sarge!"

"I'm not buying it," McGrath said, still digging through the mountain of paper. "They're on a meal break. Call them back, and this time make sure you tell them what this young lady looks like."

I was getting annoyed by all the interruptions, and one look at my partner let me know she was even more aggravated than I was. I could see her clenching her jaw, which helped keep her mouth shut.

McGrath caught the frustration. "Sorry, guys, Peltz has been here awhile. His paperwork got buried."

He kept looking while a small parade of people left the station, pushing their way through the swinging half gate that separates the front desk from the waiting area—three cops carrying oversized duffel bags; Victor, the delivery guy from Gerri's Diner; a priest; and a battle-weary older man in a rumpled blue suit who had poor man's lawyer written all over him.

McGrath's head bobbed up and down eyeballing everyone who entered or exited. Finally, he yanked a single blue sheet of paper from the pile. "Peltz, comma, Mickey," he said triumphantly. There was a yellow Post-it note stuck to the top. He squinted at it. "And his PO called at one-oh-five. He's still tied up in court. Asked you guys to hold off till he gets here."

"Not a chance," Kylie said, taking the blue

sheet. "Not after what went down this morning. Where's Peltz?"

"Yo, Sarge. *¿Dónde está la hermosa mujer?*"

It was Officer Morales, his dark eyes already zeroing in on the beautiful Colombian woman. He tightened his abs and puffed out his chest, all hot to translate.

Officer Rodriguez was right behind him. "Sarge, he's Puerto Rican. They don't even speak real Spanish down there. My father was from Colombia. I'll talk to her."

"Morales was here first, but as long as you're not busy," McGrath said, digging into his pocket and handing Rodriguez two dollars, "run upstairs and get me a Diet Pepsi."

"Sergeant," I said. "We're in a crunch. Where's Peltz?"

"Sorry," he said. "It's a zoo in here. He's..."

I heard a crashing noise, and then the Spanish woman screamed. *"Dios mío..."* She pointed over my shoulder.

McGrath's head snapped around. "What the fuck?"

I turned and saw a man staggering toward us, his arms flailing, his body in spasms, banging into walls, spewing vomit as he went. Ten feet from the desk, he pitched face-forward to the floor. Officer Rodriguez was the first one at his side, his fingers searching for a pulse.

"Peltz," McGrath said.

"He's dead," Rodriguez added, both of them confirming what I already knew.

"Shit," McGrath said, pounding his fist on the desk. Then he pointed to the front door and bellowed out an order. "Somebody stop that fucking priest!"

Chapter 65

GETTING IN TO see Mickey hadn't even been a challenge, The Chameleon thought to himself.

The cop at the front desk was busy, but it's amazing how fast you can go to the head of the line if you're wearing a black shirt, white collar, and gold cross.

"I'm Father McDougal," Gabriel said once he read the name tag on McGrath's uniform. "One of my parishioners called me. Mickey Peltz. He was recently released from prison, and he's been very careful to stay on the straight and narrow, and now he's concerned that he's in trouble with the police. What did he do, if I may ask?"

"As far as I can tell, Father, nothing," McGrath said. "He's not under arrest. He's just in here to answer a few questions for the detectives investigating an ongoing case."

"Oh, he'll be so relieved. He really is a good man. I truly believe his past is behind him. He found the Lord while he was in prison."

"A lot of them do, Father."

"My job is to make sure something like this doesn't shake his faith. Do you mind if I sit with him for a few minutes and give him some spiritual guidance, and perhaps something to quench his thirst?"

Gabriel held up a clear plastic bottle of Poland Spring.

"Is that holy water, Father?" the cop said.

"No," Gabriel said, "but at two bucks for a sixteen-ounce bottle, you would think that His Holiness Himself had blessed it."

The cop laughed out loud. *What Irishman doesn't love a funny priest?* "Donna, please take Father McDougal back to Room Two."

The Chameleon gave the cop his most sincere Christian smile. *Permission to kill Mr. Peltz granted. Hallelujah.*

Mickey, of course, was thrilled to see him. He swore up and down he wouldn't say a word about anything to anyone.

"You wouldn't lie to a priest, would you my son?" Gabe said.

Mickey let loose one of his signature raspy laughs and sucked down half a bottle of the Poland Spring.

"I'm just here for moral support," Gabriel said, "and to let you know that if you need a lawyer, don't take one of their court-appointed hacks. I have the money to spring for a real one."

"Thanks," Mickey said. "You're a good friend, Gabe."

And those were probably the last words Mickey Peltz ever uttered.

Getting out of the station was cake. Gabriel fell in behind a trio of cops and breezed right past the desk sergeant and out the front door. Less than thirty seconds later, he had peeled off his neat little goatee, the clerical shirt and collar, balled them up along with the Bible and the cross he wore around his neck, and shoved them all into a trash basket.

There was a street vendor on the southeast corner of Third Avenue and 67th Street hawking sunglasses, batteries, and "genuine pashmina" for only five dollars. His beat-up Dodge van was parked behind the stand, and Gabriel positioned himself so he could look west toward the precinct yet remain completely out of sight.

Now he was wearing a red and white Rutgers T-shirt and trying on a pair of wraparound shades as half a dozen cops came storming out of the precinct. MacDonald was in the lead. She looked left, then right, then whacked a fist into her palm once she realized she'd lost him.

She was the bitch who killed Lexi. The press didn't give her name—just "plainclothes female cop"—but that was all Gabriel needed.

He had walked right past her, no more than a few inches away. But even if he could have strangled her right there on the spot, he wouldn't have. Hot-shit Detective Kylie MacDonald was about to live through the same pain and agony she'd put him through.

This one's for you, Popcorn Girl.

Chapter 66

THE PRECINCT WAS now officially a crime scene. Technically, we couldn't move Peltz until he'd been scraped, probed, and swabbed. And since nothing says sloppy police work like a dead guy on the precinct floor, we quickly tacked up a tarp to hide the body from the public.

"If it were up to me, I'd just drag him back to the holding room," Kylie said. "Do we really need forensics to tell us that Benoit poisoned him? Probably with the same stuff he used to kill Roth."

The two of us, along with Cates, McGrath,

338

and his direct boss, Lieutenant Al Orton, were all crammed into Donna Thorson's office. She's the civilian employee who worked behind the front desk. It was hot and uncomfortable in more ways than one.

Kylie turned to McGrath. "How did Benoit get in?"

McGrath is a big man. Burly, with thick graying hair and a wide Irish grin. He can either be a welcoming presence at the front desk or an intimidating one. Like I said, an old pro. He looked straight at Kylie and spoke quietly, calmly.

"He told me he was a priest. He *looked* like a priest. He said, 'Peltz is one of my parishioners. Can I sit with him and give him some spiritual guidance?' Based on what I knew, Peltz wasn't under arrest. He wasn't even here on a parole violation. He was just cooling his heels, waiting to talk to you and his PO. So to answer your question, Detective, he got in because I let him in. I'm the wolf at the door, and I said yes, because as far as I could see, there was no reason to say no. But if you're looking for someone to take the fall, put it on me."

Orton stepped in. "Hold on, Bob. Detective, you're new here. The One Nine has worked with NYPD Red since they moved in, and by and large it works well. We've got a protocol up front. It starts with 'serve and protect.' We don't harass civilians. We don't frisk them or tell them to dispose of all liquids beyond this point. We're not the TSA. Sergeant McGrath is a decorated cop with eighteen years, and he did his job by the book. What happened was not his—"

"Al, it was my fault," Cates said. "I screwed up. I didn't want a lot of radio chatter going out, so I never told the uniforms who Peltz was or why they were bringing him in. But we ran into some bad luck. Benoit saw the pickup. Once I found that out, I should have called and had Peltz locked up. It never crossed my mind that Benoit would show up here and kill Peltz to keep him from talking."

"Talking about what?" Orton said.

"Benoit scored enough C4 to do some serious damage."

"Do we have any idea where?"

"No, but I'm sure Peltz did, which is why he is now dead."

"If it's connected to this Hollywood week, how many venues can there be?" Orton asked.

"At last count, sixty-three," I said. "And right now, K-9 only has eighteen available dogs. Without Peltz to point to the target—or targets—there's no way we can cover even half of them."

"In that case, I'm going to have to prioritize," Cates said. "Start with the functions being held at hotels or other public spaces."

"The bigger targets are more likely to be at private parties," Kylie said. "I know that the Friars Club is—"

"Detective MacDonald," Cates said sharply. "I appreciate the fact that the bigwigs are bigger targets, and I realize you may be close to some of them, but our first responsibility is to the people of New York. I want those dogs zeroing in on any event where one of our taxpaying citizens could become collateral damage. Understood?"

"Yes, Captain."

Cates didn't respond. She marched out the door and up the stairs to her office. Her mea culpa was over. She was all business.

Chapter 67

AFTER FORTY-FIVE MINUTES of weight training, twenty minutes on the rowing machine, and another forty-five on the treadmill, Spence Harrington was dripping with sweat. He peeled off his clothes and carefully studied every inch of his body in the mirror that filled one entire wall of his home gym.

He had a body mass index of twenty and was trying to drive it down to the teens. Not bad for a guy who could smell forty a few birthdays away. One of the pluses of giving up bad habits was being able to build a body that looked this good naked. He wasn't sure who liked looking at it more—him or Kylie.

He padded to the bathroom, tossed his wet gym clothes in the hamper, took a ten-minute shower, toweled himself dry, and crawled into bed.

Spence had the fifteen-minute power nap down to a science, and he set the timer on his iPhone for sixteen minutes. He was asleep before the first sixty seconds had ticked off. A quarter of an hour later, he awoke to the familiar sound of Sonny and Cher singing "I Got You, Babe," a ringtone homage to his favorite movie, *Groundhog Day*.

The thermostats throughout the three-bedroom apartment were set at sixty-four degrees, and as soon as he tossed the top sheet off, the cool air puffed playfully on his warm skin. He sank back down into the pillow and ran a hand along his belly until it settled between his legs. He cupped himself and inhaled deeply. He and Kylie hadn't had sex since she started her new job. He closed his eyes, pictured her naked in bed next to him, and immediately felt himself grow hard.

Nothing like exercise, a hot shower, and a near-death experience to get a guy horny, he thought as he removed his hand and sat up on the edge of the bed. He picked up the phone and called his wife.

"How you doing?" she said.

"I'm showered, naked, and as randy as a billy goat on a Viagra binge," he said. "How about you?"

"Fabulous. I just spent the last two hours with my masseuse. Oh, no wait, that was Internal Affairs debriefing me after the shooting to see if I'm suffering from post-traumatic stress, or if I'm still fit for duty."

"And?"

"Bad news, Goat Boy. I'm on the job till we catch this bastard. How is Shelley holding up?"

"He's as happy as Heloise on double coupon day. His doc gave him some pain meds, and he went back to the office and got a call from Electronic Arts. They're one of the biggest video game companies on the planet, and after the shoot-out this morning, they suddenly got interested in us."

"That was fast," Kylie said.

"That's the game biz. Anyway, they asked if they could send a couple of developers tonight to check out the pilot. And you know how Shelley's brain works. He said yes, then immediately called a dozen other video game developers, and now Sony and Nintendo will be there too."

"Spence, Benoit has explosives," Kylie said. "There aren't enough cops or dogs to go around, and a private party won't be one of our priorities. Make sure Shelley hires some security."

"I already told him that, but he's not worried."

"Somebody shot him," Kylie said. "Doesn't he think it could happen again?"

"No. He thinks the girl just wanted to shoot at a bunch of movie and TV people, and she figured she'd nail somebody famous at Ian's memorial. But as far as Shelley is concerned, all he's having tonight is a private meeting with a bunch of boring business guys. The real glitzy stuff with the loud music and the boldface names will be at Kiss and Fly, 230 Fifth, Tenjune—places like that. That's where you should be looking for this nut job—hold on a sec, someone's ringing up from downstairs."

He pushed star zero to get the intercom. "Who is it?"

"Hey, Mr. Harrington. It's Trevor from the Silvercup mailroom. I got a package for you—looks like script changes."

"Bring it up, Trev. Seventh floor. Thanks."

He clicked back.

"Who was that?" Kylie said.

"The escort service is here. I called them a few hours ago. Ordered up a hooker."

"How did you know I wouldn't be there?"

"I didn't. In fact, I was hoping we could make it a three-way."

"You're terrible."

"That's why you love me."

"Have fun with your hooker and your video games," Kylie said.

"And you be careful chasing bad guys. I love you."

"Love you too. Got to go."

The doorbell rang, and Kylie hung up. Spence grabbed a pillow, put it in front of him, and hustled to the door.

"Hey, Trevor, I'm not dressed," he said. "Can you just slide it under the door?"

"It's too thick," Trevor said, "but how about if I just drop it in front of the door and go."

"Perfect."

"No problem, sir. Have a nice night."

Spence put an ear to the door and listened as the envelope hit the carpet. Trevor walked to the elevator. It was already parked at seven, so the doors opened immediately. They closed, and the elevator went down to the lobby.

Still holding the pillow in front of him, Spence stepped outside, bent down, and reached for the envelope.

The Chameleon, hugging the wall outside the door, pointed the stun baton at Spence's right shoulder and squeezed the trigger. One million volts surged through Spence Harrington's body and dropped him to the floor.

"Like I told you, Spence," Gabriel said. "Script changes. Your part just got a lot bigger."

Chapter 68

"IT'S AMAZING HOW easy it is to buy one of these stun batons," Gabriel said as he pulled Spence's body across the threshold. "Only fifty bucks on the Internet. The real pain in the ass was getting it delivered. Can you believe that Tasers and stuns are legal in forty-four states, but they can't be shipped to goddamn New York? Or Jersey."

He kicked the front door shut and dragged Spence into the living room.

"But you got to love these companies that sell shit like this on the Web. Right there on their site, in big red type, it says, 'Do you live in a prohibited delivery zone? Don't worry. Give us an alternate shipping address from any legal area and we can still ship it for you!' So I drive to Connecticut, where they're allowed, except that they're restricted to in-home use. But I figure I'm legal because I'm only zapping you here in your home." Gabriel laughed.

"Anyway, I rent a box at the UPS Store in Stamford, drive back a week later, and there it is waiting for me. 'Discreetly packaged,' as promised. Like I said, it was a pain in the ass, but it's all part of preproduction."

He lowered Spence's head and shoulders to the floor, got a sturdy chair from the dining room table, and centered it ten feet from the front door.

"Now, I know you can't talk yet, but you can hear me. I need you up in this chair. I'll do most of the heavy lifting, but you got to help. Otherwise, zap, zap, zap. It's an amazing little piece of business, this baton. Twenty-four of the twenty-eight reviews on the website gave it five stars. You can see why."

Gabriel planted his hands under Spence's

armpits, grunted hard, and lifted him into the chair.

"Funny you should be naked," he said. "It wasn't in the script, but I like it. Makes you more vulnerable on camera. And the movie's already rated R, so a little nudity doesn't change anything."

It took ten minutes for Spence to come to. By that time, his ankles and calves were duct-taped to the legs of the chair, and there was more tape wrapped around his torso, trapping his arms and hands behind him. A third swath of duct tape covered his mouth. He opened his eyes and saw Gabriel hovering in front of him.

"Well, good morning, Sleeping Beauty. Your prince has been waiting."

He rested the tip of the stun baton on the chair between Spence's open legs. "I'm taking the tape off your mouth," he said. "If you yell, your voice will go up about twelve octaves."

Spence nodded, then winced as Gabe yanked hard to remove the tape. "Who are you?" he whispered.

"I'm The Chameleon," Gabriel said.

Spence stared at him in disbelief. "I don't...I don't understand. That's the name of my new show. The Chameleon is my new character."

"The one you stole from me," Gabriel said. "I submitted that idea to you two years ago. I'm The Chameleon."

The man was insane, and Spence shook his head, trying to process the information. "Okay," he said. "You're The Chameleon. I'm screening a pilot tonight. The central character is a private detective—a master of disguise. He's also called The Chameleon. It's a coincidence. I never stole—"

"I don't care if you changed him to a detective or a bus driver or an astronaut," Gabriel said, the anger raising his voice. "It's still my idea. I sent it to you. I *trusted* you."

"I believe you," Spence said. "The thing is, people send me ideas every day, but I can't read them. Most TV producers never read unsolicited pitches unless they come from an agent we work with."

"Most TV producers lie through their teeth," Gabriel said.

"I swear I'm telling you the truth," Spence

said. "The Chameleon is an idea that I had four years ago. I've been developing it ever since, and I finally—what are you doing?"

The Chameleon reached into his backpack. "Look what we have here," he said. "And you thought the cattle prod was bad? This little movie of mine is just full of surprises, isn't it?"

Spence screamed. "Help! Somebody! Help!"

Gabriel's fist connected with Spence's nose, and the screams were replaced by the sound of cartilage crunching and snapping. He pulled Spence's head back and violently wrapped the duct tape around his mouth three times.

"You not only took my idea," Gabriel said, holding up the object of Spence's terror. "You took my life. And now, guess what, pretty boy? It's payback time."

Chapter 69

THERE ARE THREE dozen dogs in NYPD's Emergency Services K-9 Unit. Half of them work narcotics, the other half are bomb sniffers. A few have been cross-trained to find cadavers. Even in a city the size of New York, on any given day, eighteen bomb-sniffing dogs would be more than enough.

But this was not any given day.

I called Sergeant Kyle Warren, the K-9 coordinator for all of NYPD. He's only thirty-two years old, but he's been training dogs since he was ten. I laid out the problem, and all he said was "I'm on it."

Two hours later, Warren called back. He had recruited dogs from the state police in New York, New Jersey, and Connecticut, and from as far north as the Ulster County Sheriff's Department. By 5:00 p.m., our K-9 contingent was up to thirty-two.

Kylie and I were at the precinct, sticking pushpins into a map of the city that was tacked to a corkboard wall. Since we didn't have enough dogs to cover every possible target, we had to decide which of them warranted a canine handler to be stationed there full-time, and which could be swept and then have the dog sent on to the next venue.

"I think Spence is right," Kylie said. "The meatpacking district has to be the prime target. It's where most of your A-listers are going to be. We should have at least half a dozen bomb-sniffing dogs working this area."

"Knowing those A-listers," I said, "I'll bet we'd hit the jackpot if we sent in a couple of narco dogs as well."

Kylie's cell rang. Except it wasn't her usual ringtone.

"Has my husband lost his mind?" she said.

"It's a Skype call from Spence. Does he really think I have nothing better to do than video-chat?"

"Consider yourself lucky," I said. "He only calls me in the middle of the night."

She held up her iPhone and connected to Skype.

"Oh my God. Zach..."

I looked over her shoulder. There on the iPhone screen was Spence, bound, gagged, and sitting totally naked in a chair.

"Spence..." was all Kylie could get out.

And then Gabriel Benoit stepped into the picture.

"Hello, Detective MacDonald. And there's your sidekick, Detective Jordan, right behind you. I don't know if you found my apartment yet," Benoit said, "but I found yours."

"What do you want?" Kylie said.

"I want you to suffer the same way you made me suffer. Do you know who that woman was that you killed this morning?"

"She was a cold-blooded murderer," Kylie said. "She opened fire on a bunch of defense-less people."

"Lexi was as innocent as a child," Benoit

said. "If she killed anyone, it's because they deserved it."

"What do you want?" Kylie repeated.

"Do you know how painful it is to lose someone you love?" Benoit asked.

Kylie didn't answer.

"You're about to find out," he taunted.

He held up a fat block of C4 to the camera. There was a digital timer taped to it with one black wire and one white wire, both connected to a detonator buried deep in the plastic.

"You have thirty minutes," Benoit said. "And then I will have taken from you, the same way you have taken from me."

He pushed a button. The digital timer flashed 29:59 and began to count down the seconds. When it got to 29:55, he removed it from view, and once again we were looking at Kylie's living room. Five seconds later, he hung up.

The screen went dark, but the last image I had seen would forever be burned onto my brain. Spence Harrington, naked, totally helpless, taped to a chair in his own apartment, alone and afraid, waiting to die.

Chapter 70

KYLIE BOLTED.

I grabbed a radio and was right behind her, taking the stairs two at a time.

"I need a PPV!" she yelled at Sergeant McGrath as she careened into the front desk and pushed aside a civilian. "Two-one-seven in progress."

McGrath didn't hesitate. If there was any bad blood from the earlier meeting, it was forgotten. A Two-one-seven was an assault with intent to kill, and Kylie was clearly a cop on a mission.

"Sixty-four Forty-two," he said. "Chevy

Caprice out front. Fastest PPV we got. Keys are in it."

Kylie flew out the door and raced for the Chevy. She opened the front door, and I grabbed her by the arm.

"We should call the bomb squad," I said.

She shoved me off.

"No. By the time they suit up, mobilize, find my apartment, and decide the safest way to defuse the bomb, Spence will be dead. It's either me," she said, "or you and me. Are you in or out?"

She didn't wait for an answer. She jumped into the driver's seat and started the car.

"In!" I yelled, throwing myself into the passenger side as she peeled out and blasted through the red light on Lexington, light bars flashing, siren screaming.

"We should call for backup," I said.

"Not until we get there and we can assess the situation," she said, swinging onto Fifth. "We can't take a chance on having some gung ho rookie showing up and deciding to play hero."

"You think it's any better to send a gung ho wife to play hero?"

"Dammit, Zach, I've got twenty-eight minutes," she said. "I know where Spence is and how to get there, and I don't have time to brief a backup unit and get them up to speed."

Kylie made a hard right onto Central Park South, the ritzy stretch of 59th Street that runs from Grand Army Plaza at Fifth Avenue to Columbus Circle at Eighth. The street was lined with dozens of horse-drawn hansom cabs waiting to take willing tourists on a twenty-minute trot through the park for fifty bucks plus tip. Kylie leaned on the siren, then hopped the double yellow line into the eastbound lane, where there was a lot less traffic.

"We went through a list of every possible target," she said. "How did we not think of Spence?"

"We were looking for the big cinematic finale," I said. "But Benoit just turned this around into a vendetta. You killed his girlfriend."

"Right," she said. She turned left onto Seventh Avenue, skidded into the fire lane, and floored the Caprice. "So if Spence dies, it's my fault."

My cell phone rang. I looked at the caller ID. "It's Cates," I said. "McGrath must have told her we took off on a Two-one-seven."

"Don't pick it up," Kylie said.

"Are you out of your mind?" I said. "She's our boss."

"Yes, right now I am totally out of my mind, and if we tell our boss what we're doing, she might pull the plug. Zach, I know that Spence doesn't mean much to you, but if you care about me, please, please, please don't answer the phone."

If I cared about her? Had I ever stopped caring? And now all that emotional baggage was threatening to drag down the only other thing I cared about. My career.

The phone rang a second time.

Cates's caller ID flashed on the screen. Below that were two buttons. One green, one red: accept, decline.

They may just as well have said: lose, lose.

I will probably regret this for the rest of my life, I thought.

I pressed one of the buttons.

Chapter 71

**EXT. 17TH STREET PIER,
NEW YORK CITY—DAY**

The Chameleon makes his final costume change and drives his rented Zipcar to the South Street Pier. His crew is waiting for him. Six men, three women, each dressed in the same uniform he is wearing—black pants, white shirt, white dinner jacket, and electric blue bow tie. He's been

working with them for three
months now, and they are happy
to see him.

"ARMANDO," ONE OF the women called
out to him as he jogged across the parking
lot. "I was worried about you. You almost
missed the boat."

It was Adrienne Gomez-Bower, the pretty
one with the curly jet-black hair, and the
blatantly obvious crush on him. He doubted
if she'd even look twice at Gabriel Benoit,
but she totally had the hots for Armando
Savoy, the brown-skinned, intense young actor, born in Buenos Aires, raised in Mar-
seilles, and trying to make it big in New
York.

"Adrienne, *ma chérie,*" he said as he leaned
toward her and gave her the traditional
French *faire la bise,* a kiss on each cheek.
"Sorry I'm late. I had a callback for the new
Mamet play. It's down to me and two other
guys."

"Oh my God, Armando—a David Mamet
play?" she said. "How awesome would that
be? I swear, if you get the part, I will be front

row center on opening night, even if I have to sell my body to pay for the tickets."

Another time and he would have enjoyed kicking up the sexual tension a few more notches. Lexi wouldn't mind. She knew it was all part of his act. But now with her gone, coming on to Adrienne felt too much like cheating.

"Anyway, boss," he said. "Sorry I'm late."

Adrienne was the crew chief, and she smiled. "I'll let it slide," she said. "But next time I may have to come down hard on you."

Gabriel pretended not to notice the innuendo and stepped to the back of one of the catering trucks. "Who's hosting this little soiree?" he asked.

"Shelley Trager," Adrienne said. "He's a multizillionaire TV producer. You see the yacht we're working on? It's not a rental. He *owns* it. He's got a hundred and twenty-seven guests, most of them connected to the biz. Maybe one of us will get discovered."

"I hope it's you," Gabriel said, wheeling a dolly under eight racks of wine glasses. He took off his white dinner jacket and laid it across the top rack. The jacket weighed eighty pounds. Lexi had sewn sixteen water-proof canvas pockets on the inside, and he'd stuffed each one of them with five pounds of C4. He'd used only twenty pounds at Harrington's apartment, so this was way more than enough.

"I'm flattered that you hope that it's me," Adrienne said. "But what about you? Don't you want to get discovered?"

Gabriel tipped the dolly and began to push it up the ramp of the waiting yacht. "Not tonight, boss," he said. "Not tonight."

Chapter 72

TRAFFIC SCRAMBLED TO get out of our way as we tore down Seventh Avenue at autobahn speed. "Thank you," Kylie said, eyes glued to the road.

I didn't respond.

"I'm sorry," she said.

"For what?" I mumbled.

"What do you think? Come on, Zach—Cates asked you to ride herd over me, and three days later, you've gone off the reservation. That's my fault."

"It was my choice not to answer the phone," I said.

"Okay. But thank you. I mean it. I owe you big-time. Spence and I both owe you."

"Great," I said. "Maybe he can help me find a job in security at Silvercup."

She turned and smiled at me, nearly plowing into a cab that couldn't get out of her way fast enough.

Under ordinary circumstances, it would have taken twenty minutes to get to Kylie's apartment in Tribeca. But with lights, sirens, and an absolute madwoman behind the wheel, we made it in eight and a half.

The Caprice screeched to a hard stop at the corner of Washington and Laight streets in front of an elegant eight-story redbrick building that had long ago been the Pearline Soap Factory. Tens of millions of dollars later, it had been transformed into a symbol of the ultimate chic that now defines lower Manhattan. No one on a cop's salary could possibly afford to live there. Spence was obviously a good provider.

"Seventh floor," Kylie said as we raced into the lobby. The elevator was right there, doors wide open, but she ran past it and into the stairwell.

I followed.

"Elevator's too slow. This is the fastest way," she said, giving the obvious answer to a question I hadn't even bothered asking.

"Do we have a plan?" I said as we got to the fifth-floor landing.

"No. Yes. I don't know. Damn it, Zach, we don't need an NYPD Red master plan for every little thing. I just want to get in, get Spence out, warn the neighbors, and get our asses out of the building. If it blows, it blows."

It made sense. *In, out, run.* Simple. There was no time to try to disarm a bomb.

We crashed through the stairwell door on seven, and turned right. There were only two apartments on the floor. Kylie's was in the front.

She pulled a key out of her pocket and jammed it into the lock on Apartment 7A.

In, out, run, I kept saying to myself. Simple. But something wasn't sitting right.

Kylie turned the key, and in that split second I knew. Nothing that came from the twisted mind of Gabriel Benoit was ever simple.

I lunged at her and threw her to the floor.

"What the fuck?" she screamed.

"It's booby-trapped," I said.

She stared at me, half believing, half in denial, because undoing a booby trap takes time, and we were running out fast.

"How do you know?" she said.

"I don't. But I know Benoit. He gave us more than enough time to get here. He *wants* us to barge through that door."

"We have to get in," she said. "Spence is in there."

"Quiet." I stood right up against the door and yelled. "Spence!"

He responded with a series of high-pitched shrieks. I knew from the Skype call that his mouth was duct-taped. He couldn't utter a word, but it was clear from the urgency and the inflection in every cry that he wasn't just asking for help. He was giving us a warning.

"Spence," I said, "is it safe to open the door? Grunt once for yes. Twice for no."

The answer came back loud and clear. Two muffled, yet distinctly separate, penetrating sounds. *No.*

"Is the door wired with explosives?"

A single grunt. *Yes.*

Every ounce of confidence and bravado drained from Kylie's face. She had made all the calls—no bomb squad, no backup, just storm the castle and save the day on her own—and now it looked like every single call she had made was wrong.

"Zach...," she said, looking as vulnerable and helpless as I'd ever seen her.

Suddenly saving Spence's life was all on me. I shut my eyes and tried to picture every square on the chessboard.

"We have seventeen minutes," she said.

No time to overthink.

"Spence!" I yelled through the door. "Can I come through the window?"

One grunt. And then...nothing.

Yes.

It was the answer I'd been hoping for.

"That's it," I said to Kylie. "I can get in through the window."

She looked back at me—fear, disbelief, disappointment, and a slew of other negative emotions in her eyes. "Zach," she said, "we're seven stories straight up. How the hell do you plan to get in through the window?"

Chapter 73

GABRIEL HAD TIMED it perfectly. The catering crew had almost finished loading in, most of the guests were on board, and Trager's yacht, the *Shell Game,* was ready to get under way.

He busied himself in the galley, artfully arranging mini crab tostadas, smoked salmon barquettes, and coconut shrimp on black lacquered trays.

"You do brilliant work, Armando," Adrienne said. "Mamet is lucky to have you."

"I don't have the gig yet," Gabriel said.

"You will. Till then, you can feed the rich

and hungry. Buffet is at seven." She walked behind him, gave him a pat on the butt, and whispered in his ear. "Dessert is at my place around midnight."

"I believe this is what you Americans call sexual harassment on the job," he said.

She smiled. "And what do you call it in Argentina?"

"Foreplay."

He winked, picked up a tray, and carried it into the main salon, working his way slowly through the crowd, smiling and passing hors d'oeuvres as he went. The guests were a typical show business mix of men and women, young and old, straight and gay, but they had one thing in common. Every one of them knew how to dress for a cruise—except for the two swarthy Latino men who were both wearing brown blazers, Kmart ties, and cop shoes.

The Chameleon smiled. *If this is Trager's idea of private security, either he has no respect for me, or he wants to help me blow up his boat.*

He walked up to one of the rent-a-cops and held out his tray. The man shook his head.

"Oh, please," Gabriel said. "You don't

know what you're missing. The shrimp are to die for."

The guy shrugged, took a napkin, plucked a shrimp from the tray, looked left and right, then grabbed three more.

"I'll be back," Gabriel said.

He worked his way to the far end of the salon and stepped through a teak-framed glass door onto the main deck. There were a lot fewer guests out here, almost all of them smoking.

He found a quiet spot on the port side and got his bearings. The Brooklyn Bridge was behind him, which meant they were headed south toward Governors Island and the Red Hook section of Brooklyn.

They wouldn't screen the TV pilot until dark, which meant the captain would sail all the way down to Sea Gate, or even Breezy Point, before circling back to catch the sunset over Liberty Island.

He had a little more than an hour to set the charges.

He found a door that said DO NOT ENTER, set down his hors d'oeuvres tray, and entered.

He took the two flights of metal stairs down to the engine room.

"Yo," a voice called out. "Hold it right there, mate."

Gabriel froze.

The man was a dark-skinned African-American, over sixty, wearing khakis and a faded denim shirt with the yacht's logo on the left breast pocket.

"Hi there," Gabriel said.

"Yeah, hi there," the man said pleasantly. "How many fingers am I holding up?"

"Three."

"Well, you've passed the vision test, so I'm assuming you saw the sign that said 'Do Not Enter.' Allow me to interpret it for you. This area is off-limits. So would you be so kind as to go back on deck where you belong?"

"It's okay," Gabriel said. "I'm with the caterer. Mr. Trager sent me down to get dinner orders from the crew."

The man laughed. "Dinner orders? Maybe for the guys on the bridge, but Mr. Trager does not make a habit of serving dinner in the engine room."

"My mistake," Gabriel said, "but hey, man,

we got food up the wazoo in the galley. You want me to bring you down a tray—shrimp, chicken, fillet of beef?"

The man frowned. "My head says no, but my stomach just chimed in with 'you can do that?'"

"Can and will," Gabriel said. "Heck, you and your buddies down here are probably the hardest-working guys on the whole boat. Just tell me what you want, and I'll bring it to you."

"Some of everything, heavy on the fillet of beef, and maybe a cold beer."

"You got it. How many guys are working down here?"

"Three. Me, myself, and I," the seaman said, laughing. "Name's Charles Connor."

"Well, Mr. Connor, you guys deserve at least two beers apiece," Gabriel said, "so how about I bring you down a six-pack?"

"Thanks, but one's my limit down here."

"This is some major setup," Gabriel said. "How do you run it all by yourself?"

"I don't run it at all. Captain Campion runs it by computer from the bridge. Normally, once we're under way, nobody even works in the engine room, but we got a full boat and the booze is flowing, so the captain sent me down here to keep an eye out for happy wanderers."

"You mean like guys who can't read the 'Do Not Enter' sign?" Gabriel said.

"More like horny couples, three sheets to the wind, who see the sign and figure they'll sneak down and join the Hudson River version of the Mile High Club."

"I'll go get your dinner," Gabriel said. "Hey, what's that big noisy thing behind you?"

Connor turned around. "That's a thruster. It's what makes the ship—"

Once again The Chameleon squeezed the trigger of the stun baton, dumping an electrical charge of a million volts into his unsuspecting victim's nervous system. The seaman dropped to the floor, numb and helpless.

"I lied about bringing you dinner," Gabriel said, putting the baton back in its holster and taking out a fresh roll of duct tape.

Gabriel had no idea how many of the crew would be working down here, so this scene hadn't been too tightly scripted. But considering it was all ad-lib, he thought both he and Charles Connor had done remarkably well.

Chapter 74

"WE CAN'T CLIMB up seven stories," I said, "but we can climb down one. What's on the eighth floor?"

As soon as I asked, I saw a spark in Kylie's eyes. Hope.

"Dino. Dino Provenzano. He's an artist. He works at home." She turned to the door and yelled back at Spence. "I love you. We're coming to get you."

We took off for the stairwell. "Dino was the first to buy an apartment here," she said, bounding up the steps. "He grabbed the top floor front, which has the best light: 8A."

Within seconds, she was banging on the

apartment door directly above hers. "Dino, it's Kylie. Open up. Emergency."

Nobody answered. Kylie kept banging and yelling. "Dino! Coralei! Anybody? NYPD. Emergency!"

Ten precious seconds later, Dino flung the door open, a paint-stained rag in his other hand.

"Dino, there's a bomb in my apartment," Kylie said, pushing her way in. "Get Coralei and get out."

"She's not here. She's out walking the dog. What did you say was in your apartment?"

"A bomb."

"Jesus," he said.

"Ring all the bells," Kylie said. "Warn the neighbors and empty the building. Then call 911 and tell them to clear the streets and evacuate the building next door. And tell them they only have fourteen minutes. You have a cell phone?"

Dino patted his pants pockets. "Yes," he said, and started to go back inside. "Just let me get my laptop."

"Get out. Now," she said, shoving him into the hallway and slamming the door.

The living room was sparse. The furniture and the carpeting were all monochromatic shades of beige and earth tones. It was the walls that brought the space to life. Three of them were filled with color. At least twenty paintings. If they were Dino's, he was damn good.

Kylie ran to the fourth wall. It was almost all glass. She pulled open a sliding door, stepped out onto a typically tiny New York City apartment terrace, and looked over the railing.

"It's a fifteen-foot drop to our terrace," she said. "I can do it. Oh shit—"

"What?"

"Rope. We need rope. Look around."

There were no drapes—nothing at all in the living room that we could use to lower someone to the terrace below.

"Check the kitchen," Kylie said. "I'll try his studio." We took off in opposite directions.

The kitchen was all stainless steel—neat, organized, orderly—not the kind of place where someone would store fifteen feet of rope. I was going through the motions of opening drawers and cabinet doors when Kylie called out.

"Zach, I've got it. In the bedroom. I need help."

I headed toward the sound of her voice, figuring I'd find her ripping the sheets off the bed and tying them together. But I was wrong. She was kneeling on a dresser, her hands under a flat-screen TV that was mounted on the wall. It was a monster, at least five feet across.

"Help me get this down," she said, grabbing one side. I jumped up on the dresser, grabbed the other side, and we lifted it up and off its mount.

It must have weighed sixty or seventy pounds. Kylie set her end down on the top of the dresser, and then, without warning, let go. I got caught off balance. I couldn't hang on to it on my own, and the TV went crashing to the hardwood floor.

Kylie didn't care. She grabbed onto the cable that was coming out of the back of the set.

"Co-ax cables," she said. "Heavy-duty, all copper and plastic. It's probably stronger than rope."

"*Probably* stronger?"

"We're about to find out," she said. "The whole place is wired, but it's all behind the wall. Help me rip it out."

She yanked the cable hard enough that three feet of it tore right through the Sheetrock.

I grabbed on, and we pulled together, chewing up the wall from one end of the bedroom to the other, then up to the ceiling and into the next room.

"Get a knife!" she yelled.

I dug a small Swiss Army knife out of my pocket.

"Bigger," she said, tearing at the thick cable.

I ran back to the kitchen, pulled a large Henckels knife from the wooden block on the counter. By the time I got back, Kylie had at least forty feet of co-ax exposed. I cut through it in one whack.

We ran back to the terrace and lashed it to the metal railing.

"You stay and secure this end," Kylie said. "I'm going down."

"No," I said. "I'm going."

"Zach, I weigh less, and it's my husband."

"Damn it, Kylie, you can't control every

goddamn thing!" I shouted. "When you get into that apartment, do you even have a clue about how to dismantle that booby trap?"

"I ... no, but I figured I could ..."

"Did you ever take a weeklong course in demolitions at Quantico?"

She shook her head. "No."

"Then shut up and wrap this cable around me," I said. "I'm going down."

Chapter 75

WE FOUND THE halfway point of the co-ax cable and wrapped it four times around the terrace railing. Kylie took one end, I took the other, and we braided them together.

I found a pair of work gloves in Dino's studio and put them on. Then the two of us grabbed the end of the cable, backed up into the living room, and pulled as hard as we could.

It held.

"Ready?" she said.

I threw one leg over the railing.

"Eleven minutes. Go," she said.

I swung my other leg over, jammed my toes into the narrow space under the bottom rail, and lowered the cable. It dropped at least five feet past Kylie's terrace. I grabbed on for dear life, wrapped my left foot around the cable for stability, looked up to the sky, and whispered the last few words of the Policeman's Prayer.

Please, Lord, through it all, be at my side.

There was no time for the rest. I lifted my right foot and stepped off into space.

The cable snapped taut. Once again, it held. And there I was, dangling eight stories above lower Manhattan, my life depending on all the skills I had learned in Coach Coviello's gym class twenty years ago.

I relaxed my death grip and began to walk monkey-style, keeping my knees bent and my hands down, using my legs to keep me from sliding.

I heard screams from the street below. Then another one from above: "Zach, don't look down! Focus."

I focused. I looked straight ahead. All I could see was red brick. I moved slowly, hand over hand, inch by inch, brick by brick.

And then I saw a glimmer of glass—the top of Kylie's terrace door. Another few feet and I was looking into her living room. Finally, my left foot connected with something solid. I lowered my right foot. Contact.

I looked down. I was standing on the seventh floor terrace railing.

I inhaled deeply, blew out hard, and with both legs on the safe side of the rail, I lowered myself to the terrace floor.

"I made it," I said, looking up.

"I'm coming down," Kylie said. "Nine and a half minutes."

The glass door was unlocked. I took off my gloves, slid it open, and stepped carefully into the living room.

The Skype image I had seen on Kylie's cell phone had been horrendous enough. But being in the same room with Spence—naked, bleeding, and taped to a chair—was that much worse. I'm not sure Kylie could have handled it on her own, which is why I lied to her about taking a demo course at Quantico.

"Spence, it's Zach," I said. "Don't even turn around."

He let out a long moan.

I stood behind him and stared at the front door. I had been right about the booby trap. Five feet to the right of the doorjamb, a block of C4 was molded to a table leg. There was a wire running from the doorknob to the charge.

Like a lot of cops, I had a few hours of basic post-9/11 bomb training under my belt. I didn't know a lot, but I knew that if Kylie had opened the front door, it would have triggered the detonator, and the three of us would have been blown apart in an instant.

Spence couldn't get out of the apartment until someone disarmed it. I sure as hell hoped I was that someone, because right now I was the only option he had left.

Chapter 76

MICKEY HAD BEEN right—rigging the explosives was not complicated. But it sure as hell wasn't easy peasy. Sweat poured off The Chameleon's face, and the white shirt under his waiter's uniform was soaked through as he inserted the remote detonator into the C4 on the starboard side of the yacht.

"One down, two to go," he said to the semiconscious seaman who was trussed, gagged, and secured to a six-inch-wide stainless-steel pipe. "According to my friend Mickey, all it takes is three perfectly placed charges, and you can sink this tub without a ripple. Let's hope he was right, God rest his soul."

The man pulled hard at his bonds, straining the veins on his neck and forehead.

"Don't do that," Gabriel said. "You'll give yourself a stroke or some kind of a brain hemorrhage. Relax. Stick around for the fireworks."

Connor stopped squirming.

"Good," The Chameleon said. "You know, if you and I had met under different circumstances—I don't know, like in a bar or something—I bet we'd have hit it off great. We've got a lot in common. You're down here in the goddamn boiler room and all the stars are up on deck. That's the kind of shit I have to put up with. I'm either a guy reading a newspaper in the back of a bus, or a businessman getting out of an elevator, or a dead soldier on a battlefield. Never the hero. Never the big star. You know what I'm talking about?"

The man's only response was the tear that streamed silently over his duct-taped mouth and onto the floor.

"I know," The Chameleon said. "It's a crying shame the way they treat us. But that's all going to change. Tomorrow morning's newspaper, you and me—we're going to be headliners."

Chapter 77

SPENCE'S BREATHING WAS labored. One look at his bloodied face and I knew why. His mouth was taped shut, and his nose had been shattered. This time my little pocketknife was more than enough. I pried out the blade and cut through the layers of duct tape behind his head.

I had no time to be delicate. "This is going to hurt," I said and yanked the tape off hard, taking hair and skin with it.

Spence hungrily sucked in a mouthful of air. "Bomb to the right of the front door," he gasped.

"I see it," I said, walking over to it. "Not very sophisticated."

"Zach, Spence, what's going on in there?" It was Kylie on the other side of the door.

"He's okay," I said, which was seriously stretching the truth. "Hang on. I'm trying to disarm the booby trap. In fact, I want you to stand in the stairwell…just in case."

"I thought you said you knew what you were doing?" she said.

"I do," I lied. "It's just a precaution. Now, back off, dammit."

"I'm going. Hurry up. We have less than eight minutes."

Spence's face was contorted with pain. I had no idea how he might help, but I was out of my element, and since I was about to do something that could kill us both, I figured two heads were better than one.

"Spence, can you focus?" I said. "I need you to track my thinking."

"I'll try."

"Okay, the front door is the trigger. Opening it pulls the trip wire. Trip wire activates the blasting cap."

"And then we're dead. Makes sense."

"Now logic would dictate that if I pinch the wire and cut the piece closest to the door..."

"You take the door out of the equation," Spence said. "No trigger."

I pinched the trip wire between my thumb and index finger.

"Do it," he said.

I cut the wire. One half fell to the floor. I opened my fingers and let go of the other half.

"We're still here," he said.

I opened the door and yelled out for Kylie.

She ran down the hall, then stepped into the apartment cautiously, eyes glued to her husband.

"Don't go in any farther," I said. "When Benoit Skyped us, the block of C4 he held up had a timer. The one I disabled doesn't. There's got to be another bomb somewhere."

"We don't have time to look for it," Kylie said. "Let's just get Spence out of here."

"You can't," Spence said.

"Yes, we can," Kylie said. "We've got six minutes and twelve seconds, and we're getting you out of this building if we have to carry you out stark naked, chair and all."

Spence's body started to tremble. "You can't get me out," he repeated.

"Why?"

His eyes stared straight down at his feet. "That's why."

I followed his gaze. I hadn't seen it before. Probably because there was almost no blood—just small dark stains where Spence's feet had been nailed to the floor.

Chapter 78

"OH MY GOD," Kylie said, kneeling down at Spence's feet.

"He had a nail gun," Spence said.

"We have to pry you loose," she said, putting a hand on his left foot.

Spence's head and shoulders jerked back hard, and he let out a gut-wrenching scream. "Don't—don't touch. Please."

"Spence, we have to get the nails out."

"No time," he said, breathing rapidly through the fog of fear and pain. "Just get yourself out."

The reality of what was happening was incomprehensible, yet Spence seemed ready to accept it.

Kylie and I weren't.

"Spence," I said. "Where did Benoit go after he started the timer?"

"Kitch-en," he said, forcing the word out in two syllables separated by a gasp for air.

Kylie and I both ran to the kitchen.

It felt like déjà vu. Only a few minutes ago I had been flinging the cabinet doors open in Dino's apartment. Now Kylie and I were doing the same thing in hers.

"I'll do the top. You get the ones on the bottom," she said.

I dropped to a squat and started opening the lower cabinets.

"Clear, clear, clear, clear," Kylie said every time she opened another door and found nothing.

And then I saw it. The top of my head was just at countertop level, and I caught a flicker of red. It was the same glowing red light I had seen when Benoit started the countdown timer. It was coming through the glass door of a sleek, stainless-steel Breville toaster oven.

"Kylie, I got it," I said, standing up.

"We only have two minutes. Can you disarm it?"

"Maybe if I had two days. I might have exaggerated my bomb experience," I said. "I can't even take a chance on opening the oven door. It could be rigged to blow. We have to ditch it—the whole thing."

"Well, we can't throw it out the window," Kylie said. "God knows how many people we'd kill."

"Do you have a safe?" I said. "That would contain some of the explosion."

She shook her head. "What about the basement?" she said. "It's like a bunker down there."

"Not enough time. Even if your elevator managed to get us down there, we'd never get out."

"We don't need the elevator," she said. "Grab it and follow me."

The toaster oven was freestanding, about the size of a small microwave, and unplugged. I picked it up and followed Kylie.

"Garbage chute," she said, bolting out the front door.

The incinerator room was just past the elevator. We went in, and Kylie pulled the chute door open.

As soon as she did, we both realized her mistake. The door was hinged at the bottom, and the hopper was designed to drop down only about sixty degrees. Plastic garbage bags could be squished and squeezed to cram down the chute. Stainless-steel toaster ovens couldn't.

"Pull hard on the door," I said. "Rip it right out of the wall."

Kylie sat on the floor, grabbed the handle, and put all her weight on it.

"It won't budge," she said. "The bomb is too damn big to shove through the door."

I stared at the red glow. We had ninety seconds.

Chapter 79

"GET ME A sledgehammer," I said.

"I don't have a sledge—no, I have something. Give me a second," she said, running back to her apartment.

"I can give you seventy-two seconds," I yelled back after her. "And then we're toast."

I watched the timer count down to 1:00, 0:59, 0:58, and I wondered how much C4 Benoit could stuff into the guts of a toaster oven. From what I knew about his style, he wouldn't skimp on the ingredients.

Kylie came back carrying a twenty-pound dumbbell. "Best I can do," she said. "Hold the door open."

I'm pretty sure I'm stronger than Kylie, but I wasn't about to debate which one of us should be wielding the dumbbell. We had only thirty-seven seconds, and I figured whatever she lacked in brute strength, she would make up for with pure adrenaline.

I set the toaster oven on the floor, pulled down the chute door as far as the hinge would go, then grabbed the handle to hold the door in place.

"I'm hoping you're as accurate with a dumbbell as you are with a Glock," I said. "Try not to hit me. We've got thirty seconds. When we get down to ten, we should run like hell for your apartment."

So we can die in there with Spence, because as sure as shit, when this blows, the blast radius is going to go a lot farther than your living room.

Kylie brought the dumbbell down hard. The force reverberated up my arm, but the door didn't budge.

"Twenty-five seconds," I said.

She swung it again.

The door hung on tight.

"Hit it again," I said. "Third time's the charm."

I was right. The door gave. Not a lot, but it gave.

"It's loose," I yelled. "Again."

She lowered the boom, and this time chunks of cinder block fell to the floor.

"One more time. Eighteen seconds."

Kylie raised the dumbbell high and brought it down with a loud grunt worthy of Serena Williams.

The steel door hit the floor with a clatter.

I picked up the toaster oven as Kylie lashed out at the cinder block wall again and again.

It crumbled, leaving a gaping hole where the door had been. I could see the garbage chute. It was round. And wide.

"Out of the way!" I yelled.

I took one last look at the clock and dropped Kylie and Spence's ultrachic, stainless-steel, countertop toaster-bomb into the abyss.

The window of time for us to get out of the incinerator room had passed.

"Seven seconds!" I yelled. "Hit the dirt."

She dropped to the floor.

"Six."

The irony of it all hit me in an instant. If

Kylie and I had been able to run back to her apartment, we probably would have had a chance. But here in the incinerator room, we were directly above ground zero.

"Five."

The bomb would explode in the basement, a fireball would travel up the chute like a cannon shot, and we would both be engulfed in flames. But maybe it didn't have to be both of us.

"Four."

We all die sooner or later. I always figured I had till much later, but if it had to be today, there was no place else I'd rather be, and no one else I'd rather be with.

I threw myself on top of her and covered her body with mine.

"Three. Two. One."

Chapter 80

"KABOOM!" GABRIEL SCREAMED at the top of his lungs.

The semi-comatose man on the engine room floor snapped alert.

"Did you hear that, Charlie?" Gabriel said. "That was the kaboom of justice."

Connor gave him a quizzical look.

"As of three seconds ago, the bitch cop who killed my girlfriend, and her asshole husband, who stole my identity, just got blown to hell. I wish I could have watched them go up in smoke, but I have bigger fish to fry. Namely your cronies on the top deck."

Connor tried to talk through the duct tape, but all that came out was a shrill whine.

"You want a speaking part?" Gabriel said. "Okay, but you raise your voice, and I will stick this stun baton down your pants and fry your junk like a Jimmy Dean sausage. Understood?"

The man nodded, and Gabriel yanked the duct tape from his mouth.

Connor gulped air. "Thank you," he wheezed.

"Don't thank me, Charlie. I'm going to kill you in about half an hour."

"Why me?"

"Don't take it personally. I'm blowing up an entire boat. You just happen to be on it."

"I don't *have* to be on it," Connor said. "Cut the tape and let me jump ship. I'll take my chances in the river. Come on, man, give a brother a break."

"Bad news, *brother.* This is just makeup. Underneath, I'm as white as Vanilla Ice."

"Even so, you said we had a lot in common. You're right. Those guys upstairs are not my cronies. I'm just a working stiff busting his balls for the man. Don't let me die down here, too."

"No can do, but kudos on presenting a noble argument. And thank you for not trotting out the old 'I got a wife and six kids' routine. It's so overdone."

"I don't have kids, and my ex won't even notice I'm gone," Connor said. "The only ones who are going to miss me are the Alley Cats."

"I hate to break it to you, but cats don't have feelings."

Connor laughed. "These cats do. The Alley Cats is the name of my bowling team. If you won't do it for me, at least do it for them."

"You crack me up," Gabriel said. "I wish I could stick around for the whole show, but I'm done here." He stepped back to inspect the final charge. "Not bad for an amateur."

"That's cell-phone-activated," Connor said. "I'd say that's a notch or two above amateur."

"Credit where credit is due, Charlie. I had a great teacher. Mickey Peltz. I hated to have to kill him. I feel the same way about Adrienne, the catering chick upstairs. You too. It totally sucks that good guys like you have to die."

"I'm touched. Your compassion means a lot to me in my final moments."

"If it's any consolation, it'll be painless. Mickey was right. Sixty pounds is more than enough to split this hull like a ripe melon. Especially with the charge I put under this fuel tank. How big is it, anyway?"

"Each one is five thousand gallons. One blows, and they'll all go."

"Then I have twenty pounds all rigged and ready to go that I don't need down here. I think maybe I'll take it upstairs and find a nice little spot for it in the main salon."

"Or maybe you could just shove it up your ass and give yourself a call," Connor said.

Gabriel laughed. "Charlie, you have no idea how much you've brought to this film," he said, tucking the remaining C4 into his jacket pockets. "When I came up with this scene, I always pictured it as high drama—me sweating like a pig, molding the plastic, scared shitless that I'd blow myself up. But you added just the right touch of comic relief. You're like the black Quentin Tarantino."

"So let me get this straight," Connor said. "You're making a movie?"

"Yeah."

"Where's the camera?"

Gabriel tapped a finger to his head.

"Oh boy," Connor said. "And this movie in your head—I die in it?"

"It's an action movie. Lots of people die in it."

"Including you?"

"Oh, no. I'm the hero. I escape."

"How?"

"That's a spoiler, Charlie. I can't tip the ending."

"First of all, the name's not Charlie. It's Charles. Second of all, there's no way in hell you'll escape. If the explosion doesn't kill you, Harbor Patrol will fish you out of the drink before you can swim fifty feet."

"Oh, I escape. It's in my script. The problem with you, *Charles,* is that you've got no imagination."

"I got plenty of imagination. You want to hear *my* script? You're no hero. You're just another one of those nut-job suicide bombers who thinks he's going to wind up with seventy-two virgins."

"I'm not one of them," Gabriel yelled,

pulling the stun baton from his holster and pointing it at Connor. "I'm the star of this whole show."

"Oh yeah," Connor said. "And nothing says 'action hero' like a young white guy using a cattle prod on a poor old black man who's duct-taped to a steam pipe."

Gabriel holstered the stun baton and knelt down next to Connor. "Charles, trust me. This is a great movie, and I really do have a brilliant way of ending it."

"But since I'll be dead, I'll never get to see it. How convenient."

"You think I'm lying?" Gabriel said. "I got the escape scene right here in my pocket. It's mind-blowing."

"Show it to me," Connor said.

"Show you? You ever even read a movie script, old man?" Gabriel asked.

"I work for Shelley Trager. He leaves scripts in the bathrooms, and believe me, that's where a lot of them belong."

"Well, mine is pure gold."

"Prove it," Connor said. "Let me read it. Right here. Right now."

Gabriel shook his head. "I don't know. I

don't usually show it around. In fact, except for my girlfriend, I haven't shown it to anybody."

"Hey, man, I'm not just *anybody*. I'm the black Quentin Tarantino."

Chapter 81

I WAS FLAT-OUT wrong. I felt a little stupid, but it's a hell of a lot better than being dead wrong.

Not only do I not know squat about explosives, but I totally underestimated the New York City Department of Buildings.

Somewhere, somehow, someone, bless his bureaucratic little heart, foresaw my predicament, and had the vision to insist that all garbage chutes in the city of New York must extend six feet above the roof and be equipped with a safety valve called an explosion cap.

The ball of flame I was afraid would travel up the chute and burn us both to hell never did. Instead, a deafening explosion rocked the building and released a pressure wave of hot expanding gases, most of which blew straight through the roof.

Some of the blowback billowed through the hole in the wall we had created, but at least the little incinerator room we were trapped in hadn't turned into a blazing coffin.

Neither of us moved for a solid fifteen seconds as ash, soot, and chunks of hot garbage fell around us.

And then, silence.

My mouth was pressed to Kylie's ear.

"Are you alive?" I whispered.

"No," she said.

"Me either," I said.

I rolled off her, and the two of us sat up. We weren't quite ready to stand.

"You have absolutely no bomb experience, do you?" Kylie said, shaking plaster dust out of her hair.

I stood up and grinned down at her like an idiot, thrilled to be alive. "I do now."

I helped her to her feet, and she put her arms around me, clasping her hands behind my neck. I wrapped my arms around her waist, and, as the dust settled around us, we stood there, gazing into each other's eyes.

I remember the first day I saw her at the academy. She was heart-stoppingly beautiful back then and, ten years later, with her face marbled with grime and her hair streaked with gray ash, Kylie MacDonald was still the most beautiful woman in the world.

"Thank you," she said softly. "If you hadn't stopped me from unlocking that front door, Spence and I—and you—we'd all be—"

She either couldn't finish, or she just decided that words weren't enough. She leaned into me and kissed me gently.

Kylie has the softest, sweetest lips I've ever kissed, and feeling them pressed against mine brought on that rush of anticipation I felt back in the days when I knew the first kiss was only the beginning of a night of tender, passionate, soulful lovemaking.

But that was ten years ago. Right here, right now, I knew that it all would begin and end with a single kiss.

"You're welcome," I said, lowering my arms from around her waist.

She stepped away, and the moment was over.

"Wish I could stay," she said, "but I've got a homicidal maniac to catch, and my poor husband's got both feet nailed to the floor."

"How many times have I heard that old excuse?" I said as I followed her down the hallway so I could aid and comfort the lucky bastard with both feet nailed to the floor.

Chapter 82

THE SECOND THAT KYLIE and I walked through the door of the apartment, Spence burst into tears.

"I thought you were dead," he said, his body still in trauma, now shaking with gratitude and relief.

"That makes three of us," Kylie said.

She grabbed an afghan throw from the sofa and draped it over his legs. Then she knelt beside him, cradling him in her arms, kissing his forehead, his cheeks, and finally his lips.

I squatted down behind him and cut away the duct tape that bound him to the chair.

As soon as his arms were free, he hugged her tight, and I watched as she quietly rocked him back and forth.

"You guys have got to stop Benoit," he said, breaking the hug abruptly.

"We will," she said. "But first we have to do something about getting those nails out of your feet."

Spence sat back in the chair. "*We*," he said, "do not have to do anything. I love you, Kylie, but I don't need a cop with a crowbar and a claw hammer prying me loose."

"I love you, too," she said, "but I can't just leave you sitting in the middle of the living room. My mother is coming next weekend, and you know what a neat freak she is."

The love between the two of them was palpable. I couldn't imagine how much pain he was in, but just having her near made him smile. She was also frustrating the hell out of him.

"Dammit, Kylie, listen to me. I'm fine. He didn't hit an artery. I'm not going to bleed to death. I can wait till the fire department shows up. They can cut the floor out from under me and take me to the hospital. After that, all I want is the best foot surgeon in New York and maybe a week on the beach in Turks and Caicos. You have more important things to do than hold my hand."

"Do you have any clue where Benoit was going next?" she said.

"I've got more than a clue. He has a shit-load of explosives, and he's headed for Shelley Trager's yacht."

Kylie was blindsided. She'd convinced herself that Shelley's little sunset cruise was a low-priority target. "Why Shelley?" she said.

"Not just Shelley. Shelley and me. Benoit calls himself The Chameleon, and he thinks we stole his persona and used it for my TV show."

"That's insane," she said.

"I think we've pretty much established that the guy is a psycho," Spence said. "He knows Shelley is screening the pilot on his yacht tonight. Benoit is planning to get on board, wait till they're somewhere out on the open water, and then blow it up."

"Did you convince Shelley to bring any security on board?" Kylie said.

"You know how stubborn he is. He finally

signed on two rent-a-cops just to humor me. I doubt if they're any better than a couple of school crossing guards."

"We have to warn him," Kylie said. "Maybe we should radio the captain."

"You do that," Spence said. "I met him. His name is Kirk Campion. He's a retired merchant marine, used to be chief mate on one of the Maersk container ships. And guess what—he pitched a movie to me about a yacht getting hijacked by a bunch of Somali pirates, and the captain and the crew take them on. You call him and tell him the madman everyone in New York is looking for is on his boat, and guess what he'll do?"

"Spence is right," I said. "The last thing we need is some civilian cowboy trying to save the day. You and I need to get on that boat. Spence, where's the dock, and when does the boat leave?"

"South Street Seaport. Pier 17. What time is it?"

"A little after six."

"By now they've shoved off, and Gabriel Benoit is somewhere belowdecks wiring it with enough explosives to blow it to Wee-hawken."

"How does he expect to get off?" Kylie said.

"Beats me," Spence said, "but after the way he escaped from half of NYPD at Radio City, I bet he won't have a hard time figuring out how to—"

There was a pounding on the apartment door.

"Police," the voice on the other side said. "Open up."

I opened the door. There were at least ten people in the hallway. All of them in uniform, except one: Captain Cates.

Chapter 83

"CAPTAIN," I SAID, "I know I should have taken your call, but—"

"We'll have plenty of time for repercussions later, Detective," she said. "Right now, I want the short version of what went down."

I gave it to her in under sixty seconds. Kylie stood by my side and didn't say a word.

"And you're sure Benoit is on the yacht?" Cates said.

"As sure as we can be, but he's fooled us before. I wouldn't pull any of the units you have covering the other events."

"Okay," she said, "what do we need to catch this son of a bitch?"

"A boarding vessel," I said. "Kylie knows the layout of the yacht, and we can both spot Benoit. Just get the two of us on board."

"Three of you," Cates said. "This time you're not going anywhere without a bomb tech."

"Fair enough, Captain."

"You see any C4, you point it out to the tech. You got lucky once, but you will not—repeat, not—attempt to disable any explosives. Your only job is to disable Benoit. Understood?"

"Yes, ma'am."

"Get moving. I'll call you with the details."

I was about to bolt when Cates held up her hand. She stared at me, stone-faced. "And Jordan...make sure your phone is on."

Chapter 84

WITHIN MINUTES, KYLIE and I were back in the PPV doing ninety on West Street barreling toward South Street Seaport.

There may only be seventy-five cops attached to NYPD Red, but there are another thirty-five thousand brothers and sisters in blue who've got our backs—and our fronts. By the time we entered the South Street Viaduct, which tunnels under Battery Park, we had two motorcycle cops from Highway Patrol clearing our path.

"Hot damn!" Kylie yelled. "We're getting a police escort."

Captain Cates had the full power of the New York City Police Department at her fingertips, and when we emerged from the tunnel, it was clear that she hadn't hesitated to use it.

The road in front of us was clear. No, it was empty. FDR Drive, which is often preceded by the words "heavy backups" on the 1010 WINS traffic reports, didn't have a single car on it—northbound or southbound.

One look at the service road, and I could see that there was plenty of traffic just waiting to clog it up, but there were squad cars with flashing lights at every entrance ramp holding them back.

Cates called, and I put her on speaker.

"We got lucky. We've got our bomb techs spread out across the city, and Jeff Ordway was on standby half a mile from the Seaport. Sergeant Ordway is one of our best. Jim Rothlein from Harbor Patrol will meet the three of you at Pier 17. He's in an unmarked boat with a plainclothes crew so you can get close to the yacht without looking like cops. I've also scrambled Scuba and SWAT, but I'm keeping them out of sight. Benoit can't know there's an armada bearing down on him. This has to run like Special Ops."

"How about the captain of the yacht?" I asked. "According to Spence, this guy Campion's lifelong dream is to take down a pirate on the high seas. I don't want him to go all Steven Seagal on us."

"Rothlein radioed him on the NYPD frequency and told him to prepare to be boarded. As far as Campion knows, you're just doing some routine follow-up on the shooting at the funeral home, and you couldn't wait for the boat to dock tonight—nothing that would set off his cowboy genes."

"MacDonald says there's a swimming platform at the stern," I said. "Can you arrange for us to board there?"

"Rothlein thinks it's too visible," Cates said. "There's a cargo hold door on the starboard side. It's harder to see from the top deck. Once you get close, the yacht will slow down, but not enough for Benoit to get suspicious. A couple of crewmen will open the cargo door and extend a ramp. The three of you will have to jump while both boats are moving at a pretty good clip."

Making a sideways leap from a moving boat onto a narrow ramp was not nearly as easy as jumping forward onto a low-hanging double-wide swim platform would have been, but Cates was right. This had to run like Special Ops.

"Getting on board won't be a problem," I said.

"Once you're on board, get Ordway to the engine room. Benoit is smart—he'll know that's where he can do the most damage. Odds are he plans to jump ship and set his bombs off by remote. Your job is to keep him from getting off that boat, because I guarantee you that as soon as he's a hundred yards away, he'll blow it up and laugh while it burns. I've got fireboats and EMS units tailing you, and I've got choppers and a chase team, but I've only got the two of you to keep him from pushing that button."

"We can handle it, Captain," I said.

"I'm counting on you, Jordan. Me and a hundred other people," she said. "Put MacDonald on the horn."

I held the cell phone close to Kylie. "Right here, Captain."

"I've got a message from your husband. FDNY cut him out of the floor, he's on his way to NYU Medical, and he loves you."

"Tell him I love him, too," Kylie said.

"I have a better idea," Cates said. "Make sure you get your ass back here in one piece and tell him yourself."

Chapter 85

EXT. HUDSON RIVER—NEW
YORK CITY—DUSK

Helicopter shot of SHELLEY TRA-
GER's yacht as it sails quietly up
the river. And there in the background, we see her, standing tall
and proud as the sun sets—THE
STATUE OF LIBERTY.

MUSIC UP: We hear THE RAT-A-
TAT-TAT OF SNARE DRUMS, followed by HORNS, and then the

track is filled with the unmistakable sound of the Greatest Musical Genius of All Time—THE LATE, GREAT RAY CHARLES, singing the best fucking version of AMERICA THE BEAUTIFUL ever recorded.

> RAY CHARLES (SOUND TRACK)
>
> O beautiful, for heroes proved,
> In liberating strife,
> Who more than self, their country loved,
> And mercy more than life.

The camera drifts in on the yacht, and we see a ramp slowly being lowered from the stern like a giant tailgate. As we move in closer, we see The Chameleon as he prepares to get off the moving ship.

James Patterson

RAY CHARLES

America, America,
May God thy gold refine,
Till all success be nobleness
And every gain divine.

The camera is in tight now as
The Chameleon unties one of two
Zodiac Bayrunners, a fifteen-foot
pontoon boat Trager uses when
he anchors offshore.

RAY CHARLES

O beautiful, for spacious skies,
For amber waves of grain,

The Chameleon slides one Zodiac
off the ramp and into the water.
He jumps in and starts it.

RAY CHARLES

For purple mountain majesties,
Above the fruited plain.

The Zodiac slowly edges away from the yacht.

RAY CHARLES

America, America,
God shed his grace on thee.

Long shot as we see the Zodiac separating even farther from the doomed yacht.

RAY CHARLES

He crowned thy good,
In brotherhood,
From sea to shining sea.

Cut to a close-up of Lady Liberty as she looks down approvingly on the scene below.

RAY CHARLES

You know, I wish I had somebody to help me sing this.

The CHORUS joins in, and now the music and the emotion build.

CHORUS

America, America,

RAY CHARLES

America, I love you, America

CHORUS

God shed his grace on thee.

Cut to a close-up of The Chameleon as he removes his CELL PHONE from his pocket.

RAY CHARLES

God shed his grace on thee.

Cut to a wide shot. Slowly the Zodiac slips out of the picture.

RAY CHARLES

He crowned thy good,
With brotherhood,

Cut to a close-up as The Chameleon dials his phone.

RAY CHARLES

From sea to shining sea.

Cut to a wide shot. The Statue of Liberty, a powerful beacon of freedom, is dominating the frame. The yacht, a symbol of greed, money, and injustice, looks insignificant in her presence.

CHORUS (MAJESTIC FINISH)
... shining sea.

The sound track is filled with the thunder of timpani and the crash of cymbals as the music reaches a crescendo, and the yacht EXPLODES into a fiery hell.

"So...what do you think, Charles?" Gabriel asked, still kneeling at Connor's side.

"I knew you could get off the ship with one of the Zodiacs," Connor said. "I just didn't know you knew."

Gabriel stood up and took a small bow. "Research. But I meant what do you think of the whole thing with the Statue of Liberty and 'America the Beautiful' playing counterpoint against a guy who's blowing up a hundred people?"

"I'd like it a lot better if I wasn't one of the hundred."

"Charles, you asked me if you could read it. I broke a rule and showed it to you. The least you could do is subtract your personal conflict of interest and give me more of a professional opinion than 'I don't want to die.'"

"Okay," Connor said. "Am I correct in assuming you had something to do with the bomb that killed Brad Schuck at Radio City?"

"I had everything to do with it."

"I saw the video. Nice. The blast, getting away from the cops—that worked. But your script reads like Amateur Night. The Statue of Liberty is 'a beacon of freedom'? The yacht is 'a symbol of greed, money, and injustice'? It's like you got the big box of clichés and you're trying to use them all."

"It's stage direction," Gabriel said. "The audience never sees it. It's only there to help the producer understand what the writer is thinking about."

"And it reads like you either think the producer is stupid, or you're so insecure that you have to spell out the message for him, or you can't decide if it's a popcorn movie with bombs going off and bodies piling up or an art house film condemning the evils of Hollywood."

"Wow, you got some balls," Gabriel said. "I'd have bet anything you'd suck up to me and try to get me to turn you loose."

"That's not who you are. You can smell a phony a mile away. The only way to deal with you is to give it to you straight."

"Thanks. I said this from the get-go. You're

my kind of guy. Another time, another set of circumstances, we'd be best buds. And Lexi—she would've just adored you."

"But you're still going to kill me."

"Charles, we've gone over this before. I've been flexible shooting this film, but this is a critical scene. I can't undo the script. My hands are tied."

"Actually, it's my hands that are tied, but let's not split hairs."

Gabriel smiled and tucked the script pages in his pocket. "I will never forget you, Charles Connor."

"Likewise," Connor said. "Just answer me one last question."

"Anything."

"Your alter ego in the film is The Chameleon. What's your real name?"

"Gabriel. Gabriel Benoit. Why do you ask?"

"Because one of these days you're going to go straight to hell, Gabriel. And I want to be able to track you down as soon as you show up and beat the shit out of you for all eternity."

Chapter 86

A LOT OF sharp-eyed New Yorkers can spot an unmarked police car. That's because most of our plain brown wrappers look a lot like our blue-and-white units, minus the department logo and the big letters on the doors that scream NYPD.

Unmarked boats are a whole different ballgame. The one that was waiting for us at Pier 17 was the water equivalent of a Ferrari Testarossa. Her name was *Kristina*, she was from Tenafly, New Jersey, and she was beautiful.

Kylie and I jumped on the sleek, fifty-foot

motor yacht, and I swear she was moving before my feet hit the deck.

Jim Rothlein, who is blond, tan, and built like a *Transformers* robot, grinned when he saw me. "Zach, they didn't tell me it was you."

Jim and I had worked together twice before. One was a homicide; the other a suicide. His team had dredged both bodies out of the river. I introduced him to Kylie.

"Since when did you guys get into Water Ops?" Rothlein said as we climbed onto the bridge.

"Today's our first day. Since when does NYPD have a budget to float this beauty?"

"She's a loaner from the Port Authority Task Force. She used to belong to some hedge fund guy in Jersey until the market tanked and he decided to supplement his income with a little cocaine trafficking. The PA nailed him on his first run. They seized the boat, and we get to use it until they auction it off next month."

"Did Cates tell you what's going on?" I said.

"She told me enough to know you're stark, raving, out-of-your-gourd nuts," Rothlein said. "Do you know anything about the boat you're about to risk your lives on?"

"I've been on it three or four times," Kylie said.

"And how much of that time did you spend in the engine room?" Rothlein asked. "Because I doubt if he's going to be planting a bomb in a champagne bucket on the promenade deck."

"You'd be surprised the places some people plant bombs," a voice said. "Hi, I'm Jeff Ordway, and as you can tell by my outfit, I'll be your bomb tech this evening."

Ordway was tall, lean, with an ingratiating smile that was contrasted by his dead serious eyes. He was dressed in thick black canvas military fatigues and a tactical vest loaded with more paraphernalia than Batman's utility belt. As bulky as it was, it was a lot more streamlined than I expected.

"Where's your Kevlar moon suit?" I asked.

"Captain Cates said your bomber was an amateur," Ordway said, "so I figured there's no point wearing an extra hundred pounds of gear on the open water just to disarm a device I could defuse in my sleep."

"Let me show you guys what you'll be looking for," Rothlein piped up. He walked us to a console and turned on a TV monitor. The screen came alive with the image of a vast space filled with high-tech equipment that could have belonged to NASA, but which I assumed was the guts of Shelley Trager's yacht.

"Where'd you get that?" I said.

"The manufacturer's website," Rothlein said. "Every one of these two-hundred-footers is customized, but that's just the living quarters. The engine room doesn't change."

"If our boy is determined to rip it apart six ways to Sunday, I'm thinking these are the most likely places he would plant his explosives," Ordway said, pointing out half a dozen vulnerable spots.

"Let me give you a quick tour of the whole enchilada," Rothlein said.

He took us through a series of architectural drawings that laid out the ship's levels as well as the doors and staircases that connected one to the other.

"It's a lot to process in a short time," he said. "Are you sure you don't want to take some of my team with you? We do this kind of thing for a living."

"Jim, if this guy sees a mob storming the boat, he'll blow it to hell before anyone can stop him. Cates is giving us a shot at doing it our way."

"I don't know what your way is, but do me a favor," Rothlein said. "Don't try to do it in those Florsheims. At least let me fit you out with a couple of pairs of deck shoes."

"And radios," Kylie said.

"And while you're at it, a little Dramamine," I said. "I've never been much of a sailor."

A voice came from the cockpit. "Target is in sight, Lieutenant. I'll radio the captain of the yacht to reduce speed. We'll be alongside in three minutes."

"You guys ever jumped from one boat to the next?" Rothlein said as I slipped on a pair of Sperry Top-Siders. "It's a lot easier than it sounds. It's like hopping on an escalator at Bloomingdale's. The hard part is all being done by my guy at the wheel. It's his job to get close enough so you can jump, but not so close that I have to apologize to the

Port Authority for putting a big hole in their shiny new boat."

"Well, then I guess we've got the easy part," Kylie said. "All we have to do is make sure Benoit doesn't send a raging fireball through two hundred feet of Shelley Trager's yacht and a hundred of his dinner guests."

Chapter 87

THREE MINUTES LATER, we had dropped our speed and were cruising alongside the *Shell Game.*

Rothlein radioed Captain Campion. "We're in position."

A section of the yacht's massive steel hull opened like the door on the fuselage of a jetliner. An aluminum ramp telescoped out about six feet.

"Is that as far out as it goes?" Kylie said.

"It was designed to be lowered onto a dock," Rothlein said. "Not for changing horses in midstream."

There was an even shorter ramp extending over the side of our boat, and I stood on the edge waiting for the two ramps to line up.

"Zach, if you're waiting for them to lock together like a couple of Legos, it's not going to happen," Rothlein said. "This is as close as we're going to get."

It was only a three-foot jump. Half my height. Easy on dry land. Not so easy when point A and point B are bobbing and weaving like two staggering drunks trying to cross Broadway against a red light.

"Go," Rothlein said.

I watched the rhythm of the two ramps as they moved back and forth, up and down, hoping to pick up on a pattern. There was none. The water was too choppy.

"Don't think about it, Six," came the familiar taunting voice from behind me.

I jumped just as the *Kristina* caught some chop, and what had started out as a graceful leap turned into a flailing lunge. But both feet hit the ramp, and I stumbled into the arms of two crew members who broke my momentum and lowered me to the steel floor of the cargo hold.

Within seconds, Kylie was right behind me.

"Have you ever tried to get on the escalator at Bloomie's during the Christmas rush?" she said. "This was actually easier."

"I hate you," I said.

Ordway stepped to the edge of the *Kristina*'s ramp, sized up the gap, took a few steps backward, and got a running start.

Just as he was about to spring off, a cross-current caught the *Kristina,* tilting it, and dropping the front end of the ramp into the river. He didn't have a chance. He pitched forward, and his chest slammed into the hard steel of the opposite ramp.

He slid into the water, floundering against the weight of his equipment to keep from going under.

I could hear Rothlein yell "Kill the throttle," and the *Shell Game* zipped ahead, leaving the *Kristina* in its wake.

I radioed Rothlein. "Is he okay?"

"One of my guys dove in after him as soon as he hit the water," Rothlein said. "We'll have him back on board in two minutes, and if he's game, we can line up another pass. Five minutes tops."

If he's game? Five extra minutes for Benoit to get off the boat? Another pass for him to spot us?

I keyed the mic. "Negative. Hang back. I'll call you as soon as we have Benoit in custody."

I turned to the two crew members. "Lock it up," I said.

They retracted the ramp, and I took one last look at the *Kristina* as it slowly faded into the distance.

The steel door clanged shut.

Kylie looked at me. "Good call, Zach," she said. "Let's go find Benoit."

Chapter 88

GABRIEL STOOD ON the main deck looking out at the splashes of red and orange in
the western sky. "Magic hour," he whispered,
using the time-honored film term reserved
for sunsets as glorious as this one.

No director could ask for more perfect
lighting. And there in the distance was the
star of the scene. She was still just a gray
shape, but he could make out the torch held
high in her right hand, welcoming the tired,
the poor, the huddled masses yearning to
breathe free.

"Sorry to disappoint you," he said, "but

you're going to have to settle for the rich, the oppressive, and the toxically greedy."

The yacht had turned around and had just sailed under the Verrazano Narrows Bridge, which links Brooklyn to Staten Island. Miss Liberty would be ready for her star turn in about ten minutes. Plenty of time to plant the final bomb in the galley, go back downstairs to the Zodiac, and line up the parting shot.

He stood at the rail for one last lingering look, quietly marveling at the sun-streaked horizon, when he felt the first tear trickle down his cheek.

I can't be crying. It wasn't in the script. Everything was going so perfectly. It was all coming together as writ, but the tears—that caught him by surprise.

"Damn you, Lexi. You're ruining my makeup," he said, laughing into the warm evening breeze. "I miss you, baby. I should have let you have a bigger role. Maybe you wouldn't have gone out on your own and—what the hell?"

It was another boat.

The river was filled with all kinds of fishing

vessels and pleasure craft, but this one stood out because it was coming straight at them. The guy at the wheel was probably some millionaire, either drunk, stupid, or both.

It drew closer. But this guy wasn't drunk. He was a pro, and Gabriel watched as he swung around and pulled up parallel to the bigger yacht.

He looked around to see if any of his shipmates saw it, but the buffet must have opened because there were fewer than a dozen people on deck, all of them too absorbed in themselves to notice the world around them.

Gabriel watched as the smaller boat kept pace with the bigger one, wave for wave, side by side, with military precision. And then, out of nowhere, a ramp extended from the yacht. A boarding ramp.

It was just at the waterline, and within seconds the other boat lowered its own ramp.

Impossible, Gabriel thought as he watched Detectives Zach Jordan and Kylie MacDonald pull an Evel Knievel across the makeshift bridge and disappear into the cargo hold of the *Shell Game.*

Im-freaking-possible. They were supposed to be dead, but there they were. Coming for him.

A third cop, decked in black fatigues and weighted down with a vest full of gear, stepped up to the edge of the ramp. *Bomb squad goon here to put me out of business.*

But the man in black wasn't so lucky. Just as he was about to leap, the boat tilted, and he bounced off the ramp and into the water.

One less cop to worry about, but now there was no time to plant the bonus bomb. The three in the engine room were more than enough.

Gabriel had no idea how the two cops had managed to avoid getting blown up and then track him here. But it didn't matter.

He stormed down the metal steps to the lower deck. "Glad to have you on board, Detectives," he said, the tears in his eyes now replaced with white-hot rage. "You'll be dead before the sun sets."

Chapter 89

"ENGINE ROOM," I said to the two crew members who helped us board.

"We can take you," one of them said.

"Just point," I said. "Then leave."

They were trained not to argue with authority. One pointed, and they both left.

"This is my first time on a yacht," I said to Kylie. "I hope they weren't expecting a tip."

We drew our guns and found the metal door that warned us to stay out in five languages.

The engine room looked exactly like the picture Rothlein had showed us, but it wasn't nearly as loud as I expected. I was prepared for the clanking and banging I've heard in the movies, but this was more like the low rumble of a high-performance car.

We headed straight for the forward section, and there, molded to the hull, exactly where Ordway predicted it would be, was a thick gray block of C4, still bearing Benoit's handprints. There were red, white, blue, and yellow wires buried inside the plastic along with a cell phone waiting to be triggered by a signal from a cell phone.

"It's armed," I whispered.

"Then we better find him before he jumps ship," Kylie said. "We'll split up. You go upstairs, and I'll—"

The thud was loud, clear, and completely out of sequence with the steady rhythmic beat of the engine.

Kylie mouthed the word *Benoit*.

A second thud.

Engine rooms are not known for their acoustics, and we couldn't tell exactly where the thuds were coming from. I went left, Kylie went right, and we slowly advanced in the general direction of the sound.

And then, a new sound. This one was human, but muffled. Déjà vu. It was the same thing I had heard from Spence less than an hour ago. Only this time, I couldn't trust the source.

Benoit was smart, and for all I knew it could be a trap. He could have heard us come in and figured a muffled cry for help would get us out in the open.

I motioned for Kylie to stay down.

"NYPD!" I yelled. "Come out with your hands over your head."

The voice came back loud now, desperate, angry, and totally unintelligible. I pointed my body and my gun in the direction of the sound. And then I saw him. An older guy, obviously a crew member, duct-taped to a pipe.

"Over here!" I yelled to Kylie, and I dropped down and peeled the tape from the mouth of Benoit's latest victim.

"NYPD," I repeated.

"Bomb squad, I hope," the man said.

"No."

"Then cut me loose and get me the hell out of—Mother of God—Kylie? Kylie Harrington? Is that you?"

"Hey, Charles. Right now, I'm Detective MacDonald," she said as I slashed the tape from the man's arms and legs. "Are you okay?"

"I'll be fine as soon as I get the hell off this ship. There are three bombs down here, and somewhere topside there's a maniac with a cell phone who's planning to set them off."

"Benoit—how long ago did he leave?" I said.

"Maybe five minutes. He's crazy. He thinks he's making a movie. No camera, but this whack job is making a movie."

"He can't blow these till he's off the boat," I said. "Do you have any idea how he plans to get off?"

"He's going to steal one of the Zodiacs, put some distance between us and him, then speed-dial us all to kingdom come."

"Not if we can stop him first," Kylie said, helping the man to his feet.

He was a little wobbly, and he grabbed onto a thick chrome pipe.

"Charles, you're on your own," she said. "What's the fastest way to where Shelley keeps the Zodiacs?"

"Staircase D. Red door," he said, pointing.

We took off.

"Kylie, wait!" he yelled out. "One more thing you should know."

We stopped.

"Benoit showed me his script. He wants to blow up the ship with the Statue of Liberty in the picture," Charles said.

"What does that mean?" Kylie said.

"It means that once he's out on the river, and he can see the statue in the background, we are dead in the water."

Chapter 90

RICH, POWERFUL BUSINESSMEN always have an exit strategy, Gabriel thought as he raced down the steps toward the stern. In Shelley Trager's case, it was the Zodiac Bayrunner, a fifteen-foot yacht tender with a sleek, fire engine red fiberglass hull and a forty-horse Yamaha outboard engine. At about twenty thousand bucks a pop, it was the rich man's dinghy, and Trager, of course, had a small fleet of them.

Two were waiting for him at the swimming platform. He untied one, slid it into the water, and got in, taking care not to do anything stupid that might get his cell phone wet.

The evening light was picture-perfect, bouncing off the wake of the yacht as it slowly pulled away from him. But the statue was still too far in the distance. He had to get closer.

He started the Zodiac's engine and, with about a hundred feet between him and the yacht, followed her, cupping one hand to his forehead to block out the sun. With both eyes fixed on Liberty Island, he waited for the perfect shot.

"O beautiful, for spacious skies," he half talked, half sang. But he was so wrapped up in the visual that he wasn't even aware of the sound track.

The first bullet snapped him out of his reverie. The gunshot rang out, instantly followed by the cracking of fiberglass as it bounced off the hull.

"It's a rigid inflatable, you idiots," he yelled at the two cops standing on the swimming platform of Trager's boat. "You think you can sink this baby like it's a rubber raft?"

Another gunshot. And another.

He crouched low in the Zodiac and yelled over the gunwale. "Keep shooting, assholes. You're only making this movie better."

Chapter 91

BY THE TIME we got to the swimming platform, Benoit was following the yacht in one of the Zodiacs. He was far enough away to survive a blast, but close enough for us to open fire.

"Shoot out the pontoons!" I yelled. "Sink him. He can't detonate with a wet cell phone."

The Zodiac was going fast enough to raise its nose, and the blazing red sausage-shaped tubes that peeked just above the waterline made perfect targets.

We both fired. We both hit a pontoon. And we both expected the Zodiac to deflate like a balloon when the air is let out.

But it turned out that we knew as much about watercraft as we did about explosives. The bullets made direct hits, but nothing happened.

"Shit, it's an RIB," Kylie said. "The pontoon is rigid. It's like shooting into Styrofoam."

Benoit sat up and yelled at us. All I could make out was the word "assholes."

"He's slowing down," Kylie said as our yacht started to draw away from the Zodiac. "He's drifting out of range."

"The hell he is," I said, untying a second Zodiac and dropping it over the side. "Get in. I'm driving."

I dove into the boat, yanked hard on the starter cord, and the Yamaha engine sprang to life. With my right hand on the throttle, I extended my left to help Kylie climb aboard.

She grabbed on, set one foot on the hull, and I leaned back to pull her in. It was a classic case of the right hand not knowing what the left hand is doing, because as soon as I leaned backward, my right hand moved the throttle. The Zodiac lurched forward, and I pulled Kylie into the drink.

She was underwater for less than five seconds, then popped up, sputtering. "I lost my gun."

I maneuvered the boat in a circle, and when I got close enough to Kylie, I killed the power just to make sure I didn't chop her into fish bait with the propeller.

She put her fingers on one of the fiberglass sides, but it was slippery. I grabbed her hands to pull her in, but there was no leverage. I leaned over the side of the boat and put my hands under her arms. "On three," I said. "You jump up. I'll pull.

"One, two, three." Kylie bobbed up, and I threw my body back hard. Her clothes were drenched, and the water felt like it had added another hundred pounds, but I managed to drag her halfway over the side of the boat. I hung on tight as her hands found a chrome grab bar, and she pulled herself all the way in.

"I lost my gun," she said again.

"My fault. I'm an idiot. I'm sorry."

"Where's Benoit?" she said, sitting up and pushing the wet hair out of her eyes.

Anyone else would have turned his boat around and tried to get away. But not Benoit.

He had cut the engine and was letting his Zodiac drift. He'd had a front-row seat to every murder he'd committed so far, and he wasn't going to miss the grand finale.

He sat up and raised his cell phone in the air.

Like a mime in the spotlight, he held up his middle finger. It hung there, silhouetted against the twilight, mocking us, defying us to stop him, and knowing we couldn't.

And then, he turned the finger downward and pressed it hard on the dial pad of the cell phone.

I wasn't sure if Kylie and I were far enough away from the yacht to survive the blast.

We were both on the floor of the Zodiac. I rolled over on top of her and covered her with my body.

"That's twice in one day," she said.

"Old habits die hard," I whispered in her ear. "Brace yourself."

Chapter 92

THEY WERE MAKING a mockery of his movie.

Another time, another place, and The Chameleon might have found it funny. But this was the climax of his film, and instead of acting like worthy opponents, MacDonald and Jordan had showed up and were floundering around in the water like a couple of Keystone Kops.

Liberty Island was not as close as he would have liked, but it was close enough. He had to act now. He waited for Jordan to haul MacDonald up into the Zodiac. This was the last scene, and he didn't want them to miss it.

"And action!" he yelled.

He raised his cell phone in the air, angling the glass face so it reflected the light of the setting sun. They'd see it, and they'd know what it meant.

He held up his other hand, slowly gave them the finger, then pointed it down and rested it on the number 1 button of his speed dial.

The cops knew exactly what was coming next. They ducked for cover, but The Chameleon no longer cared about them. He gazed out at the horizon. It was just as he and Lexi had imagined—the doomed yacht, the all-knowing statue, the orange glow of the sun as it slipped into the water.

He pressed down hard on the button. He heard the beep of the auto-dial, then a single ring, and then . . .

"Kaboom."

The word was followed by a deep throaty laugh.

"I said 'kaboom,'" the voice on the other end of the phone mocked. "Sorry it isn't any louder, but I cut the phone wires to your detonators—all three of them. What's the matter, Mr. Chameleon? You suddenly at a loss for words?"

"Charles?" Gabriel finally said.

"You sound surprised. Didn't you see the last-minute script changes? The cavalry showed up, cut me loose, and upgraded me to hero status."

"Those sons of bitches," Gabriel said.

"That's show business," Connor said. "Your movie doesn't always turn out the way you—"

"My movie will turn out amazing!" Benoit screamed. He hung up. Charles Connor was an extra. Not worth talking to. The talking was over. This was an action movie, and the action was about to kick into high gear.

He gunned the engine and drew his Glock.

"Alternate scene!" he yelled as he barreled down on the other Zodiac.

Chapter 93

KYLIE AND I were pressed flat to the bottom of the Zodiac, waiting for the inevitable.

She kept count. "One-one-thousand, two-one-thousand, three-one-thousand..."

By fifteen-one-thousand the inevitable still hadn't happened.

"Something went wrong," she said. "Take a look."

I lifted my head and peered over the gunwale.

"Game changer," I said, ducking back out of sight. "I don't think he can get it to blow. He's talking to someone on the cell phone."

"Maybe he's calling tech support," she said. "Don't give him a chance to figure it out. Let's take him."

I sat up and reached for the starter cord.

The first bullet tore through the Yamaha engine, and I hit the deck. Three more shots flew over our heads.

I heard Benoit's Zodiac race past us. I rolled over, grabbed my gun, and fired back, all noise and no accuracy. He did a one-eighty and came back at us. I yanked at the starter cord, but his first shot had taken out the engine.

He opened fire, and I flattened out yet again.

"Zach, I don't have a gun," Kylie said.

"I have a backup. Ankle holster." I could hear the Zodiac bearing down on us again. "I'll get it as soon as he passes."

He didn't pass.

He rammed us.

He clipped the front corner of our Zodiac, catching it at the perfect angle to lift it high and pitch me overboard. I flew out of the boat backward and hit the water headfirst.

It felt like somebody came up behind me

and whacked me with a two-by-four. All I could see were blue spots on a field of black, and then I went under.

I'm not a natural-born swimmer, and I thrashed my way back to the surface, coughing up river water and jerking my throbbing head in all directions looking for Kylie. Our Zodiac had righted itself, and she was still in it, but there were at least thirty feet of open water separating the two of us.

Benoit made another U-turn, saw the gap between us, and roared straight down the middle, firing at me as he came. Somehow I had managed to hang on to my piece, and, keeping it above water, I fired back wildly without a prayer of hitting him.

His bullets were much more on target, cutting through the water to my left, my right, and one striking less than a foot in front of me. He barreled right past me and swung the Zodiac into a wide arc so he could make another pass. I knew it was only a matter of time. I was a fish in a barrel, and Benoit was hell-bent on shooting fish.

And then, over the roar of the engine, I heard Kylie yell, "Zach, fake a hit! Go under."

Benoit was bearing down on me again, but much more slowly so he could line up his shot.

He fired once. I grabbed my right shoulder, stopped treading water, and dropped straight down. The last thing I saw before I let the river swallow me up was Kylie kneeling in a shooter's position on the hull of the Zodiac, both arms outstretched, aiming straight at Benoit.

Aiming? Aiming what?

As of two minutes ago, her gun was at the bottom of the Hudson River.

Chapter 94

GABRIEL HAD SEEN it a hundred times in the movies. In a high-speed chase scene, the cop car turns into the back wheels of an escaping vehicle, causing it to spin out of control.

He used the exact same concept to flip the cops' Zodiac around and send Jordan flying into the water. The cop landed flat on his back.

By the time he got his bearings, he was totally separated from his partner, and now Gabriel could take them out one at a time.

Jordan first. Benoit closed in on him, firing

as he went. At one point he was less than ten feet from his target, but the water was choppy, and none of his shots hit the mark.

Slow down, a voice said.

It was Gabriel the director.

Gabriel the action hero eased up on the throttle and circled the boat for another run.

Steady, steady, steady, the director said. *Now.*

He fired.

Jordan grabbed his shoulder, flew back, and went under.

"One down," Gabriel said. He turned to Kylie. Her boat was disabled or she'd have come at him. She had no place to go.

He slowed his Zodiac to a crawl and stopped twenty feet from her.

It was dark, but her body was clearly back-lit by the setting sun. She was kneeling in a shooter's stance.

"NYPD!" she yelled. "Drop your gun and hold your hands up high."

"You don't have a gun, bitch!" he screamed. "Otherwise you'd have opened fire on me before I nailed your partner."

"Final warning!" she called out. "Drop your gun and get your hands in the air."

Shoot her, the voice said. This time it wasn't the director.

It was Lexi. She was here for the final scene. Uninvited, but of course she showed up anyway. He laughed. That Lexi—he never could control her.

Shoot her for me, Gabe. Shoot her.

He pulled the trigger.

Click.

He was out of bullets.

Ram her. Run her down. Cut her in half. Kill her.

Gabriel put his hand on the throttle. MacDonald's Zodiac was directly in his path. She was still aiming at him. And then he saw it in her hand, silhouetted against the sky.

It was boxy with a square front and yellow stripes on the side.

She squeezed the trigger.

Chapter 95

I SURFACED JUST in time to see the stand-off. Kylie and Benoit, about twenty feet apart, neither of them moving.

And then the river exploded. A heart-stopping, earsplitting volcanic bang shattered the serenity of the Upper Bay and reverberated from Brooklyn to Bayonne. For an instant, the world turned a blinding bright orange. Then a geyser of boiling hot white water shot up, followed by large plumes of thick black smoke that blossomed out across the sky, showering down pieces of flaming Zodiac and human body parts.

Benoit, who had been at the center of the explosion, was vaporized. Kylie was only twenty feet away, and the seismic waves lifted her boat out of the water. One second she had been on her knees drawing a bead on Benoit, and the next her body was arcing through the air.

She hit the water fifty feet away from me and went under.

I called her name and started swimming through the oil slick and burning remnants of the fiberglass hull hissing in the water. I waited for her to pop her head up, but she didn't, which meant she was either unconscious or worse.

My clothes and my shoes were dragging me down, and I felt like I was swimming in a dream—no matter how hard I pushed myself, I never seemed to get any closer.

When I finally got to the spot where I saw her hit the water, I dove down. It was dark and murky, and the best I could do was search frantically by sweeping my arms in front of me. After a minute, I shot up, gulped down some air, called her name again, and looked in every direction.

Nothing.

And then something broke the surface. A shoe. I dove back underwater and swam toward it. Ten feet. Twenty feet. I had lost all sense of direction. I no longer knew where I was or where Kylie had gone down.

Then I saw it. Swirling in the black water were strands of gold. Blond hair.

I kicked so hard I collided with her, then I grabbed her and pushed my way to the top. I sucked in some air, pressed my mouth to her mouth, and forced whatever oxygen I had in my lungs into hers.

She threw her head back and let out a loud gasp. I held on to her as she coughed up most of the water she had gulped down.

"Breathe," I said.

She breathed.

"Just keep breathing. Don't try to talk."

She talked. "What happened?" she said.

"I saved your life. Second time today."

"No, with Benoit.

"You blew him out of the water into bite-size chunks."

"I was only trying to stun him."

"He must've had a pocket full of C4. You

couldn't light it up with a bazooka, but if he had it primed with a blasting cap, all it took was one good Tase."

I could hear the sirens. Then I saw them coming at us from all angles—Harbor Patrol, fireboats, Coast Guard, and at the front of the pack, Jim Rothlein in the *Kristina*.

The last traces of sun were disappearing into the water, and there in the distance, wrapped in a purple and pink New York City twilight, I could make out the Statue of Liberty.

"I guess this is how Benoit's movie ends," I said.

The water was cold, and Kylie, shivering, pressed her body as close to mine as she could get. "As they say in the biz," she said, "'fade to black.'"

I wrapped my arms around her, held her tight, and whispered in her ear, "Roll credits."

EPILOGUE

END CREDITS

Chapter 96

NEW YORKERS LOVE a hero, and when they woke up Thursday morning, they had two new ones. Splashed across the front page of the *Daily News* was the headline "Dynamic Duo Foils Hollywood Killer."

Below it was a picture of Spence Harrington in his hospital bed with Kylie sitting at his side.

The headline on page 3 said "Bomber Nails Producer. Producer's Wife Nails Bomber." The story was accompanied by a shot of Kylie in an evening gown and Spence in black tie which had been taken just a few days before at Radio City.

There was also an inset photo of me, my official department head shot, captioned "Kylie MacDonald-Harrington's other partner, Detective Zachary Jordan."

It was hard to believe. On Monday, I had woken up wondering if teaming up with Kylie MacDonald would be career suicide. By Thursday, she was a hero, and I had become the Other Guy.

I got to the office at 7:30, and Kylie was already there waiting for me.

"Zach, I'm mortified," she said, holding the paper in her hand.

"Don't be," I said. "You took down Lexi, you took down Benoit, you deserve the glory."

"But you and I are partners. We were in this together. You've been with NYPD Red three years. I'm here all of three days. I don't know what the press was thinking when they spun the story the way they did."

"They were thinking that you and Spence are a celebrity couple, and that a picture of the two of you on the front page would sell more newspapers than one of me sopping wet, dragging my ass off a police boat."

"I'm sorry," she said. "I can have Spence call the studio publicist and have her get the press to clarify—"

I jumped in fast. "Absolutely not. I'm a cop. I don't have a publicist, and I don't want one."

"Is there anything I can do to make it up to you?" she said.

"Well, yeah, if you don't mind," I said.

"Anything."

"I'd really be honored if you and Spence would autograph my copy of the *Daily News*."

She punched me in the shoulder. "Asshole."

"Speaking of Spence," I said, "how is the other half of the Dynamic Duo this morning?"

"He's on heavy doses of antibiotics, so they're keeping him in the hospital for a couple more days, but the surgeon says he'll be fine. He'll need crutches for a while, but in about six months, it'll be like nothing ever happened."

My phone rang. It was Cates.

"You and MacDonald," she said. "My office. We have some unfinished business."

It was time to bite the bullet.

"I just watched the mayor's press conference," Cates said when we got there. "He blew the usual smoke up Hollywood's ass. Something on the order of 'it can get ugly wherever you shoot, but if it happens in New York, you'll get the fastest, smartest, bravest police force in the world. Nobody backs up the film industry like NYPD Red.'"

"Those are the same exact words Shelley Trager said to him yesterday when the mayor was thinking about canceling the rest of Hollywood on the Hudson week," Kylie said.

"Nobody ever said our mayor was an original thinker. Anyway, it doesn't matter what he said. I doubt if it convinced any of the LA crowd to bring more of their business to the city, but I'm sure the sweet tax package Irwin Diamond offered them will work wonders. Bottom line, the mayor is happy. So is the commissioner. He said I should congratulate the two of you on your 'extraordinary heroism while engaged in personal combat with an armed adversary.'"

"Thank you," I said.

"His words, not mine," Cates said. "I, on

the other hand, am not happy. I have a problem with cops who work off the reservation. What the hell were you thinking when you blew off my phone call?"

Before I could say a word, Kylie jumped in. "It wasn't Zach," she said. "I blew it off."

"I didn't call you," Cates said. "I called Jordan."

"Yes, but I practically ripped the phone out of his hand," Kylie said, taking more than her fair share of the heat. "I wasn't thinking. My husband's life was on the line, and I was going to save him."

"And did you think I would have stopped you?" Cates said. "I will back up any detective under my command who operates on guts, instinct, and initiative. You have a lot of authority in this unit, but it's only because I give it to you. If you ever cut me out of the loop again, I don't care how many front pages your faces are on, I will transfer your asses right the hell out of NYPD Red. Understood?"

"Understood," Kylie and I responded in unison.

"That said, I can't deny what you've done.

You brought down a serial killer who was on the verge of blowing up a boatload of innocent people."

"We had help from someone on the boat," Kylie said. "Charles Connor."

"Mr. Connor is brave and articulate," Cates said. "And if I know anything about public relations, somewhere in the next news cycle, he'll be standing on the steps of city hall, where the mayor will award him the Bronze Medallion for exceptional citizenship. But don't kid yourselves; Connor would be dead if you two hadn't showed up. You're heroes. You did the unit proud, and I'm sure when Detective Shanks gets back he'll understand why I'm making the two of you a permanent team."

"Us?" Kylie said. "Permanent?"

"As permanent as things can get in this department," Cates said. "I myself am always looking over my shoulder to see who's after my job. It's a lot easier if one of the contenders works right here, where I can keep an eye on her. Congratulations, Detectives. Dismissed."

We walked out of the office, and Kylie gave

me a high five. "Did you hear what she said, Zach? We're a permanent team."

"As long as you don't piss her off again," I said, feeling a twinge of remorse over Omar's impending reassignment.

"Me? You're the one who blew off her phone call. Shape up, partner." She punched me in the shoulder again, laughing this time. "Is this cool, or what?"

Her face radiated with joy and triumph. The beautiful, confident, unpredictable young cadet I fell in love with the first day of academy was now a beautiful, confident, unpredictable NYPD Red badass supercop—my partner.

And I was still in love with her.

"Yeah, it's cool," I said.

Chapter 97

KYLIE AND I spent all of Thursday and Friday buried in paperwork and psych evaluations. Having killed one person with her service revolver and blown another one to bits with her Taser, Kylie got to spend a lot more quality time than I did with Cheryl Robinson, but I was looking forward to a different kind of quality time on the weekend.

"Are you still game for the opera on Saturday?" she asked me when I ran into her at the office.

"Sure. What does one wear to the Met anyway?"

"Black tie, top hat, and maybe you could bring along a pair of those opera glasses on a stick like Mrs. Thurston Howell III had on *Gilligan's Island*," she said.

"You don't know anything about the dress code either, do you?"

She shrugged. "I'll just wear what I wear to the office. I'm planning an evening of Giuseppe Verdi and Chinese food. Why don't you meet me at Shun Lee Café on Sixty-fifth across from Lincoln Center at seven o'clock."

"I'll be there," I said. *Let the post-Fred renaissance begin.*

Saturday afternoon, I went to Kylie's apartment to visit Spence. Both Laight Street and Washington were lined with double-parked vans and trucks.

"Emergency repairs," Spence said. He was in a wheelchair, and his broken nose was taped, but all things considered he seemed pretty chipper. "The real renovation doesn't start till the insurance guys figure out who pays for what."

"Do you think the insurance guys will pay for a new flat-screen TV for your upstairs neighbor?" I said.

"If they don't, it's on me," Kylie said. "Along with a new bedroom wall and dinner for Dino and Coralei at the restaurant of their choice."

"Zach, do you mind if I pick your brain?" It was Shelley Trager. He had been sitting there, uncharacteristically quiet. No doubt he was still in some pain after breaking his ribs.

"There's not much left of it," I said, "but sure."

"With Benoit dead, nobody owns the rights to his story, which means that anybody can take it and adapt it. Spence here wants to turn it into a movie."

"It's a natural," Spence said. "We could get Kevin Spacey as Benoit. Nobody does crazy like Kevin."

"I flat out refuse to do it," Trager said. "Benoit always planned for someone to turn his script into a film, and if we do it, then he wins. What do you think?"

"It all depends on who plays me in the movie," I said.

"I'm serious," Trager said.

"Shelley, I'm not a producer, but I can tell

you this—if you make the movie, a lot of people will go to see it."

He shrugged. "True."

"But I definitely will not be one of them."

He smiled. "Me either. Thanks."

Chapter 98

I DECIDED THAT gray pants, blue blazer, tattersall shirt, and a yellow tie were as opera-worthy as anything I had in my closet. I took the number 1 train to Lincoln Center and walked to the restaurant.

Cheryl was waiting. She was wearing a sleeveless black dress that showed off her flawless caramel skin with a V-neckline that provided just enough cleavage to drive a man crazy.

"You look amazing," I said.

"Thanks. You clean up pretty well yourself," she said.

"But you lied," I said. "That is definitely not what you usually wear to work. If you did, you'd have a lot more cops showing up for counseling."

Shun Lee Café is perfect for pretheater dinner. Pretty young waitresses push rolling carts of bite-size dim sum in steamer baskets from table to table. The customers pick out a few to share, and then the cart moves on, magically reappearing just when you're ready for your next course.

"The seafood dumplings with chives are to die for," Cheryl said, holding one in a pair of chopsticks and passing it across the table. She popped it into my mouth, and I had to lean over to keep the juices from dribbling down my chin and onto my tie.

"That older couple over there is staring and smiling at us," she said. "I think they think we're adorable."

"We are," I said.

When the check came, I reached for it. Cheryl put her hand on mine. "I've got it," she said.

"You got the opera tickets," I said.

"I didn't pay for them. They were a gift."

"Even so, I'm old-fashioned," I said. "Guys pay for dinner."

"My father's a guy. He's paying."

"I thought daddies stopped paying for their daughters' dates right after senior prom."

"He bet me a hundred bucks you'd never show up for the opera," she said. "He lost, so he can pay."

"Your father bet I wouldn't show? How did that even happen? Do you always discuss your dating plans with your parents?"

"When you called me Tuesday night, I was having dinner with my father," she said.

"You said you were with a cop."

"Daddy was a cop. Didn't you know that?"

I shook my head.

"Anyway, he's very old school. Doesn't think a cop could listen to a woman screaming without jumping onstage and arresting someone. I told him you were much more enlightened, and it cost him a hundred bucks."

I took my hand off the check. "Thank him for dinner and tell him I'm sorry I let him down."

La Traviata had been nothing short of mesmerizing.

"Did you really like it?" Cheryl said as we left the opera house.

"Are you kidding? It was the classic love story. Boy meets girl. Boy loses girl. Boy finds girl. Girl dies of consumption in the third act. It doesn't get any more romantic than that."

She took my arm, and we walked through the plaza and stopped in front of the Revson Fountain, one of the city's most recognizable landmarks.

"Turn around," she said.

I turned, and I was facing the opera house. It was like a cathedral with its crystal chandeliers lighting up the Chagall murals on the inside and the five soaring floor-to-ceiling arched windows on the outside. The fountain was putting on its own show with multicolored lighting effects and a perfectly choreographed water ballet.

"I take it back," I said. "This is even more romantic than a girl dying of consumption."

"People come from all over the world just to stand where we're standing right now," Cheryl said.

I turned to face her and put my arms

around her waist. "It just might be the best place in all of New York for a first kiss."

She leaned in even closer. "You may be right," she whispered.

Our lips met and lingered while the water danced around us and covered us with a fine mist.

"I live right here on the Upper West Side," Cheryl said. "Walking distance."

"Would you like a police escort?"

"Definitely. Some of these operagoers look menacing."

We walked uptown to Lincoln Towers, a sprawling complex of six high-rise apartment buildings on West End Avenue. It was yet another New York City neighborhood where most cops can't afford to live.

"I got the condo. Fred got the bimbo," she said, reading my mind.

We stood in the shadows, away from the bright lights of her lobby. I wrapped my arms around her. She was exotically beautiful, her skin was soft and warm, and the lingering traces of her perfume set every male hormone in my body on point.

We kissed. The second kiss was longer,

sweeter, and even more electric than the first.

"Thank you," she said. "I had a wonderful evening."

"Me too. Except for the part where I didn't get to pay for dinner."

"I'll tell you what," she said. "I'll let you buy me breakfast tomorrow."

"Tomorrow?" I said. "Are you really sure you want to trek over to the East Side and have breakfast with a bunch of cops at Gerri's Diner on a Sunday?"

"No," she said, taking me by the hand and walking me toward the lobby. "I have a better idea."

She certainly did. Much, much better.

But that's a whole other story.

Acknowledgments

The authors would like to thank Undersheriff Frank Faluotico and Jerry Brainard of the Ulster County, New York, Sheriff's Department, NYPD Detective Sal Catapano, Dr. Lawrence Dresdale, Michael Jackman, Jim Rothlein, Gerry Cuffe, and Jason Wood for their help in making this work of fiction ring true.

About the Authors

JAMES PATTERSON has created more enduring fictional characters than any other novelist writing today. He is the author of the Alex Cross novels, the most popular detective series of the past twenty-five years, including *Kiss the Girls* and *Along Came a Spider.* Mr. Patterson also writes the bestselling Women's Murder Club novels, set in San Francisco, and the top-selling New York detective series of all time, featuring Detective Michael Bennett. James Patterson has had more *New York Times* bestsellers than any other writer, ever, according to *Guinness*

About the Authors

World Records. Since his first novel won the Edgar Award in 1977, James Patterson's books have sold more than 240 million copies.

James Patterson has also written numerous #1 bestsellers for young readers, including the Maximum Ride, Witch & Wizard, and Middle School series. In total, these books have spent more than 220 weeks on national bestseller lists. In 2010, James Patterson was named Author of the Year at the Children's Choice Book Awards.

His lifelong passion for books and reading led James Patterson to create the innovative website ReadKiddoRead.com, giving adults an invaluable tool to find the books that get kids reading for life. He writes full-time and lives in Florida with his family.

MARSHALL KARP has written for stage, screen, and TV and is the author of *The Rabbit Factory* and three other mysteries featuring LAPD detectives Mike Lomax and Terry Biggs.

Books by James Patterson

Featuring Alex Cross

Kill Alex Cross • *Cross Fire* • *I, Alex Cross* • *Alex Cross's* Trial (with Richard DiLallo) • *Cross Country* • *Double Cross* • *Cross* (also published as *Alex Cross*)• *Mary, Mary* • *London Bridges* • *The Big Bad Wolf* • *Four Blind Mice* • *Violets Are Blue* • *Roses Are Red* • *Pop Goes the Weasel* • *Cat & Mouse* • *Jack & Jill* • *Kiss the Girls* • *Along Came a Spider*

The Women's Murder Club

11th Hour (with Maxine Paetro) • *10th Anniversary* (with Maxine Paetro) • *The 9th Judgment* (with Maxine Paetro) • *The 8th Confession* (with Maxine Paetro) • *7th Heaven* (with Maxine Paetro) • *The 6th Target* (with Maxine Paetro) • *The 5th Horseman* (with Maxine Paetro) • *4th of July* (with Maxine Paetro) • *3rd Degree* (with

Andrew Gross) • *2nd Chance* (with Andrew Gross) • *1st to Die*

Featuring Michael Bennett

I, Michael Bennett (with Michael Ledwidge) • *Tick Tock* (with Michael Ledwidge) • *Worst Case* (with Michael Ledwidge) • *Run for Your Life* (with Michael Ledwidge) • *Step on a Crack* (with Michael Ledwidge)

The Private Novels

Private Games (with Mark Sullivan) • *Private: #1 Suspect* (with Maxine Paetro) • *Private* (with Maxine Paetro)

Stand-alone Books

Zoo (with Michael Ledwidge) • *Guilty Wives* (with David Ellis) • *The Christmas Wedding* (with Richard DiLallo) • *Kill Me If You Can* (with Marshall Karp) • *Now You See Her* (with Michael Ledwidge) • *Toys* (with Neil McMahon) • *Don't Blink* (with Howard Roughan) • *The Postcard Killers* (with Liza Marklund) • *The Murder of King Tut* (with Martin Dugard) • *Swimsuit* (with Maxine Paetro) • *Against Medical Advice* (with Hal Friedman) • *Sail* (with Howard Roughan) • *Sundays at Tiffany's* (with Gabrielle Charbonnet) • *You've Been Warned* (with Howard Roughan) • *The Quickie* (with Michael Ledwidge) • *Judge & Jury* (with Andrew Gross) • *Beach Road* (with Peter de Jonge) • *Lifeguard* (with Andrew Gross) • *Honeymoon* (with Howard Roughan) • *Sam's Letters to Jennifer* • *The Lake House* • *The Jester* (with Andrew Gross) • *The Beach House* (with Peter de Jonge) • *Suzanne's Diary for Nicholas* • *Cradle and All* • *When the Wind Blows* • *Miracle on the 17th Green* (with Peter de Jonge) • *Hide & Seek* • *The Midnight Club* • *Black Friday* (originally published as *Black Market*) • *See How They*

Run • Season of the Machete • The Thomas Berryman Number • santaKid

FOR READERS OF ALL AGES

Maximum Ride

ANGEL: A Maximum Ride Novel • FANG: A Maximum Ride Novel • MAX: A Maximum Ride Novel • Maximum Ride: The Final Warning • Maximum Ride: Saving the World and Other Extreme Sports • Maximum Ride: School's Out—Forever • Maximum Ride: The Angel Experiment

Daniel X

Daniel X: Game Over (with Ned Rust) • *Daniel X: Demons and Druids* (with Adam Sadler) • *Daniel X: Watch the Skies* (with Ned Rust) • *The Dangerous Days of Daniel X* (with Michael Ledwidge)

Witch & Wizard

Witch & Wizard: The Fire (with Jill Dembowski) • *Witch & Wizard: The Gift* (with Ned Rust) • *Witch & Wizard* (with Gabrielle Charbonnet)

Middle School

Middle School: Get Me Out of Here (with Chris Tebbetts, illustrated by Laura Park) • *Middle School: The Worst Years of My Life* (with Chris Tebbetts, illustrated by Laura Park)

For previews and information about the author, visit JamesPatterson.com or find him on Facebook or at your app store.